Books by David Griffith

The Freedom Series

Free to Run

Vengeance is Mine

Sacrifice

The Border Series

Blackwater Crossing

The Death Dealers

Without Redemption

Brothers of the Blood

The Fugitive

Sacrifice

BOOK THREE IN THE

FREEDOM SERIES

DAVID GRIFFITH

Sacrifice

Book 3 in The Freedom Series

David Griffith

<u>**Chapter 1**</u>

Thirty years old, pregnant, and single, had never been my childhood dream. Mind you, I doubt any eight-year-old girl acts out that scenario with her favorite doll. Nevertheless, that was now my life, and I had to make the best of it.

My husband was not at fault. He is a good man, and I'll go to my grave defending him. It's just that we lived different lives. Our personalities, our goals, and our love had somehow diverged from whatever had been the pole star of our marriage.

We had so many things against us. Though at work, Frederick made lightning fast assessments of agents, operations, or anything else that threatened the security of those he was responsible for, about us, he was agonizingly slow to make *any* decision. My spontaneous and volatile nature is total Latin, completely at odds with the makeup of the man I married. From the first day we'd met, our relationship had been a clash of wills. Despite that anomaly, we fell in love, and though there had been moments of peace, nothing had changed. The resentment built, layer upon bitter layer, until in the end, it engulfed both of us. By the time we split sheets, home, and assets, there was little to discuss. The lives we'd known, and the future we'd hoped for were nothing more than a pile of cold ashes.

It was a stifling, hot June afternoon with thunderclouds building in the eastern sky when the divorce papers arrived at the ranch in Agua Prieta. Our division of assets was more civil than most. Frederick would keep our home in Albuquerque. It had never meant anything to me, and I didn't want it. He gave me a hundred thousand dollars, most of which he'd borrowed from the bank, and I kept the training facility my parents had owned in Cave Creek. We'd upgraded it over the years, and so it seemed a fair division. I, of course, also kept my parents' vast property south of Agua Prieta, in the Mexican state of Sonora.

As I scanned the papers Frederick's lawyer had sent me, I couldn't suppress a bitter laugh. Though we were both people driven by ambition, we hadn't done very well financially. Other than the home in Albuquerque and a very modest bank account, there was little in the way of monetary reward to show for our ten years of marriage.

I shoved the papers into the top drawer of my desk. I would sign and send them back to my attorney after I had time to sit down and read each line. Not that I was worried. It would be uncharacteristic of Frederick to try to pull anything underhanded. Besides, there was nothing to contest other than the child who grew inside me. We'd long tried to make that happen, and it seemed ironic that now our marriage was over, the event we'd so longed for had come to pass. I'd not told Frederick, and though it seemed underhanded, I wouldn't, at least not until the divorce was final. There seemed little virtue in discussing a continued relationship just because we'd finally been successful in producing offspring. At the time, I doubted the child would be any better off if we stayed together and fought.

Later, I was to change my mind, but back then, I hadn't the benefit of knowing the future.

For me, that day had been another difficult one. Mornings, I spent retching over the toilet. Afternoons were easier. Those were consumed with me lying in bed, trying to recover. It was not an easy pregnancy—if there is such a thing. Like all trials in life, it eventually came to an end. When the doctor handed me little Luis, my life changed in a way I could never have foreseen. He *became* my life.

With a ranch to run, I had little time to spend recuperating. Daily decisions were necessary in order to keep our horse and cattle operations running smoothly. Fortunately, I had the best *segundo* anyone could ever have. Raul had been with my father before I'd been born. Once, after the death of his wife, he'd taken some time off, but after spending a winter in Nevada, he'd come home, and for that I was incredibly thankful. Though he was getting up in years, he still ran the ranch with a gentle but firm hand.

Luis was barely a month old when I took him to meet his grandmother. I trudged down to the big coulee, then up the worn trail to the bluff on the other side, trying not to joggle him too much. I'd dressed him in a bright blue, one-piece sleeper with tiny red galloping horses across the front. Then I'd wrapped him in a light, silk blanket. Though he still seemed foreign and strange in my arms, I loved him with a fierce passion I'd never thought possible.

When we reached Mama's grave, I sat on the edge of the sarcophagus and told my little son about his *abuela* and how proud and excited she would have been to hold this little grandson. And then I cried, because my Mama had often longed to hold a grandchild, but the cancer had taken her long before Luis came. I still missed her so much, a heavy hurt that would never go away.

For a long time, I sat and talked to Mama. As I had so many times before, I avoided any mention of my divorce. She'd always been stern when I'd broached the subject—or perhaps that was my own conscience. Somehow, she seemed to always stand in front of me, gently telling me I'd been wrong. She and Papa would never have considered anything as disgraceful as leaving their spouse. For one thing, the church would have forbade it, but it was more than that. They were as much in love the day Papa died as the day they'd married—probably more so. And even if they hadn't been, the divorce word was not in their vocabulary. So today, as always, I avoided that topic. Besides, this was not a time to dwell on anything negative, or for that matter, any issue that would displease Mama. Today was a day of joy, and I cuddled and played with little Luis until he gave his first smile for his *abuela*. Above us, I could almost hear Mama laugh with pure joy. It was a fun time with her, even though I was sad.

I stood and said good bye, and even picked up Luis's little hand and waved it at his grandmother's grave. She wasn't really there, but up in heaven, she would look down and smile. She would know about all the other bad things happening, and would make a petition to our Savior and Lord. God knows, I needed it. Tomorrow, if I had time, I would come back and talk to her about the other issues that had brought fear and discord to the ranch.

<u>**Chapter 2**</u>

Managing a world-class horse facility at our Agua Prieta ranch in Sonora had never been easy. Though our costs were lower than they would have been north of the border, we had other difficulties. Nevertheless, through the years, Papa had made it work, and after he died, Mama and I had carried on with little change. In some ways, the situation was ideal. We were adjacent to the American market, which is what we targeted, and were only a few hundred miles from the tony Cave Creek ranch which Papa had bought shortly before he died. Cave Creek was our sales center and American training headquarters. It was where we sent the three and four year olds after they were well-broke, and ready for the final phase of their training.

Our line of horses were bred to run, and when we sent them to Cave Creek, they went one of two directions. Either they became top rope horses, or if they were very fast and talented, they were started on the barrels. The rope horses that we sold paid the bills, but it was the higher dollar barrel racing horses that had vaulted the Rodriguez horses to stardom. The challenge in our business was that from the time a mare foaled until there was a colt that might be salable was usually five to six years. It was a long and expensive process, and there were only a few who made it to the top tier. Though we'd always managed those challenges of raising and training performance horses, what we now faced seemed insurmountable.

The Mexican border is divided into sections by the drug cartels. All are bitterly fought over, and defended with the latest and best weaponry in the world. My home town of Agua Prieta is one of the prized plazas, and had long been held in an iron grip by the Sinaloa Cartel. But leaders don't last forever, and as soon as it appeared that Joaquin 'El Chapo' Guzman was weakening, the Jalisco New Generation thugs moved in. Actually, they didn't have to move in. They were already there. The Sinaloa Cartel had long used them as an enforcement arm against the even more violent Los Zetas criminals, especially in the border city of Juarez. It was hard to say which of the three cartels were the bloodiest, but the Jalisco gang was doing everything possible to earn that coveted mantle.

We'd long lived with violence. Like everyone along the border, our lives varied between unpleasant, and terrifying. Most of the time, we coped with the occasional veiled threat, and avoided trouble wherever we could. Many of our relatives and close friends had acquaintances or even family members who had disappeared with no trace, victims of cartel violence. We had been fortunate. But now, our town of Agua Prieta had turned into a battleground. Shootings, often in broad daylight became common. Pitched battles between the Sinaloa and Jalisco Cartels opened up nightmares the residents of our state of Sonora hadn't seen since the Mexican Revolution. Our only line of defense was to stay away from town until we absolutely had to have supplies. When we did have to stock up, it was a hurried, nervous affair. One did not linger. And then it hit us in a way I could never have imagined.

We needed groceries, and a ton of rolled oats. Raul had gone to the Cave Creek Ranch, and everyone else was busy, so I took one of the pickups and made the trip into town. I stopped at the feed store for the ton of bagged feed, then pulled into the parking lot of the Super del Norte grocery store. As I left the pickup, I glanced at the rolled oats stacked in the back of the truck. I should have bought the groceries first. It wasn't smart to leave something as easy to steal as bagged feed, but there was little I could do now. I grimaced at my lack of forethought as I walked into the air-conditioned building. It would be all right. The store wasn't crowded. I'd get what I needed and be through the check-out in record time.

When I wheeled my grocery cart out to the truck, a man lounged against the side of the pickup. He smirked, his insolent eyes roving up and down my body. "You shouldn't leave your truck unattended." He nodded his head toward the feed.

"Yes, you're right. Thank you." I unlocked the pickup and started loading groceries onto the floor and back seat.

"Hey Dina girl, we need to talk."

I whirled, surprised that he knew my name, quite sure I'd never seen him before.

My eyes darted around the parking lot, hoping for help. It was then I noticed the black Cadillac Escalade parked two spots over. The windows were opaque green, the wheels top-of-the-line expensive. Where we live, Cadillac Escalades might not be a calling card of the cartels, but they're a good indicator. Suddenly wary, I hurriedly loaded the rest of my groceries and slammed the pickup door. "What do you want?"

He stepped forward. Out of nowhere, his hand snaked out and rammed me up against the side of the pickup.

"A little more respect." A shiny blade suddenly appeared in his right hand. "Or should I just cut that pretty face."

My throat tightened with fear, and I stuttered a protest.

"Shut up. Now listen. We're the new boss of this plaza, so whatever you've been giving to the Sinaloa scum for protection? That's over now. My name is Ovaldo Ramirez. Jalisco Cartel. Can you remember that?" His face moved closer. The deadly blade now slipped lower, invisible to any but the most curious passerby. "Repeat it. Ovaldo. Jalisco."

"Ovaldo." My voice quavered. "Jalisco Cartel."

"Good, you've got it. Now, you need to make the first payment. Twenty thousand pesos. That's kind of an initiation fee for the rich." He leered, his heavily jowled face no more than six inches from mine. I recoiled from the expensive aftershave and body odor. It didn't mix well.

The smirk left his face. "After that, there's a monthly fee. Five thousand."

"We don't have that kind of money."

His hand now held the knife handle hard against my crotch. Suddenly he flicked it the other way, and I felt the point.

I sucked in my belly and tried to meld further into the side of the pickup. "I will try to get it."

"No, you don't understand. You need it now. We don't have a credit plan." The point of the blade pressed harder, and this time, I knew it was drawing blood. I nodded mutely. "I will get it. Let me go across the street to the bank."

His eyes bored into mine. "If you play games with me, I will kill you." He stepped back and motioned with his head for me to leave.

Without a backward glance, I reached into the pickup, scooped up my purse and stumbled away. What should I do? We'd never been forced to pay a toll charge to the Sinaloa Cartel. Now, everything had changed. I pulled the glass door of the bank open and stepped into the cool, air-conditioned room. A line snaked toward the two tellers. Mexican banking at its best, and never had I been so glad. I had plenty of time to execute a plan.

Two federal soldiers, both armed with AR-15's, stood on either side of the door, a common sight since the drug cartel war had started. My mind raced. Should I trust them? If I told them my story, would they believe me? They might just hand me over to the Jalisco gang of thieves. It wouldn't be the first time that had happened. Before I reached the front of the line, I'd made my decision.

I stepped out of the line and walked over to the oldest soldier, who I hoped might have the coolest head. Quickly, I related my situation. He maintained a grim, expressionless mask. When I'd finished, he inclined his head toward the line of customers.

"Go back to your place in the line."

I glared at him. I'd been prepared for rejection, but I hadn't expected the curt dismissal I'd just received. I rejoined the line, but not before I'd given him the most withering glance I could summon. Once, I glanced back. He was on his cellphone, probably talking to his girlfriend.

When my turn came at the wicket, I asked the teller for twenty thousand pesos out of the ranch account. She counted it out, and I stuffed it into an envelope. I turned and headed for the door. Scowling my disgust at the soldiers wasn't an option, because they were no longer there. I pushed through the glass doors and out into the hot Sonora sun— and then I understood. The whole parking lot swarmed with police. My pickup seemed to be the focal point of whatever was happening. With dread in my heart, I walked toward it, terrified of the consequences. Ovaldo and two other goons were spread-eagled against the Cadillac Escalade. Three semi-automatic rifles, along with various other illegal weaponry, lay on the pavement. I had to pass the Escalade to get to my pickup. Ovaldo turned his head as I hurried past. His smile was slow, and completely evil. He didn't need to say a word. I knew what was coming.

<u>**Chapter 3**</u>

When it came to brood mares, Papa's motto had always been "buy the best," so that's what he did. We'd continued to purchase the leading bloodlines in the industry, and the outstanding broodmare band we'd built over the years was the reason why we sold some of the top barrel racing horses in the nation. There wasn't a mare in the five section pasture south of the house for which we'd paid less than ten thousand dollars, and most had cost many times that amount. Papa had always felt if we were going to develop a respectable breeding program, we had to have mares that produced superior babies. Many times, we couldn't afford them, but when the right mare came on the market, no matter the cost—my father bought her. So far, his decisions had paid off.

Every morning, one of our cowboy crew was designated to ride the pasture where we kept the forty head of valuable, and mostly irreplaceable mares. Every horse was scrutinized for health problems or injuries.

Though to some it would have seemed foolish for mares of that caliber to run like wild horses, Papa had been convinced that his strategy was part of our success. The rocky Sonora range helped the colts to develop hard, flinty feet. Running the canyons and hills of the south pasture while dodging cactus and rattlesnakes gave them strong, muscular structure and cat-quick reflexes. We occasionally lost a colt, but those that survived were the best in the world.

My little Luis was no more than a few months old the morning Raul sent Paco to the south pasture. It was a job he split between the men. Everybody took a turn, and more often than not, it took most of the morning, simply because the mares were not always easy to find. The pasture was over a thousand acres, much of it covered in mesquite, desert thorn, and catclaw, and often, the horses were never quite where you thought they should be.

Paco didn't return until late in the afternoon, which was unusual. I'd left Luis in the house with Lupita, our long-time housekeeper and cook, while I did a few chores, so I happened to be at the barn when he rode up and wearily stepped off his horse.

Raul eyed Paco carefully. It was at least three hours later than what it usually took to adequately check the broodmares.

Then Paco dropped the bombshell. "Five mares and colts are missing."

I was puzzled, and mildly alarmed. Horses are herd creatures. It almost never happens that a band will split. Though I wanted to discount what I'd just heard, I knew I couldn't. Paco had been with us for a long time. He was a good man, conscientious, and if he said the mares weren't in the pasture, I had to believe him. Still, I had to ask. "Where all did you check for them?"

"I rode the rim and went clear to the back fence."

"And you found nothing?" I asked.

"No, they weren't there." Then he destroyed every vestige of our cocoon of safety. "I know where they went. Somebody loaded them in a trailer at that back gate next to the spring."

Raul glanced my way, his stricken eyes a reflection of what I felt in my heart.

"Who would do this—and why? Paco asked.

Raul clenched his jaw, his rising anger a growing volcano. "The new guys in town put the squeeze on Dina the other day. She was able to notify the Federales. They arrested those involved, but we all are aware that the arrest means nothing. This is their first reprisal." His calloused hands clenched as he turned away. "I'm afraid there will be more trouble."

Paco slipped the bridle off his horse and haltered him. "I don't understand. Those mares are valuable, but without registration papers and signed transfers to the new owner, they are worth no more than mustangs."

"You're right," I said. "And they don't have registration papers because those are in our safety deposit box at a bank in Tucson. But they didn't steal the mares for their monetary worth. They took them to send a message to me."

Fear twisted everything inside me into a writhing pit of worry. My decision back in the bank in Juarez to refuse to buckle to the cartel had endangered my life and the lives of everyone around me. If I hadn't realized that before, I certainly did now. Through the years, the names had changed, but in our town, the drug cartels had been the law for as long as I remembered. Stealing the mares was simply a cryptic note from the Jalisco Cartel. Do not defy us, because we can reach out and hurt you—anytime and anywhere.

In years past, we'd survived by treading softly, though I must admit that often we'd turned a blind eye to drug cartel depredations. Now our lives—and everything we'd worked for was in danger, and I had no answers. A hundred thousand dollars' worth of horses had disappeared. For the ranch, that was devastating, and the Jalisco Cartel knew it. So what next? How could I capitulate to their strong-arm tactics in front of my employees? And what would happen if I was too cowardly to stand up to their brazen theft of our mares? I pretty much knew. What would come next would be more violent.

I squared my shoulders, wanting to be seen as the boss, in control—only I wasn't. Nevertheless, I did my best. "Go ahead and put your horse away, Paco, and thank you for taking the extra time to discover who stole the mares. We'll all get together this evening.

Whatever decision we make regarding future action should involve everyone."

After Paco left, Raul momentarily placed a hand on my shoulder. "Dina, be careful. If we respond in any way, they'll target everyone on this ranch."

"You're right, and thanks." I crossed my arms and hugged my chest, trying to ward off the fear building inside me. "So many others have faced this. Now, it's our turn. Back in Juarez, I should have just given them the twenty-thousand pesos and kept quiet. Any one of those mares is worth ten times that, not to mention the lives of our people at the ranch I may have endangered."

Raul scowled. "But that's why the scum are so powerful. We're all afraid of what they will do."

I had no answer or argument to that, but "being right" in our country means little. Too many of my countrymen were right—and dead.

We both leaned over the top corral rail and watched as Paco unsaddled his sweat-stained horse. He turned him into one of the spacious pens on the backside of the main barn and trudged past us to place his gear in the tackroom.

Raul spoke softly to Paco as he left the barn, reiterating my earlier announcement. "We'll meet after supper. With all the crew."

Paco nodded wearily, then trudged toward the bunkhouse. I matched Raul's pace as we walked to the house. Mentally, I ticked off each man who made up our team. Most were long-time employees, as much a part of the ranch as I was. None of them would be afraid, and I couldn't think of any that would quit over this. They were family.

"What do you think we should do?" I asked.

Raul sighed. "I wish I could tell you. The older I get, the angrier I become over what has happened to our country, and every year, it only gets worse. What you tell the crew must be your decision." He stopped on the trail, and I turned and studied the face of this, my oldest friend and mentor.

I shook my head. "All I know is that this is our home. If we want to keep it, we have to fight for it. So many of our people have spent their lives here. How do we tell them that the cartels have now made it too dangerous, and we're selling the ranch? I can't do that."

Raul's eyes hardened. "I'm glad you think that way. As much as I'd like to find a safer place, I could never live with myself if we gave up and ran away."

"Tell the crew we will meet in the dining room after *cena*."

Raul nodded. "Sounds good. Paulina and Lupita probably should be there as well."

"It's Paulina's day off, but I'll tell Lupita."

The graveled path from the barn led to the side door on the east side of the house. I pushed the door open, kicked off my barn boots, and padded into the kitchen in sock feet.

Lupita glanced at me. "*Cena* will be ready in ten minutes."

"Sounds great. What are we blessed with tonight?"

Lupita shrugged. "The usual. Some fruit, maybe a tortilla, and a few vegetables."

"Sounds great. Let me wash my hands . . . and Lupita?"

"Yes?"

"We're having a meeting with the crew after supper."

"Why? What's wrong?"

"It's about what happened in town the other day."

"At the grocery store?"

"That, and now five of the mares are missing."

Lupita's eyes widened. "Five? They . . . somebody took five of our mares?"

As I pushed back my sleeves at the door of the bathroom, I suddenly realized what Lupita had said. She'd referred to the five missing mares as "ours," which encapsulated everything I'd tried to convey to Raul. Lupita had lived at the Rodriguez ranch since I'd been a toddler. She, like so many of our other employees, took personal ownership in the horses, cattle, and well-being of everyone who lived here. I walked up behind Lupita and slipped my arms around her. "Yes, they took five of our mares, and we need to have all of our family together to decide what our response should be."

Lupita turned, tears in her eyes. "The cartels are so dangerous. All they know is destruction and death. What are we going to do?"

"That's why we're having a meeting. Maybe among all of us, we can find an answer, though I certainly don't know what that might be."

"Oh, Dina, neither do I. Our country is in such a mess. They say there are now fewer deaths from the cartels, but I don't think this new government in Mexico City is going to save us—or anyone else, for that matter."

I jammed my hands into the shallow, cheap pockets of the faux designer jeans I'd been unwary enough to buy on my last trip to Tucson. Before I escaped to the bathroom to wash up, I replied with all the frustration this day had brought. "You're right, Lupita. We need a government that will solve the drug cartel problem that afflicts our country—no matter the cost."

Minutes later, I slipped into my regular seat at the table. Now, it was so different. In days past, *cena* used to be a time we spent together as a family, Papa, Mama, and in the early days, my brother Alejandro. But Alejandro left, then Papa had died. Finally, the cancer had taken Mama. Before our divorce, there had been Frederick. Now there was only me, Lupita, and sometimes Raul. The few men who had stuck with us through good times and bad either ate with their families, or if they were single, in the bunkhouse dining room. Though at times I grieved for the past, there was nothing that would bring it back.

Lupita's evening fare was simple, but as always, delicious. When we'd finished, I helped clean up. Precisely at seven, a knock on the door announced the outside crew. I hurried to open it. The whole bunkhouse, plus the married men, stood on the veranda with Raul at the front. They trooped in, and I ushered them to the big dining room table. It wasn't like it was anyone's first time here. Meetings on ranch policy and direction were a regular occurrence, an exercise in which every man was involved.

When they'd all seated themselves, I informally called the meeting to order.

"As all of you know, I had a run-in at the *mercado* with the Jalisco Cartel. The decision I made to involve the federal police has now backfired, and we've lost five mares."

"For sure, it's them?" Sandy asked.

"No, but I suspect before the end of the week, we'll find out."

"And, of course, they'll remind us of our responsibility to pay our share now that they're here to protect our interests," Raul scoffed.

Paco shook his head. "What can we do? We've all seen what happens if we don't pay."

None of the other men spoke. Each averted his eyes, refusing to meet mine. That, as much as anything, was my answer. I glanced at Lupita. Her face mirrored the poorly concealed fear in the eyes of the men. Every person in that room had seen the devastating consequences to any who tried to buck the demands of the cartel. And what she was seeing from the crew in front of her was a microcosm of what was on the face of nearly every man and woman in our country. Too many had loved ones or friends whose bullet-riddled bodies were a testament to the power of the cartels. That creeping, insidious message had infiltrated the national psyche.

As I looked around the room, I didn't see the faces of the men who worked and lived on the Rodriguez Ranch. Instead, I saw the collective despair of my country. My people were survivors, but to endure was to internalize the message of fear the cartels drilled into every man, woman, and child. Do not deny us. Do not flout our commands. And most of all—never, ever betray us.

<u>**Chapter 4**</u>

Nervously, I glanced at Raul. His face betrayed no emotion. He was the one the men respected. I needed his help. Only he could sway their opinion. If they all quit, there wouldn't be any ranch left. He knew that, so why wasn't he saying something? Was it because he understood their fear better than I did?

I studied each of the eight faces around the table, and for a moment, their features blurred into a single entity of fear, akin to the debilitating panic I'd faced in that parking lot at the *mercado*. Ovaldo Ramirez had left no room for doubt. Either I followed the cartel's bidding, or I needed to prepare for the consequences. The anxious faces around the table reminded me with stunning clarity how naively American I had become.

With a Mexican mother and American father, it is very easy for me to live on both sides. In America, life is good, as it has always been. My days are spent driving sculptured and pristine interstate highways to rodeos held in quintessential towns and cities across the length and breadth of America. On the whole, they are safe, and if you want a reprieve, you can pull into one of the busy enclaves, small towns, or minor cities where the rule of law is the accepted norm. If by some outside chance a bad event occurs, all one needs to do is call 911. Paramedics, ambulances, and mostly honest law enforcement immediately swarm to the rescue. In America, there is a backstop for every misfortune, and Madam Justice, though sometimes tipsy, prevails.

South of the border, everything changes. Here, much is twisted, and Americans will never in a thousand years understand the difference. Inside the bank in Agua Prieta, I hadn't been certain of any help. The police might have simply turned me over to the cartel, and I, like so many thousands of others, would have quietly disappeared. Here, protection is a commodity that has to be bought, which meant that my decision to involve the police had affected every one of my employees. As I studied each face around the table, I understood their reaction. To defy the cartels was to place your life, and everyone you loved, in danger.

I swept an arm to indicate the employees around the table. "I want to hear what you think. But keep in mind—once we start paying for protection, it will never end."

Instant silence as three of the men on the farm crew cast glances at each other. Finally, Antonio, the oldest of them, stood. "Señora, we have all loved working at the Rodriguez Ranch. You have treated us fairly, and there is nowhere we could ask for more. But we cannot fight the cartels. They rule our country, our state, and now our town. If this new gang of thieves demands that we pay, then that is what we must do. We are not strong enough to resist—and, Señora, my family must come first. If I die, my children will go hungry. I must try to survive—for them. If that means we have to pay *mordida* to the cartels, then so be it."

I watched Antonio fall silent, then lower his head. I glanced from one employee to another, but there were only downcast eyes and an ominous silence, which probably meant I had to accept that what Antonio had said was what they all felt.

What I'd heard was not a surprise. By my actions, I'd endangered their lives. Maybe

I'd been wrong. The problem was, what to do now. How did I protect our people from the storm that was sure to come? Though five of our mares had been stolen, it wasn't likely the cartel would take more. That had been an unusually gentle warning. If there was another message of the cartel's power and displeasure, it would consist of bodies—possibly horse, but more likely human. I folded my hands on the table. I didn't have the luxury of waiting to see what might happen. We needed a plan, and we needed it now, not tomorrow or next week.

"Okay, we must make a decision. Thank you, Antonio, for saying what I think everyone here feels in their heart. The ranch must survive, or none of us will be able to feed our families. But maybe we need to restructure. I propose that we send the rest of the horses to Cave Creek, along with any of you who have the proper papers to work in the United States. Those who don't will carry on as we always have until this all goes away."

Raul raised an eyebrow. "And we will pay the cartels?"

I'd dreaded that question. However, I was thankful it had been Raul who brought it up. "As much as I despise buckling to their evil, we have no other choice. At least for now—we will pay."

"And then?" Paco asked.

"We will leave that to God. Surely someday, the government will drive the cartels into the ground, and we will be free."

Lupita sputtered with obvious anger. "How can that ever happen when the Americans provide such a huge and ready market for their evil products?"

I scrubbed at my eyes, weary and discouraged. "We can't fix the Americans, or their failed policy." I threw my hands in the air. "For the record, they're convinced we're not doing our share either."

The faces around the table remained expressionless.

"Okay, unless somebody has something more to add, let's call it a night. Raul, can we move the mares as soon as the blood work is done?"

"Yes, I have scheduled that we draw blood on the day after tomorrow, which means we should have the necessary paperwork by the end of next week." He consulted his cellphone calendar. "I will personally accompany the samples to Hermosillo. With a proper monetary consideration, I am sure we can convince the lab that we need the paperwork completed quickly."

I rolled my eyes at the always expected *mordida*, but nodded anyway. To do business in our country, there was always a kickback.

"Sounds good. Can we bring the mares in tomorrow morning?" I asked.

"Yes." Raul turned to Paco. "Take Tomás with you."

Paco stood and glanced at the young man sitting beside Antonio at the end of the table. "It will be hot tomorrow. We should leave at dawn."

Tomás nodded. "I will be ready."

Raul stood, then nodded a dismissal to the men. After bidding goodnight to Lupita and I, he made his way toward the door.

For tonight, that ended the debate on our future. After I'd bid goodnight to Lupita, I trudged upstairs, took my son from his nurse, and cuddled him to my breast. Should I just sell the ranch and buy a nice house in Tucson or Phoenix? Or perhaps try to lease or purchase a larger ranch, something adequate for the rest of the young horses and the mares? Though Mama and Papa had dreamed that this ranch would be a place of refuge and delight for their grandchildren, they had no idea how powerful the cartels would become. Was it time for me to leave Mexico forever? That thought nearly made me cry, and I'd never been prone to tears. How could everything in my country have gone so wrong?

Eventually, Luis fell asleep. A fierce desire to protect my son washed over me, and not for the first time, I realized how difficult and dangerous it was for those who battled the cartels. For Luis, I would make any compromise to guarantee his safety. But did that mean I would have to abandon the ranch and everything my family had worked to attain? Wearily, I tucked my son into his crib, then trudged to my own bed, less sure than ever that escaping to the safety of America and our Cave Creek ranch was the answer to my problems.

<u>**Chapter 5**</u>

Shortly after midnight, Luis started fussing. I stumbled out of bed, changed his diaper, then slumped into the rocker to nurse him. He was an easy baby to care for, not that it would have mattered. This was our time together, and I treasured these moments in the middle of the night when I'd gotten to know and develop a fierce love for this new little person. Eventually, Luis dozed off. I tucked him under his blanket, but I had a hard time falling asleep. In the morning, I had to make a decision, one that might affect all of us on the ranch for a very long time.

Dawn eventually lightened my room. I was as undecided as ever, and I knew that I would have to call Frederick. We were still on speaking terms. When it came to Luis, whatever problems we had between us were set aside. Though our son lived with me, we had joint custody. There were not specific times for Frederick to visit, and I think we both hoped that later, we would be civil enough toward each other to share him without mandated court orders on visitation rights. At this point, that wasn't looking hopeful, but perhaps with time, that would improve.

The fault was at least partly mine. It started with the child's name. Frederick had always hoped to name a son after his father, Michael. Both his parents had been killed in an airplane crash when he was thirteen years old. Instead of respecting his wishes, I wrote Luis Miguel on the child's birth papers. Miguel, the Spanish equivalent of Michael, was as much as I would give. Frederick's angry and resentful response was nothing new. He'd carried plenty of both emotions for a long time before we actually went our separate ways. And as if Miguel instead of Michael wasn't bad enough, there was my son's first name. That was a grenade I should not have thrown.

Luis Mendoza Valencia had been one of our long-time employees. He'd come to the ranch as a child and had a crush on me since our early teenage years. I admit there had been a short time where the infatuation had been mutual. However, I'd chosen to marry Frederick. In the ensuing years, though I suspected Luis still had feelings for me, nothing happened between us that was inappropriate. We remained good friends. Whatever there had been in our past remained firmly in check.

Though he'd never made any verbal accusations, Frederick apparently hadn't been so sure. When he learned the name of our son, the matter was closed as far as he was concerned. I had loved, and probably had an affair with Luis.

Though I'd not admit it even to myself, I knew in my heart that I'd considered breaking my marriage vows, though only once. It was one of the numerous times Frederick and I were battling. We did that a lot, and in a moment of anger at my husband, I let a completely innocent ranch conversation veer into forbidden territory. However, nothing happened, and for that I will be forever grateful to God. Both Luis Valencia and I would have regretted it immensely.

It wasn't long after that, during a botched robbery at the ranch, when our loyal employee and very good friend Luis was killed in an attempt to save me from death.

His selfless act of love had moved me deeply. Possibly, naming my son after him was not the best way to signal my gratefulness, but by the time our little boy was born, and though it was wrong of me, I cared little for what Frederick thought. My impulsive decision only brought more bitterness and distrust, and God knows, we already had enough of that for any broken marriage.

As I dressed, I tried to shake off the accumulated weariness, though like any new mother, I was learning to cope with the frequent sleep interruptions. After feeding Luis, I turned him over to his nurse. Gracicla was an old friend who often had filled in at the ranch. When she found out I needed someone to help with Luis, she begged for the job. So far, she'd been fantastic, and I was grateful for her tender care of my son.

Downstairs, Lupita had breakfast on the table. Most mornings, Raul joined us, as he had since his wife had died, another casualty of the drug cartels. We, like so many families in our country, would always bear the scars from the lawless reign of our own made-in-Mexico Mafia Dons.

Raul and I sat across from each other. It was my turn to say grace, a ritual to which we'd long adhered. Lately, I'd wondered if we only did it out of habit. Was it that I was afraid that if we didn't say a prayer over the food, God would drop the big hammer on me? Though I'd sometimes mulled through that theological conundrum, I quickly dismissed the thought and reverently mumbled through my standard meal-time prayer. "Bless Us, O Lord, this food to our use, and us to thy service, and keep us ever mindful of the needs of others. In Jesus' name, Amen."

Lupita had declined to join us, which left Raul and me alone to discuss our multitude of current ranch problems. Nevertheless, for most of the meal, we ate in silence.

After Raul had finished, he poured coffee out of the insulated pot in the middle of the table, then leaned back in his chair. "You should go to Cave Creek. It makes sense for me to stay here to look after things. I can keep a few of the less valuable colts here to train. We'll get through this."

I finished the last bite of scrambled egg and pushed my plate away. "No, Raul. We have always made decisions together, so I hope you'll agree. In a way, this ranch belongs to all of us, but ultimately, I am responsible. I am staying here. You are going north with the horses."

Raul's face darkened. He set his cup down and leaned forward. "Why? That doesn't make sense. A woman alone cannot battle the cartels."

"A few have."

"And they are dead."

"If the Jalisco Cartel comes calling, they will kill me no matter which gender I am. Besides, did you forget? We're going to pay them off. We will try to buy peace and safety for our people. That's the only way we can survive."

I stood and turned toward the window that looked out into the side yard in a desperate attempt to hide the fear I felt inside. Raul was right. I would be alone, with very little protection if trouble came. Nevertheless, my responsibility was to the crew and the ranch. I turned and folded my hands in front of me, if only to keep them from shaking.

"Raul, there's another reason for you to go. We need to look for a larger ranch. There's more grass over toward Show Low, but the horses might do better down in those rocky breaks near Benson. See what's out there that would fit our expansion needs. As soon as you find something suitable, we'll put the Cave Creek property on the market. If the cartel problem gets worse, which seems likely, we'll need to have more land north of the border."

Raul nodded, but his eyes flickered from the ceiling to occasional glances at my face as I talked. He knew me well, which meant he saw the fear that laced through everything I'd said. Nevertheless, I'd made up my mind, so I just kept talking.

"We will always keep this ranch that my parents worked so hard to build. Our people here depend on us, which means that for now, I need to stay."

Raul crossed his arms. "You know I can do that just as well, and I don't want you to be in danger. Think of the little one. Take him away from this cesspool of crime. He needs to grow up where it's safe, where he has more opportunity."

"Luis can go to the same school I did. And if we stay here permanently, he can go to high school in Douglas."

"That's not ideal, and you know it."

"And why's that?"

"You will still spend many months of the year barrel racing in the United States. How will that work once Luis starts school?" Raul scooted his chair back and walked to the door. With his hand on the knob, he turned toward me. "Take him and go."

I gathered the condiments and dirty plates to take to the kitchen. "Raul, you are like a father to me, and I respect your opinion. But on this my mind is made up. I'm staying, and I need you to go and take care of our interests in Cave Creek."

"And, my little one, what if I refuse?"

"Please don't. There is nobody else capable of doing what we need done there."

Raul scowled. "Your mind is made up then?"

I nodded. Though I tried to appear more confident than I felt, my stomach churned. I wished Raul would tell me I had to go, that I had no choice. I didn't want to stay and face the brutality and bloodthirsty viciousness of the Jalisco Cartel. But for whatever it cost, I'd had my say.

Raul met my eyes and held them. With a set jaw, I returned his gaze. Finally, he turned and walked through the door. Before he closed it, he turned back. "I will take the first load. Felipe can go with me. I will stay up there, and he can come back and haul the other horses with the big trailer. It will probably take three trips, but he'll get it done."

"That will be great, Raul." I folded my arms and tried to be the manager in control. "I'll make sure the right paperwork goes with each mare when they're loaded."

Raul nodded, then without further comment, he softly stepped outside and closed the door.

My shoulders slumped as I walked to the dining room window and watched Raul stride purposefully toward the barn. He was a big man with hardened muscles from a lifetime of handling horses. His long-legged stride was paced by arms that swung gently at his sides. Despite the gravity of my decision, I smiled, grateful for his calming presence. Raul had always been a cowboy. Others looked up to him. The younger men almost worshipped the ground he walked on. I swallowed the lump in my throat. Now, more than ever, I needed him. This morning had been hard, and I had no idea whether I'd made the right decision.

<u>**Chapter 6**</u>

Three days later, Raul and Filipe left with the first load of mares. We were all nervous about the arrangement. Mares with colts are more difficult to transport, and Raul and I had several discussions on possible configurations so we could move them without making four trips. In the end, we decided it would be safer to take fewer at a time, even if we had to make the extra run north.

Four of the men had Green Cards, which allowed them to live and work in the United States. I'd tried to attain U.S. Residency status for all of our people, but the process took time, and for some of them, because of differing circumstances, it was not possible. The four men that had the proper paperwork were sent immediately to Cave Creek. Two of the men had families. That made it more difficult, but we started the necessary paperwork to move their families to Cave Creek as well. In the meantime, Raul would run the training facility there and begin searching for another ranch with more acreage and carrying capacity.

After the men left with the last load of mares, life settled into a slower routine. Luis seemed to grow every day. It was fun playing with him, and hearing his first giggles. Then, Frederick called. He wanted to come and see our son. I immediately agreed, though I was not at all sure how I would handle his visit. After all, because I was nursing the baby, it wasn't like Frederick could take our son for the weekend or even a day, for that matter, which meant he and Luis would have to visit at the house. I told Frederick it would be convenient for him to come on Friday at noon. Secretly, I hoped he'd have meetings, which meant he'd have to immediately return to Albuquerque. Nobody had more of those than Frederick. Surely, his week would be filled with debriefings, orders for the following week, and who knew what else. To my surprise, he said that would be fine, and that he'd be at the ranch precisely at one o'clock.

Throughout all our tumultuous years of marriage, Frederick had never been anywhere *precisely* at any time of the day—if it concerned me. I'd been stood up more than any wife in the world because suddenly some agent or problem at the office needed his precious time. Do I sound bitter? I guess I am, which meant I wasn't looking forward to being in the same room with him.

As the day approached, I grew progressively more nervous, and of course Luis picked up on that, which affected *his* mood. By the time his father arrived, he was a fussy little boy, which wasn't at all like him.

When Frederick's car pulled into the yard, I took a deep breath and answered the door with Luis cradled in my arm. "Hello. You're right on time. Unusual, to say the least."

Frederick appeared crestfallen. "Dina, I'm sorry for my part in the failure of our marriage. For now, let's just try to be civil. We have many years to regret what might have been."

"Regret?"

"What I mean is, maybe if we'd have tried harder—"

"I think I did. I have nothing to—"

"I know." Frederick sighed. "It's all *my* fault—as usual."

"I didn't say that. You, *as usual,* jumped to your typically erroneous conclusions."

By this time, our voices had risen toward the ninety-decibel level, and Luis had gone from a whimper to a full-fledged howl. He didn't like conflict.

I pointed to the right. "Wait in the living room while I try to quiet Luis. You've upset him, so this may take a while. I'll bring him to you in a few minutes." I turned and strode out of the room.

In the kitchen, I hugged Luis closer to my breast as I mentally shot arrows through the wall at my baby's father in the living room. Nothing had changed, other than I liked him even less. As I marched back and forth, patting and cooing to Luis, I counted the days until I could file for divorce. This was the last of the last straws. I'd had more than enough.

Twenty minutes later, Luis was mostly asleep. I could hardly put off his meeting with his other parent any longer, so I tiptoed into the living room. Frederick stood at the far wall next to the window. Gently, I slipped our son into his father's arms. Once, our hands touched, and I remembered the electric shock I'd felt when that first happened. Now, there was nothing. It was as if my hand had touched a piece of marble or wood. I withdrew my arms from our blanketed child and walked out of the room. Whatever my problems with my soon-to-be ex-husband, I trusted him. He would never hurt our child, and he was too honorable to try to steal him away. Briefly, the thought crossed my mind that a lot of women would think that those were quite redeeming features in a man. I scowled. They could have him—with my best wishes.

Luis lasted longer than I'd thought he would. Frederick was obviously gentle with him. Once, I peeked in to see how they were doing. Frederick walked back and forth, from one end of the room to the other. His big, blond head was tipped down as he gazed at the child. He spoke softly, his deep baritone voice soothing Luis toward sleep. He might be a crappy husband, but he was a good father. Luis was as much Frederick's as he was mine, and I needed to be fair. Whether I liked it or not, my little boy needed his dad. I suspected that mostly, I wouldn't like it, nor would it be convenient. But regardless of what happened in the future, we had a lot of years ahead, and we needed to get along, at least when it came to our son. I shoved my hands in the pockets of my jeans and stared out the kitchen window. Yeah, this wasn't Barbie doll country. Never could I have imagined that this would be my life.

Luis let out a howl, which meant the dad and son bonding time was over. I walked into the room. "He's hungry and probably has a wet diaper."

"I would change him if you'd bring me a diaper." Frederick's look was hopeful, and again the thought occurred to me that even if he wasn't around all that much, he'd be a really good dad to our son.

"You can do that if you want, but I'm afraid I have to feed him."

"Sure—okay. Let me change him, though."

I shrugged. "Whatever." There were diapers in a bag in the dining room, and I went to fetch one. Frederick did a passable job of removing the soiled diaper and fastening on a fresh one. Then he picked Luis up, kissed him gently on the forehead, and handed him to me.

"Thank you, Dina. Let's not fight in front of him—ever. It's not his fault we don't get along, and I want to make his life as good as I can."

Anger boiled up in my chest. Then I saw the tears in Frederick's eyes, and I realized how difficult this afternoon had been for him. He wouldn't watch his son grow up, at least not the way he'd pictured. Their relationship would consist of Saturday afternoons, weekends, maybe some holidays. It was not what any dad would want, and for the first time, I felt his pain. It was intense—and it hurt.

Frederick walked to the big double doors in the entryway. By the time he reached it, he was again composed, apparently devoid of emotion, which was so typical of the man I'd known. "Good-bye, Dina. Thank you, and I appreciate your efforts immensely."

"You are welcome to come next weekend, if you'd like."

"I'm afraid I can't. I would love to, but —"

"There's no need to make excuses." There was an edge to my voice, and I hadn't intended it. "Call when you want to see him again."

He nodded. "I will—soon." He turned and slipped through the door. I walked slowly to the dining room window and watched him drive away. He clearly wasn't happy, and neither was I.

<u>**Chapter 7**</u>

The following Monday, I trudged down to the barn, more to just check on everything than to do any chores. After all, there was little enough to do now in the way of chores. I considered what to do next. Though determined to stay at the ranch, if I was to survive, I needed a plan to keep busy and stay productive. I'd sent most of the young horses in training up to Cave Creek, along with the mares. Sandy couldn't legally immigrate, so Raul had left the five colts he was riding, but they would go as soon as we found a larger ranch to purchase.

The day was still early, the barn pleasantly cooled by the big overhead fans. I walked down the alley, the familiar smells of fresh hay and leather mixed with the more pungent odors of horse sweat and manure. Though most of the stalls were empty, they were freshly bedded and ready for new occupants. Mentally, I went through the two-year-olds that were left. Sandy would ride three or four of them. I would take a couple of the more advanced and quieter ones and work with them. I'd always had my hands full with the older horses when we started them on the barrels. Now, those who were at that level would be in Arizona. For the foreseeable future, we would do nothing here but feed the few colts left while we tried desperately to stay out of the gun sights of the Jalisco Cartel. I glanced at my watch. It was time for Luis's mid-morning feeding. I'd better get up to the house.

When I closed the barn door, I immediately spotted the gun-metal gray pickup in the driveway. A heavy-set man stood beside the open passenger door, his eyes riveted on whoever stood on the veranda talking to Lupita. She blocked the entry, her arms crossed in front of her. As I walked up the path toward the driveway, I could hear her telling the man before her that she didn't know where I was, and that if he'd leave his name, I would call him.

The man seemed disinclined to leave, so I guess it was a good thing I showed up at that moment. He turned and walked toward me when he heard my feet crunch on the gravel.

"Ah, Miss Rodriguez, I don't believe we've met. I am Carlos."

I nodded disdainfully. His smoldering, insolent eyes ran up and down my body. He was either from the government or the cartels. Either one was going to cost me plenty. "What can I do for you, Carlos?" I made no effort to inject any friendliness or welcome into my voice.

"Perhaps it's more what I can do for you, . . . Dina, isn't it?"

"That is my name. I suspect you know it well. Now, what was it you were going to do for me?" I made no attempt to hide the sarcasm in my voice.

His toothy smile faded. "Perhaps I can instruct you on how becoming less insolent might save you hundreds of thousands of dollars. I believe you met a colleague of mine who was treated quite badly. We would like to give you an opportunity to rectify that oversight." The smile had now completely vanished.

Icy fingers of fear trickled right to my fingertips. Why had I stayed? Raul hadn't been gone for more than a few days, and the cartel was already here. Momentarily, I wished I'd not sent him away, but I knew in my heart that his staying would have changed nothing. Involving Raul, or any of the men, would only compound the problem. This, I would have to face alone.

"And if I become less insolent and perhaps offer an apology for the way I treated your colleague, does that mean we get our mares back?" I had no intention of doing either one, but it didn't seem like a good time to tell him that.

Carlos's face gave nothing away. I couldn't tell whether or not I'd guessed right about the mares. He swept his arm to indicate the barns and nearby pastures. "You have a prosperous ranch, Señora. I'm sure you understand that every business decision has consequences. You, of course, have made some regrettable ones, but I am sure we can build an amicable relationship—starting today. I would hope you agree."

"And what about our mares?"

"You must consider their loss a result of your own bad judgment."

Behind me, the other man was rustling around in the pickup. I wanted to turn and see the gun he was no doubt searching for before the bullet smashed into my body, but I refused to look. Never would they see the terror bundled up inside me. However, my head, almost of its own volition, bobbed up and down in agreement.

The smile returned, larger than ever. "When a first offer is refused, the price we must charge is then doubled." He stepped forward to lay one of his greasy hands on my shoulder. I backed away. His eyes flashed with instant anger, and his mouth formed a hard line. "I see no reason to change our policy. The money that guarantees your protection must be paid on the first of every month—ten thousand pesos."

Mentally, I calculated the cost in dollars, simply because that was the currency of our income. Ten thousand pesos meant seven or eight hundred American dollars every month.

"We could never afford that much."

The man's sardonic mouth twisted downward. "Yes, that is expensive, but Ovaldo is now in jail. Because of your actions, someone must now look after his family. I would think that you, Señora, would understand your civic responsibility. I will send a person to collect your donation on the first of every month." He walked across the driveway to the pickup and turned as he opened the driver's side door. "Oh, I should inform you that if your payment is not on time, there is a late fee of another ten thousand pesos."

Like a wooden puppet, I nodded, then folded my arms as if to protect myself from the onslaught against everything we'd worked and strived for. Now, it all meant nothing. The cartels had found us. Our lives would never be the same.

Woodenly, I clumped up the sidewalk to the door. Lupita held it open. She squeezed my shoulder as I stumbled over the sill. Luis was crying, and I kicked off my barn boots and scurried upstairs, too numb and afraid to even think, but I had to. I had a son who needed to eat.

Graciela handed Luis to me.

"I'm sorry for being late. Those men who came? I had to deal with them."

Graciela shook her head in disgust. "The one with the gun is from the town. His parents are my neighbors. He was a good boy, though I think he is trouble now. The other one I have never seen."

"Thank you, my friend. I don't know what I'd do without you."

I rocked Luis, and eventually my heart beat returned to something near normal, which I suspected was much better for my little boy.

"Graciela, you can have the rest of the day off if you want. There's office work to do, so I will be in the house for the rest of the day."

"Oh, that would be nice, but are you sure? Should I stay with Luis, just in case something else happens?"

"No, I'll be fine. Just come in the morning at the usual time."

After Graciela left, I continued to rock my baby boy. Had I been too much of a pushover for Carlos's demands? Should I have insisted the mares be returned if I had to pay? And ten thousand pesos—every month? That was more than I'd heard of anyone ever having to pay, but what could I do? As much as I wished for things to be different in our country, nothing had changed. Once in a long while, a shopkeeper or businessman decided to rebel and not pay *mordida* to the ruling cartel. As I had today, they received a visit. If they refused to see the error of their ways, their brutalized, bloody bodies soon served as a warning to others who might be so foolish. No. As much as I despised the thought of buckling to the terror and extortion of the cartels, they were the law. Here, there was no other.

<u>**Chapter 8**</u>

Though we'd lost five of our best mares, I was grateful that at least the others were now safe from anymore cartel activity. Those that the Jalisco Cartel had stolen produced excellent offspring, and their loss would do serious damage to a breeding program that had taken many years to build. Their monthly extortion was bad enough, but to lose those mares was devastating.

Dejection and a building anger dogged my every step as I strode down to the corrals. Most raw emotions dissipate when challenged by everyday life. Mine did as well. Sandy was in one of the corrals saddling a two-year-old. It was the colt's first day in the round pen. So as not to distract the young horse from his trainer, I stayed well away from the fence. Sandy had already worked the colt for a couple of hours, because the sorrel gelding, though watchful, was calm and comfortable with this man who was now doing things to him that had never before happened in his young life.

Under Raul's careful tutelage, Sandy had become an absolute master. He'd come to us from some tiny pueblo I'd never heard of up in the Durango mountains. In spite of his American moniker, Sandy was all Mexican. His real name was Salvatore. However, anybody at our ranch who had a three-syllable birth name generally got a nickname. Salvatore got his shortly after he arrived. On a rainy, cold morning, a colt he'd pushed a little too hard had caught him off-guard and bucked him off. Salvatore had skidded through the wet sand face-first. It was his bad luck that half the crew had been around to watch the incident, and when he struggled to his feet, his whole face was coated in a thick layer of sand. Only his dark, flashing eyes were visible through the thick mask of sand. From that day on, Salvatore became Sandy. Short and thick-chested, with an unusually dark complexion and curly hair, Sandy now handled horses almost as well as Raul. When two-year-old colts were brought in for their first lessons, Sandy was the one who started them. He built a quiet trust into the young horses, and when the colts were moved on to the trainers who schooled them in the finer points of roping or barrel racing, there was never any doubt who had been their first mentor. They were done right.

Sandy put some weight in the stirrup and immediately stepped back to the ground. He then did it from the other side. Time after time, he repeated the process. Then he'd swing a leg over the horse's back so his whole weight was in the saddle before he immediately dismounted. The gelding cocked a hind leg and let out a big breath of air, now bored with the whole procedure. Eventually, Sandy stayed in the saddle, but by this time, the colt was used to his weight in the saddle. I watched as the horse ambled forward. Sandy petted and praised him, building trust that would last a lifetime.

Minutes later, Sandy was asking the colt to give to the bit. Within the hour, they'd be in the big arena. I grinned and spoke quietly to him before I walked away. "Great job. You're making another exceptional horse."

He smiled, pleased with the compliment. "It is always fun to work with good horses. They are more intelligent, and they learn so fast."

"That is true, but they can also be quickly ruined. I'm so glad we have you."

He shrugged. "I must do my best with each one. That's my job."

Later, while I nursed Luis, I remembered Sandy's rather profound statement. *"I must do my best, because that's my job."* It seemed the whole world would be a better and more productive place if everyone had Sandy's attitude.

On the first of the following month, a hard-faced young man drove an expensive King Ranch Ford pickup into the yard. He swaggered up to the door and announced that Carlos had sent him. I handed over the cash without comment. Receipts, of course, were out of the question, so I had to hope that Carlos really had sent him, and that the Jalisco Cartel wouldn't send someone else to collect again. Nothing further happened, and I breathed a sigh of relief, but I often thought about the missing mares and wondered if there was some way to get them back. Two of them were older mares with big bellies from raising colts. It would take a discerning buyer to recognize their quality. Without knowing their breeding, most buyers would give no more than meat price for them.

For the next couple of days, every time I sat and fed Luis, I thought about the missing mares and colts. Where would the cartel have taken them? The possibility of getting them back intrigued me. The more I thought about it, the more certain I became that whoever had stolen them would have taken them somewhere close until they could dispose of them permanently. Paco had said they'd been loaded in a trailer. Stock trailers large enough to accommodate five mares were still a rare commodity where we lived.

Suddenly, it came to me, and I wondered why I'd been so dense. The Garcia Ranch bordered ours. At one time, our families had been reasonably good friends, that is until Eduardo Garcia asked my parents for my hand in marriage. In our culture, and especially in my parent's generation, that was how it was done, especially in the upper caste society my mother was raised in. At the time, my mother thought my marrying into the wealthy Garcia family was a grand idea. I did not. I didn't love Eduardo, never had, and never would. Later, he became involved with the cartels, and it was rumored that he was now very influential in the Jalisco gang.

I was not privy to Eduardo's rising criminal career, nor did I care. But right now, I had a pretty solid hunch I would find the missing mares right next door on the Garcia Ranch. Twice, I'd scorned Eduardo's offer of marriage. The last time had been bitter. For him, taking the mares would be a small down payment for the humiliation I'd heaped on him. But what was I to do? I couldn't drive into his yard and tell him I thought he was a thief and a crook. Besides, he already knew I thought that of him. And if the mares were on the Garcia ranch, they would be well hidden. The only point in my favor was that we were a ranching community. Eduardo was a part of it, and if life-long neighbors discovered that he was holding our stolen horses, it would give him a pariah status he'd not want.

I finished feeding Luis, then cuddled and walked with him until he fell asleep. When I gently transferred him to Graciela's arms, I kissed his soft forehead. I would have liked to have spent more time with him, but I needed to get back to work.

When I arrived at the barn, Sandy was saddling a sleek, well-muscled brown colt he'd started a week ago.

"That's the two-year-old out of Carmen?" I asked.

"Yes, he's a very quick learner."

I ran a hand over the horse's long hip. "What an amazing colt. I would hardly have recognized him."

"Yes, he really grew over the winter. He will go to Cave Creek next year. Raul can start roping on him. Not too many, of course, and only very light steers. He is going to be very fast."

"Do you think he's too big to run barrels?"

Sandy shrugged. "Who knows? Even the big ones can sometimes be agile and fleet enough. For now, it's important that he get the right start so he is ready to go wherever his talent leads."

"Sandy, can I ask you a question?"

"Of course."

"The Garcias . . . do they have a large stock trailer?

Sandy slipped the breast collar around the brown colt's muscled chest. "Yes, I believe they do." He glanced sharply at me. "When I was in town last week, I saw Eduardo pulling a new aluminum gooseneck."

"How big was it?"

"Oh, about twenty-four feet."

"A trailer that size would hold five mares."

"Easily. So what are you saying?"

I stroked the colt's neck and ears. "Nothing. I just wondered."

Sandy watched me from the corner of his eye as he tightened the cinch. "I don't think we want to have any more of a war with the cartel than we already have. Perhaps we should forget the mares. We've escaped with nobody hurt. We might survive if we just go about our business." He untied the colt, slipped the halter off his head, and eyed me as he gently coaxed the snaffle bit between the horse's teeth.

"I know you're right, but it makes me so angry that they'd just be able to walk away with a hundred thousand dollars' worth of horses with no consequences."

"Are they worth your life?" Sandy paused. "It is not my place to argue, Señora, but the mares can be replaced. Your life cannot."

"Oh, I know, but it makes my blood boil—especially if that sleazy Eduardo had anything to do with it. Anyhow, I'm keeping you from your work. Talk to you later."

I turned and trudged back to the house. Sandy was right. The country was saturated with the blood of those who poked around in what the cartels considered their business. I was well aware of the danger involved, especially after I'd angered them once already. For me, there would be no second chances. Nevertheless, I found it hard to submit to the terrible injustice that had upended our lives.

The five-section pasture on the southwest corner of the ranch was where we'd kept the mares. This was a good day to check the available grass. Now that the rest of the mares had left for the Cave Creek ranch, the pasture might carry a few yearling steers. Besides, at the far end, a high mesa gave a wonderful view for miles, which included much of the Garcia Ranch.

I checked on Luis, then grabbed a pair of binoculars out of the house and jumped into one of the oldest of the ranch pickups. A horse would have been better, but with Luis needing to be fed at regular intervals, I didn't have time for that.

A rough trail wound through the top end of the mare pasture, then dropped down into a dry wash. After a couple miles of bouncing over boulders and debris left by the infrequent floods, I reached the south gate. A half-mile later, the mesa came into view. I parked at the bottom, grabbed the binoculars, and angled up a shale slope to a chute that was barely passable. At the top, I paused while I panted from the exertion. To the north, the slash that delineated Mexico from the United States ran straight as an arrow until somewhere toward Nogales it disappeared in the haze. To the west were the mountains, but it was the flatlands to the south which drew my attention. A few hundred yards from where I stood, the vast Garcia property swept away to the south and east. Occasionally, a sparsely brushed coulee created a gentle ripple in the rolling flatlands. I scanned every inch through the binoculars. Heat waves shimmered in the distance, and a commercial jet far to the west droned its comfortably boring message of safety and sameness. Nearer to me, a couple of white-winged doves cooed their pastoral messages of peace.

A pickup loaded with hay kicked up a cloud of dust along the road that separated our ranch from the Garcia's. Minutes later, the pickup left the border road and turned south along one of their fence lines. There were precious few fences on either of our ranches. The animosity between Eduardo and I had changed a lot of things. Now, there were fences that in the past had never been needed, and not all of them were barbed wire.

In the last few years, we'd lost some cattle, and though there was nothing we could prove, I was fairly certain they'd not died or been pulled down by predators. I moved the binoculars along the track the pickup had taken. Suddenly, it disappeared into a coulee. I perched on a rock and scanned the surrounding area. Twenty minutes later, the pickup reappeared. I raised the binoculars to my eyes. There was no hay in the back of the truck. A tremor of excitement competed with twinges of fear as I watched the pickup follow the road toward the Garcia headquarters. What were they keeping in that canyon that required hay? I was pretty sure of the answer to that question. By the time I parked the truck alongside our other two ranch pickups, my fear had been replaced by a building corrosive anger. I had a plan.

<u>**Chapter 9**</u>

When I arrived back at the ranch, I told no one of my scheme, though I asked Graciela if she could spend the night. Her eyebrows nearly collided with the bottom of her hairline as she harumphed her way into the nursery. My face turned red with embarrassment, but if she figured I had a romantic assignation, so be it—at least for now. She knew I had long-held beliefs on that subject, which made it even harder to walk away without an explanation. But it wouldn't do for her or any of the other ranch employees to know what I'd planned. Graciela's misconceptions would have to be dealt with later.

I hoped what I was going to do wouldn't hold any danger, or at least not much. My hunch could turn into nothing. Just because a Garcia pickup had delivered some hay to one of their remote canyon pastures didn't mean that's where our mares were, but I had to know for sure, and there was only one way to find out.

Just before midnight, I latched the side door silently behind me. I would have liked to have started earlier, but I couldn't leave until Luis awoke for his eleven o'clock feeding. He'd be fine now until just after six in the morning, which should give me plenty of time.

I'd made sure Cholla was in the corral by the barn. Tonight would require a sure-footed and trustworthy horse. I hurried down the rocky path to the barn, saddled up, and rode quietly out of the yard. When I reached the big coulee, I broke Cholla into the little jog-trot he did so well. A half-moon rose in the eastern sky, for which I was grateful. It wasn't enough light, but it would do for my purpose.

Like all our horses, Cholla had spent his early years running through the rough country of the pasture we were soon going to ride through. He never made a bad step, for which I was thankful. I had enough to worry about without having him step into a badger hole or stumble into a barrel cactus.

By the time we reached the rusty back gate at the west end of the mare pasture, the moon had risen to nearly straight overhead. It would have been faster if I'd used the same gate the thieves had used, but I would have left tracks on the road. If I used the wire gate under the mesa, I could cross the road in a place of my choosing and then ride south, far from the road. I wanted no one from the Garcia Ranch to know I'd been here, especially if I was wrong.

When I reached the gate, I dismounted and tried to open it. It hadn't been opened in years, probably since before Eduardo and I had clashed. Since then, the posts had sagged, which tightened the gate even more. It wouldn't budge. I threw all my weight against the gate, trying to pull it close enough to the gate post to release the latch loop on the top, but my hundred and fifteen pounds wasn't enough. I mouthed a few words for which I'd need forgiveness and stepped back. It wasn't the first gate on our ranch that our stupid cowboys had made too tight. I mounted Cholla, unslung the rope on my saddle, and side-passed him up to the gate, then dropped a loop over the gate post and the stay that held the latch loop. I took a half-hitch on the horn and backed Cholla away. The loop tightened and pulled the gate toward the post. Quickly, I jumped down and flipped the latch loop up and out of the way. Once again, I was glad I'd brought Cholla. Though I might have done the same on a colt, it would have taken three times as long, and time was a commodity I didn't have. I threw the gate back and mounted. I'd close it when I returned. There wasn't time now, and the odds of anyone seeing the open gate at this time of night were slim.

Though I knew there was some danger in doing so, I broke Cholla into a slow lope. The sound of drumming hoof beats travels a long way in the desert night, but at this late hour, it was worth the risk. After crossing the road, I angled back toward the south-east and the track which led to the canyon where the pickup had dropped the hay. A half-hour later, when I figured I was getting close. I dropped Cholla back to a walk. The terrain was now rough and broken, and I kept a sharp eye out for any human activity. If the mares were actually here, the cartel may have left someone to feed and guard them.

As I tried to picture what might lay ahead, Cholla quietly picked his way through the rocks and cactus. The only advantage I might have is that the cartel wouldn't expect anyone to come looking for the mares. After all, it *was* the brutal Jalisco Cartel. Their word was law, and absolutely nobody defied them. I grimaced as I followed that thought to its logical conclusion. Only a complete fool would defy them twice.

Cholla suddenly stopped. I needed no more moonlight than what I had to assess the situation. Fifty feet below me, a canyon formed a perfect box with a spring at the far end that fed into a fair-sized pool. The old-time horse hunters had used this canyon to capture wild horses, and I remembered being here once before with Eduardo and a half-dozen other kids. It had been a swimming party, probably somebody's birthday. We'd all ridden our horses out from the Garcia Ranch headquarters to swim in the pond. Everybody had a great time, not at all like tonight. On the far side of the pool, five mares and colts stood in a group. I didn't have to read their brands to know they were ours.

I scanned the area near the mouth of the canyon. A small, adobe cabin squatted against the wall on the south side. A rock fence ran from the cabin to the north wall. A few feet from the cabin, several stout logs served as a gate. I had no illusions. The cabin would be occupied, which meant that any effort to drive the horses out of the canyon would be a problem. Mares and colts make noise—lots of it. If I started them running, the mares would whicker at their babies, and the colts would whinny in panic at their moms. The crazy plan I'd formulated this morning on the mesa to drive the horses back to our ranch now appeared suicidal. What should I do?

I've never taken well to defeat, but there would have been many times when my life would have been easier if I'd recognized that there really is a time to abandon bull-headed stubbornness. It wasn't something I was proud of, and at times I'd asked God to help me overcome it. On that subject, He seemed to have abandoned me. Tonight didn't feel any different. God stayed silent, which meant in the end, my old habits carried the most weight.

I reined Cholla to the right and followed the slope of the land until I could pick my way to the bottom and reach the fence that guarded the entrance to the box canyon. Though I had no idea who I was dealing with in that dark cabin, my fiery Latin blood was up and running strong, which was not necessarily good. I dismounted and quietly slid the heavy poles back that formed the gate. Then I mounted and rode through the opening, and around behind the mares. They eyed me suspiciously. I gave them a few minutes to nervously mother up with their babies as I rode around behind them. When I'd reached the far side of the pond, I repeatedly slapped my nylon rope on my leather chaps, which sounded nearly as loud as gunshots, then whooped and hollered, wishing mightily for my Papa's revolver. I'd have fired it over the mare's heads, and then, if whoever was in that cabin had appeared, I might have blown his brains out. Well—maybe not that, but I would have wanted to scare him badly.

The mares swept through the gate, and they were as noisy as I'd thought they'd be. Mares whickered. Colts whinnied in distress. And me . . . I yelled like a Comanche Indian.

Once, I saw a face at the door of the shack. When I rode by, whooping and yelling, the face disappeared. My gamble had worked. They'd placed a caretaker here, but he wanted no part of a war. I'd tried to make it sound like there was an army outside. It seemed to have worked. I pushed the mares north and to the open gate as fast as they could run. Unfortunately, they ran right up the middle of the road, leaving tracks a blind man could have deciphered. There would be consequences, but tonight I couldn't think about that. I'd rescued our valuable mares. Tomorrow would be soon enough to deal with whatever consequences there might be.

Just after five-thirty in the morning, I pushed the five mares and their colts into a hidden corral in the deepest part of the big coulee. Then I unsaddled Cholla and rubbed him down. By six, I was in the house, just in time to feed my son. The night had been as successful as I'd hoped it would be. But when I slipped my nightie over my head and padded into Luis's room, I wondered how soon I would have to deal with the fallout. Those who ran the cartels weren't stupid, and neither was Eduardo. They'd figure out where the mares had gone. With all those tracks, it would be relatively easy to see they'd been driven back through the west pasture gate. I hoped the cartel would drop the whole issue. They'd stolen our mares. I'd taken them back. Deep in my heart, I knew that hoping the dispute was dead was akin to wishing for the moon and stars to fall from the sky.

<u>**Chapter 10**</u>

After I'd fed Luis, I crawled into bed. Several times, visions of all that might happen for my daring theft of the mares awakened me in a cold sweat. Finally, as the first rays of dawn lightened the window on the east side of my room, I fell into a deep sleep.

What seemed like moments later, the sound of a vehicle rolling onto the driveway brought me instantly to my feet. I stumbled to the upstairs window in the hall. My heart stopped. Two men stepped out of the same black pickup that had been in the driveway yesterday. I recognized the driver immediately. The other man was Carlos. There was only one reason he was here. Quickly, I pulled on pants and a blouse, hurriedly sponged my face, and brushed my teeth. Makeup would have to wait. I slipped on a pair of leather thongs, then hurried downstairs. Lupita had been unable to keep Carlos at bay. He stood inside the entry, so I walked forward with my most welcoming smile.

"Carlos. To what do we owe the pleasure of this visit?"

Some might have been taken aback at my phony greeting. Not him.

"Do you always sleep this late?" he growled.

I regarded him coolly. "I have a baby who is not well. I was up in the night with him."

"Sure you were." He stepped forward, his face only inches from mine. "Do not lie to me. I am well aware of why you slept late." He cocked his head. "Do you think for one minute that you won't be punished for this?"

I refused to look away. "I'm afraid I don't understand. Perhaps you could tell me what you're referring to."

"You, or one of your people, were on the Garcia property last night."

"And—"

"Do not anger me further, Dina. You fail to understand the consequences of your actions."

I backed away from his fetid breath and folded my arms. Inside, dread seeped through every capillary of my trembling body. "And what might that be?"

"I have neither the time nor the inclination to bandy words. I convinced my people to be lenient. We took those horses—instead of your life. Your decision to take them back puts me in an unfortunate position." His eyes smoldered as they dropped to the front of my blouse. His hand moved to my shoulder. I knew the look, the move. Every woman does. His fingers traced down toward my breast.

I stepped back, acutely aware of what this was about. Fear scuttled any semblance of bravery I might have possessed. I shouldn't have gone after the mares. One last time, I attempted a defense. "We have paid, and will continue to pay. Isn't that enough?"

As his fingers dropped to the pockets of his expensive slacks, the smile faded. "Not any longer. Actually, Dina, you can keep the mares. We will consider it an arms-length sale."

His oily voice seemed to slither around me, and even on this hot day, I shivered.

"After all," he continued, "you already have the Quarter Horse registration papers for them, so we're willing to sell cheap. A cash payment of fifty thousand dollars will smooth things over with my people quite nicely."

"That's ridiculous."

He snickered. "Consider the alternative. You have much to live for: a nice ranch, people who depend on you, a little boy who will grow up to be your heir."

My shoulders slumped. Even if we could scrape up that much cash, it would put us into an insolvent operating position. We wouldn't be able to pay wages or buy the necessary feed for the horses. I crossed my arms, determined not to let him see the desperation surging through my brain. "How soon do we need to have the money?"

"Well." Carlos rubbed his hands together as if he was in deep thought. "The horses in question have already been returned to you. I would think that tomorrow evening would be a good time to finish the transaction —in cash, of course. You and I will have dinner at the Bonanza Steakhouse. That venue seems appropriate for such a large and propitious agreement. As the fortunate seller of such good horses, I will, of course, buy dinner. I hope that is acceptable."

I couldn't imagine spending an evening with this killer, but he seemed resolute. Fifty thousand dollars and an evening spent with him. I dared not push the issue further. I'd already angered him. To refuse his demand would either mean my life or the lives of any number of our people. From the beginning, the decision to buck the cartel had been mine. To risk the lives of any of my employees was unacceptable.

I stood as straight and tall as my five-foot-four frame would allow. "I will meet you there—with the money. But I will not be able to have dinner. I need to be home by eight to feed my baby."

"Oh, but you must. That is part of the deal." He reached up and caressed my cheek. Again, I recoiled from his touch. It didn't discourage him, and why should it? He was from the cartel. One way or the other, they got what they wanted. Inside, I trembled. I'd been so sure that my staying here was the right thing to do, and that it should be Raul who went to Cave Creek. Now, fear and a loneliness I'd never known washed over me. Carlos had been abundantly clear. An integral part of the payment was "the evening." He would not be content with dinner and fifty thousand in cash. He expected sex. From the beginning, I'd been in way over my head, and my taking the mares back had made my position a hundred times worse.

Carlos leered one last time, turned, and strode down to the black pickup without another word.

I closed the door behind him, then trudged up the stairs. Even though I'd only taken back what was mine, I now wished I'd left the mares where they were. I'd been forced into a situation from which I might not be able to extricate myself—for any amount of money.

At the top of the stairs, I clung to the banister in a vain attempt to calm my rapidly beating heart. When I picked up Luis, he immediately sensed my distress. Consequently, there wasn't enough for him to eat. I took deep breaths, and tried to sing both of us into a more peaceful mood, which was dumb. He didn't want songs. He wanted food. It all took longer than usual, but eventually, I settled down enough that my physiology worked the way a nursing mom's is supposed to. Luis got sufficient milk to make him a happy baby again. I walked the floor with him until he fell asleep, only partly for his well-being. I needed that extra bonding time to quiet my own heart, to convince myself there was still a God in Heaven, and that He might even be in control of Carlos and the drug cartels. But did He care? That was another question. Would God save me from actually having to give my body to that evil man? And if I had to succumb to that humiliation, would it rescue those around me from further evil? I shuddered with fear and grief. There were no good options. Lupita and Paulina, Graciela and Sandy. Each one was as dear to me as blood family, and Carlos had left little doubt in my mind that if I caused any more trouble, the next lesson would consist of terror and death.

Insubordination to the cartels has always been met with a heavy and brutal hand. At the ranch, we'd been treated gently. Now I understood why. Carlos knew what he wanted. As long as I slept with him, those dear to me would be safe. Never in my life had I ever dreamed I would be in this situation. I put

Luis back in his crib and walked to my bedroom. A small statue of Jesus and the Blessed Mother stood on a shelf in the far corner next to my dresser. Years ago, I'd removed them. Frederick had scornfully called them idols, because in his Protestant-Baptist world, that's what they were. Later, after a thousand arguments and discussions, he mellowed, though I don't think he ever quite understood what they meant to me. They weren't idols; they simply gave every room a focal point, a daily reminder that intercession with God was possible and ongoing. I'd never needed that privilege more than now, and I fell to my knees, pleading for deliverance.

Downstairs, the house phone interrupted my desperate prayer. The caller obviously didn't want to leave a message, because the phone immediately rang twice more. When I couldn't stand the ringing any longer, I picked up the receiver and growled into it, exasperated at whoever thought they were too important to talk to an answering machine.

A deep male voice introduced himself as Errol Carter, an old friend and colleague of my father's. Papa had acquired a reputation as one of the premier smugglers along the Arizona-New Mexico corridor. Valuable contraband, or anybody important who wanted to slip into the United States unobserved, came to the best—my father. Few were aware he was a CIA agent, and that they were monitored from the moment of contact. Even my brother and I had not known of our papa's work with the CIA until after his death. In the ensuing years, there had been occasional visits from people who had worked with my father. Mostly, they were just social occasions to reminisce about the old days, or at least that's what I presumed. Certainly, before her death, Mama had never indicated anything to the contrary.

I held the receiver away from my ear as Mr. Carter prattled on. Apparently, he was in Douglas and wondered if it would be convenient if he dropped in tomorrow afternoon. That was the last thing I needed. It was the end of the month—payroll time. Worse, tomorrow I would have to go to at least three different banks to gather up the cash I would need to make my payment to the cartel. As if that wasn't enough, I had the evening meeting with Carlos the cartel goon for dinner and—and what? Tears welled up in my eyes. I wiped at them as I told Mr. Carter that tomorrow afternoon would be inconvenient. He insisted he would only take a few moments of my time, which was strange. The last 'old friend" of Papa's had stayed all afternoon, eaten with us, and then after Mama insisted, he had stayed the night. To her credit, she did put him in the "blue room." No guests stayed more than a night in that ghastly nightmare of a paint job. Finally, I agreed that three o'clock would be a good time for him to come, but that I had an appointment at four. That was a half-truth, but I did have to put everything together for the evening. I still had no idea what that consisted of, and I continued to mutter prayers to our Father in heaven for deliverance.

After I'd disposed of Mr. Carter, I called each of the three banks where I had accounts and ordered the cash. Most times, it would have taken at least three days to pull out that much money. However, my family had a long relationship with all of them, and each of the banks promised that the currency would be available. I would have been more impressed—and pleased—to have been turned down. It didn't happen, and the night found me tossing and turning, searching for the sleep that would not come. What if I just headed for the border? I had American citizenship. I didn't have to stay here. There was a way out, and yet I knew that for me, there was no escape. If I fled to the United States, the Jalisco Cartel would torch everything that would burn. And then they would start on our people. They would kill somebody as punishment for my sins, maybe two or three. How could I live with that on my conscience? I couldn't.

At one point, I considered calling Frederick. He might have an option I could consider. After all, the company he headed was one of the premier intelligence operatives in Mexico. Whatever failings he had, there was little he didn't know about the drug cartels. But I couldn't do it. Frederick and I had made our break. It wasn't in me to run back to him and ask for help at the first sign of trouble.

The next afternoon, a few minutes before three, a white Avis rental car crunched onto the gravel in our driveway. I was upstairs feeding Luis. When I finished, I handed him to Graciela, then straightened my blouse and hugged her. "I appreciate your devotion to Luis. What would I do without you?"

Graciela smiled. "I hope you never have to find out. I love looking after this baby. I wish you had a husband so you could have more little ones."

"Well, that's not going to happen," I huffed. "Luis will have to do."

I stomped down the stairs. A husband? I didn't need another one of those. Before I reached the bottom, my mind careened back to the night Frederick had proposed. It seemed a century ago, back in Miles City, Montana. I'd driven there to escape from my parents and the Mexican life of my childhood, which included my neighbor and newest enemy, Eduardo. Now, I wondered. Had I really been in love, or had I married Frederick because he'd been my protector and friend at a time in my life when I was especially vulnerable? It didn't seem productive to go there. Besides, there wasn't time.

Mr. Errol Carter stood in the middle of the living room gazing through the expansive windows down toward the barns and training arena. He turned at my approach.

"Dina?"

"Yes, and you're Mr. Carter?" He was younger than my father would have been, had he been alive. Though the deepening tracks around his mouth and eyes, along with sparse gray hair, placed him in the fifth decade of life, he was as trim as any thirty-year-old.

His response was immediate and warm. "I am, and so glad to meet you. Call me Errol, if you would?

"Errol, then. We're always pleased to meet any of my father's old friends and colleagues."

I seated my guest on one of the sofas in the living room. "What can I get you to drink? Would you perhaps like a soft drink, or a beer? Or I will order coffee, if you'd like."

"I would love a cup of coffee, if that's not too much to ask."

"Not at all."

I stepped into the dining room. "Lupita, could Mr. Carter and I have coffee in the living room?" As always, my orders to Lupita were phrased as a polite request.

Lupita wiped her hands on her apron. "I will bring it as soon as it is ready."

I winked at her, then smiled. Lupita and I did our best to do the servant-master routine when we had company. We'd been close friends since I was a little girl. Since then, nothing had changed, nor would it in the future.

I returned to the living room and sat across from my guest on a straight-backed chair, one of the three that Mama had bought for a small fortune at some antique show in Mexico City.

Errol scooted forward on the couch, his hands locked together in front of him. "So, you're a busy young lady. I guess we don't have much time." He peered around the room, but I was observant enough to see his eyes dart back to me at near millisecond intervals. In some quarters, he'd need a badge. He didn't here. He was like my very intelligent brother, Alejandro, and my Papa—typical CIA. I wanted to prod him forward, to tell him I was waiting for whatever message he'd come to deliver. Instead, I sat with my hands folded demurely in my lap, my face as expressionless as I could make it.

"Dina, ongoing support from the agency is one of the benefits that was a part of your father's legacy. Though there have been periodic visits from the staff, I don't believe that has happened for awhile."

I nodded. "Yes, we have had several visits, but none since my mother died."

"I'm sorry. We should have done better. Though we're mostly concerned with the spouse, it doesn't mean we walk away from the rest of the family. I might add that your case is even more of a concern because of your brother's ongoing involvement with the agency. Anyhow, my reason for coming this afternoon—"

At that moment, Lupita walked through the door, her arms laden with goodies. She unloaded it all on the coffee table in front of the couch where Errol sat. "Is there anything else you'd like, Señora?"

I glanced at the tray. It was filled with sugar cookies, two plates with generous helpings of Tres Leches cake, cream, sugar, and of course, a whole pot of coffee. I glanced at my friend out of the corner of my eye. "No, Lupita, that will be more than sufficient." I hoped this Mr. Carter didn't plan to stay long enough to eat all of Lupita's goodies. I didn't have that much time, and so far, I'd heard nothing from him I didn't already know. I offered a plate with cake to Mr. Carter, then poured the coffee.

He accepted gracefully and continued to talk. "As I was saying, I came here not only to reiterate our support, but to let you know that we are aware that the Jalisco Cartel has put some pressure on you. That is of great concern."

I munched on a cookie while I considered how to answer, but my decision was instant. To tell this man of Carlos's demands would put everyone on the ranch in even greater danger. We would have to handle this without any outside help. It was the only way we could survive.

Errol set his coffee cup on the table in front of him and leaned forward, his hands clasped together. "We'd like to help."

"How did you know?" I asked. It was a stupid question, one I would have liked to take back. No CIA agent would ever divulge that kind of information. However, Errol was polite.

"It's our job to know."

My already clenched hands tightened. "I appreciate your concern, but we don't need help—yet."

Errol studied my face, and I knew he saw through my fear. Slowly, he stood. "Please, Dina, don't wait too long to ask." He smiled down at me. "You're your father's daughter, no doubt about that, but we both know how dangerous these people can be. Just be careful."

I wondered what "careful" meant. If I'd ever needed help, it was now, but for this man to call in the long arm of the CIA would undoubtedly cause more trouble than we'd ever seen. Those agents didn't live here, nor could they protect our people, the ones like Lupita, who didn't have an American green card or passport. She couldn't run. Her only choice was to stay and face the horrors that

were sure to come. It wasn't in me to abandon
her.

Chapter 11

Despite turning down Errol Carter's offer of help, I had at least a small amount of hope that if our situation at the ranch became desperate, we weren't alone. But my hands trembled as I thought about tonight. I would have to pay the fifty thousand dollars in American greenbacks, but to have anything more to do with the detestable Carlos was unthinkable, especially now that we had an offer of outside help.

I hurried upstairs, fed Luis, and tucked him in bed before I put on clean clothes for the evening. I chose my usual ranch attire. Dressing up for dinner with a drug cartel goon I despised was *so* not going to happen. I stood in front of the mirror and daubed my usual minimal amount of lipstick and eye liner for going to town. Makeup and I maintained a distant relationship, and certainly tonight, I wanted to appear as unappealing as possible.

I stopped by the pantry and fished through the plastic bags for one of the larger ones. Would one bag be enough to carry fifty thousand dollars? I calculated the number of hundred dollar bills I would need. It seemed sufficient.

After visiting the three banks, I had a mixed wad of American hundred-dollar bills and Mexican one-thousand peso notes. Nervously, I stuffed the money in the bag, then stashed it under the seat, the only place in the pickup I could think to hide it. I had an hour before I had to meet Carlos at the Bonanza Restaurant, but even if I'd had shopping to do, it seemed foolish to leave that much cash unattended in the pickup. For lack of another plan, I drove home. After I'd spent a few minutes with Luis, I trudged downstairs. Lupita sat at the small kitchen table, making a list of grocery items prior to her weekly shopping trip.

She glanced at me as I entered the room. "I thought you said you would be in town this evening?"

"I'm just leaving. I wanted to run home and feed Luis first." I tried to keep any fear or worry out of my voice. It didn't work, at least not well enough to fool Lupita.

"What's wrong?" She laid a hand on my arm.

"I can't tell you." My voice cracked. "Just say a prayer for me."

Instant concern clouded Lupita's eyes as she followed me out the front door. I couldn't have told her what I was facing, even if I'd wanted to, at least not without breaking down completely. If she knew what I might have to do tonight to protect her and the others at the ranch, she would never let me go. But there was no other way. I started the pickup while Lupita stood on the veranda, her features dark with worry. I waved and pulled out of the yard before I lost what little resolve I had.

The restaurant parking lot was crowded when I arrived, not unusual on a Friday evening. I found a place to park off the street and stepped out of the truck. Carlos and another man immediately appeared out of the darkness.

"Ah, Dina." Carlos's voice was even more ingratiating and oily than before, if that were possible. "You're right on time."

I reached into the cab and pulled out the bag.

"No, leave it there for now." He nodded at the other man. "You, Sebastian, must make sure the lady's money is safe."

Carlos turned to me. "Now is a time for pleasure. Business can be conducted later." His lips pulled back to reveal his large, white teeth. Though they appeared menacing in the dark parking lot, he held out his hand. "Come, we have a table waiting for us."

A table? Reservations had never been necessary at the Bonanza, but perhaps he'd made one, anyhow. He walked me inside, his hand on my elbow. I moved away from it whenever I could. When I couldn't, I steeled myself not to recoil at his touch. He headed toward the back of the restaurant, his arm now at the small of my back as he steered me to a private alcove. Two waiters nearly ran backwards in front of us as they cleared the way for our arrival. I couldn't help it. My lips flattened in anger at their obsequious behavior. Their fear was why the cartels had so much power, but then, I guess it was no different than my own. We all kowtowed to the cartels—because we wanted to live.

One of the waiters seemed to recognize me, and as he pulled out my chair and waited for me to be seated, a shadow flickered over his face. He hadn't needed to speak. His denunciation of my companion was written large across his features, and my face flushed. As quickly as his censure had appeared, it vanished. Even so, Carlos had noticed. He scowled and dismissed the waiter rudely.

"You." He pointed at the other one. "I will have a Tecate." He named a popular Mexican brand of beer.

The waiter nodded politely, laid out menus, and glanced at me. "And for the Señora?"

"I will have a Coke."

"Certainly."

The waiter left to fetch the drinks, which left me alone with Carlos. It would be a long and fear-filled evening, and I sent up my own prayer that God would deliver me. The sooner this could end, the better I'd like it. I crossed my arms and leaned as far away from the man across the table as I could. "I have your money, but it's not all in U.S. dollars.

Some of it, I had to get in pesos. I hope that is okay."

He waved his hand as if to dismiss the subject. "We can discuss that later. Let's get to know each other. I hope this will be the first night of many."

My heart dropped into my shoes. It wasn't that I hadn't expected this, but to actually hear it verbalized made me want to jump up and run to the far end of the continent. One night of degrading misery was one thing. What if there were more? I couldn't do that.

I'd never been a good actor, so I'm sure the horror I felt scrawled across my face like graffiti on concrete. I swirled the ice in my glass and stared into my coke. If I looked at him, he would see the revulsion. I couldn't let that happen. For the sake of those who depended on me, I had to go through with this.

Music blared in the background, one of the many *narco-corrido* songs that had gained notoriety along the border, songs that glorified the exploits of those like the man who sat across from me. I tried to concentrate on wht Carlos was saying as he commented on my hair. The last thing in the world I cared about was what this man thought of my hair, or anything else. However, I nodded and forced a frozen smile. Had Raul been right? Should I have gone to Arizona while he stayed here at the ranch? Inside, I wailed at my vulnerability. Raul would have been much better equipped to deal with the scum that sat across from me.

The waiter arrived. I ordered a salad. Actually, at the Bonanza, if you didn't like what we referred to as *carne de res*, you were in the wrong restaurant. They had every cut of beef imaginable, including tripe, which was a local favorite, but not much else. I had no appetite for any of it, but I had to order something.

Carlos signaled the waiter to bring him another beer, then continued regaling me with his importance. I had no doubt that in the world of the Jalisco drug cartel, he was a rising star. After all, he had the authorization to make fifty thousand dollar cash deals. He likely also had the authority to order my execution, as well as every other person on the ranch. That was the only reason I was here, and as much as I wished the situation was different, I had to accept reality. The cartels were more powerful than any local police force, and though there were rumors that we were going to receive a contingent of *Federales,* so far, it hadn't happened. When it did, there would be war, and everyone in the surrounding area would be caught up in it. In the meantime, we had to survive, and going to the police was probably the fastest way to earn a cartel bullet. Rampant corruption and a nearly non-existent justice system were the order of the day. The sooner one realized that, the better chance you had at survival. Fortunately for me, Carlos liked to talk about himself. Intelligent answers from me were not required. He wanted me for one reason only. Brilliant conversation was not a prerequisite.

Both waiters arrived with copious quantities of food. No one ever left the Bonanza hungry. The waiter I'd been acquainted with had my large bowl of salad. Carlos watched him closely, his mouth sullen and hard. Both men set the dishes on an adjoining table while they moved napkins, condiments, and drinks out of the way. As in all fine restaurants, setting the food in front of us was a ceremony. It was done at precisely the same moment. Both waiters backed away. Carlos nodded his approval and dismissed them.

Tonight, a piece of lettuce would have been more than sufficient, although I doubt Carlos cared whether I ate all or any of what was put in front of me. His eyes were more focused on my cleavage than the food in front of him. I picked at my salad, forcing a few bites down, but my stomach felt like a war zone, with the bad guys winning.

Three tables to my left, two men signaled for their bill, paid it, then left their seats and walked by our table. Probably because I was so scared and looking for any possible escape, I noticed that one of them had shown more than a passing interest in Carlos after we'd sat at the table. As they passed on their way to the door, neither of the men looked our way. Then they disappeared into the night, and I slumped further into my chair. I'd hoped . . . no, that was unreasonable. I shouldn't have expected any outside help. For a few moments, I concentrated on my salad, but after a few bites, I could eat no more. My stomach churned with dread. I prayed to God for deliverance. Wasn't there some way to escape? What if I refused Carlos's advances? Yes, that's what I would do. I would find some other way to protect our people. To let this man violate me was more than I could do.

I pushed my chair back and stood.

"Restroom?" Carlos's eyes slid down my body.

I would have gladly used the restroom for an excuse and then bolted, but they were at the back of the restaurant, which meant there was no way outside except past our table. That dodge wouldn't work. "No, I'm afraid I'm sick. I have to go home."

Carlos set his fork and knife down, then pushed his plate away. "Good try, Dina girl." He threw several hundred pesos on the table, stood and kicked his chair back, taking my arm. Resistance seemed futile as he hustled me outside and into the dark parking lot.

His malevolent chuckle and following words sealed my fate.

"I guess if you're sick, we must get our business over with as quickly as possible, but I doubt there's anything wrong with you." He grabbed me by the shoulder, spun me around to face him, and jammed his fingers into my throat. "I wanted to be gentle with you, but you're a lying little witch. Your kind are best handled with spurs. Get in." He punched the key fob in his hand and opened the passenger door of a late-model pickup. I bit back a sob as I crawled into the passenger seat. How could this happen? Now, my decision to stay at the ranch and protect my people seemed like foolhardy bravado.

The smart thing to do would have been to pay very careful attention to where Carlos was taking me, but I was too distraught and scared as he drove through the back streets of our town. Eventually, he pulled through the gates of a walled compound, which made me realize I might be in even bigger trouble than I'd thought. What if he wouldn't release me? What would happen to Luis—my baby?

"Get out."

I pushed open the door and stepped onto the concrete.

Carlos walked around the front of the pickup and took me by the hand. "Let's go."

My heart pounded in a resounding drum beat of defeat as he pulled me up the stairs and through the marbled entryway. My boots clicked dully on the polished floors as he led me to a massive bedroom on the main floor. He locked the door, kicked off his shoes, and pulled his polo shirt over his head.

"We can make this easy or hard. Your call." He stepped in front of me and pointed at my blouse. "Take it off—now."

Tears of anger stung my eyes. "No."

I never saw his hand until it rocketed my head sideways. "You really don't understand. Do you know who I am?"

I staggered back, trying to stop the exploding Roman candles in my head.

He strode forward and I cowered against the wall. "Please don't do this. I will give you more money."

His open hand shot out and connected with my jaw. I dropped to the floor, now barely conscious. Somewhere in another world, I watched my bra and panties slip away from my now naked body. The violation started. It went on and on, and I could do nothing about it. Tears streaked my face, and once I called out for Frederick. Where was he? More important, where was God? What had I done to deserve this? All I'd wanted to do was protect those who depended on me. Eventually, Carlos rolled off me. Like a wounded animal, I crept across the floor and searched for my underclothes while he dressed.

"Get your clothes on. You're the worst piece I ever had."

I didn't reply. There was no response I could think of to the violent rape I'd endured. Would he let me go, or was my fate now to join the thousands of other women who had disappeared and died at the hands of the cartels? I found my pants and blouse and pulled them on as quickly as I could. My body now seemed reprehensible, a disgraceful object to be covered and hidden away, even from my own sight.

"Come on. We still have business." Carlos opened the door of the bedroom and beckoned me to follow.

I pulled my boots on and stumbled after him, unable to think or function, other than by direct command. He led me back to the pickup.

"Get in."

I scrambled into the passenger seat. This time, I forced myself to pay more attention. The house was in the south sector of the city. Though I didn't get a street name, I was sure I would never forget its location.

Ten minutes later, we arrived at the Bonanza parking lot, and suddenly a thought ricocheted around my brain. After I handed Carlos the money, would he kill me? Was that all he was waiting for?

Carlos parked in an alleyway, a few steps from the ranch pickup I'd brought to town. "Get the money."

I nodded like my head was on steroids. If the money would give me freedom, I wanted him to have it. To get away, to never see this man again, was the agonizing cry that spewed from my innermost being. I stumbled to the ground and hurried toward my pickup, fumbling through my pockets for the keys. Like all modern vehicles, when I punched the button, the parking lights came on and the driver's door unlocked. I opened it and scrabbled for the bag under the seat. My hand touched it, and it was as if I'd pulled the trigger on a whole arsenal of guns. The night erupted with gunfire. I whirled in time to see two gunmen pouring bullets into the white Silverado. Carlos, the Jalisco Cartel goon, died in a hail of lead. The *Sicarios*, whoever they were, stepped into a gunmetal gray Nissan pickup and disappeared down the street. As they passed me, I could have sworn they were the two men who had been in the restaurant, but I may have been wrong. The point was—I didn't really care. I shoved the plastic bag of bills back under the seat and walked over to Carlos's still idling pickup. Carlos's head and upper body were slumped over the console. Blood and spattered body material ran down the steering wheel and dripped onto the upholstery. I am a Catholic and a Christian. I try to follow my Savior. He says to love your enemies. Tonight, I could not do that. I hated that dead piece of cartel crap with every fiber in my body. I wanted to spit on him. I didn't, but I spit on his pickup.

<u>Chapter 12</u>

I wasted no time in putting plenty of distance between me and the Bonanza parking lot. When the police arrived, there was no telling whose side they'd be on, and I wasn't about to take any chances, not with a sack full of cash under the seat of my truck. From town to where I turned off onto the track that led to our ranch, I let the tears flow. It was the only breakdown I could afford. When I got home, I had a baby to feed, people who needed my attention, and a ranch to run. What crying I had to do would have to be on my own shoulder.

I parked in my usual spot, and slipped into the house. I wanted to see no one. Luis would be okay for a few more minutes, so I slipped into the shower and tried to scrub away the shame and loathing. It didn't work, but for a few moments, I felt better. Later, when I sat with my little boy in the nursery rocking chair, I wondered if he'd ever find out his mama had been raped. I hoped not. More than anything in the world, I wanted this night to go away, for the memory to forever die. I knew in my heart of hearts that wouldn't happen. What had transpired in that house on the south side of Agua Prieta would never go away, and unless God did a miracle, it had the potential to destroy my life.

I kissed the top of my little boy's soft, downy head and tucked him in his crib. In the hallway, an avalanche of tears once more broke through my hastily constructed bulwark against a complete breakdown. It was as if my whole world, the carefully constructed story of who Dina Rodriguez really was, had only been built of cheap packing crates and twine. Why had God abandoned me? What had I ever done to deserve the degrading violation I'd experienced tonight? I had no answer, and no banner rolled out across the night sky to inform me where I'd gone wrong. I needed peace. I needed answers, and when I needed them the most, there were none.

When Luis woke me for his early morning feeding, the events of the previous night all seemed like a nightmare until I clambered out of bed. My whole body felt dirty, as if I'd been violated all over again, and I had to wipe tears of resentment and anger away before I forced myself to walk into the nursery. This was not a time for *my* feelings. My son needed me.

In the days that followed, I slogged through each hour, trying to hide the turmoil that threatened to overwhelm me. Though I'd determined not to dwell on what had happened, I was seldom successful. For hours on end, I sat huddled in the upstairs rocker, my arms wrapped around my chest.

On one level, I understood that if I was to survive, I had to let go of the bitterness and anger from Carlos's rape. Sadly, it didn't matter what I knew to be true. The deluge of emotions wouldn't go away. Once, I wondered who had killed my rapist. Had it just been a cartel hit? After all, the Jalisco and Sinaloa Cartels were bitter enemies, and assassinations were as common as petty theft. Or was there more to it? Had that Errol guy from the CIA been involved? I wasn't to know. He never called, so a week later, I called my brother, Alejandro, in Washington. He never answered his phone, but he would usually return my call if I left a message. I asked him to call my cellphone number and headed for the barn. There were too many neglected chores, and it was time I pushed aside what had happened.

When Alejandro called, I was in the barn office checking employee schedules and reassigning work projects. Two of our regular stable hands were off. Pancho's wife was having a baby, and Mateo had a sprained ankle. He would be back tomorrow, though probably only capable of light work. I glanced at the number on the call display and quickly answered the phone. "Hey, brother."

"How you doing, sis?"

"I've been better."

"Oh, no. What's wrong?"

"We're having some issues with one of the cartels."

"Which one?"

"The new one. Jalisco. They stole some horses."

"Horses. Why would they steal horses? What did they want?"

"I had a run-in with one of them in town. They put the squeeze on me and I refused to pay. So they took some mares. Anyhow, we got them back." I couldn't tell Alejandro anymore, or I would start crying, so I just kept talking. "What's happening in Washington?"

"Same old stuff. They're talking about a transfer. I guess they figure I need some overseas time."

"Oh,no. Where will they send you?"

"Right now, it sounds like Venezuela. Not a good posting, but better than Iraq or Libya. Anyhow, I gotta' run. How about I call you tomorrow evening?"

"Sure, but one thing before you go. Can you find out if someone actually works for the CIA?"

"Absolutely. Why?"

"A man called me last week and said he'd worked with Papa. He came to the house, and we visited."

"Did he show you his credentials?"

"No, I never thought to ask."

"What was his name? I'll check him out."

"Errol Carter."

Alejandro chuckled. "Him? I don't have to check anything. He's more than legit. In our father's era, he was a legend. Anyhow, how's the little guy?"

"Luis is doing great—getting big fast."

"Good. Give him a hug from his uncle. Talk to you soon."

"For sure. Be careful, and start looking for a better job so you don't have to go to Venezuela."

I slipped the phone into my pocket and strolled out into the alleyway, glad that whatever reservations I'd had about my CIA visitor had been answered. Today, all the stalls were empty. The few horses we still had here in training were quartered in the outside pens. I leaned over one of the stall doors as the familiar smells of fresh bedding, alfalfa hay, and horse wafted into my lungs. I would never be able to tell Alejandro about the degrading violation I'd suffered. What had transpired in that house on the south side of our town was a wrapped-up ball of hurt buried deep inside me, an ulcerating tumor of shame and anger I could never expose—to anyone. For me, to even speak of the rape was impossible, because it would instantly bring back all the horror and shame, and that I could not do. That was all fine, but no matter how hard I tried to erase that evening from my memory, my every waking moment was haunted. I gripped the boards of the stall in front of me as deep, sobbing breaths wracked my whole body. If I was to survive, I had to leave this place forever. If I didn't, it would only be a matter of time until I succumbed to the growing tumor of guilt and shame. If that happened, my life would be over, and I would be of little value to those here at the ranch who depended on me. The choice before me lay stark, unforgiving. I'd never been one to take the easy way out, but though I had no vision of the future, I knew I had to make decisions I'd not have ever considered before if I was to remain in the land of the living.

The following morning, I entered a couple of rodeos, both well within driving distance. When I hung up the phone, I packed up everything Luis and I would need and left the ranch—for how long, I did not know. Though I hadn't figured out how I was going to compete when I had a baby to care for, it didn't matter. My need to be far away from here had catapulted far above every other commitment. I would deal with ranch decisions that needed to be made when they came.

My barrel racing horses were always kept at Cave Creek, so getting horses across the border wasn't a problem. At the ranch, I left Sandy in charge. Though I phone-coached him a few times a week, he showed exceptional skill in handling everyday problems. I didn't know how long that would be necessary, but for now, I had no choice. If I was to survive, I had to leave Mexico and the ranch.

Though I still didn't know who had killed the Jalisco Cartel gangster who had raped me, when I crossed the U.S. border, it was as if a huge weight was lifted from my chest. It would have been nice if that would have lasted, at least to Tucson. It didn't. When I drove into the yard at Cave Creek, the guilt and horror had all returned, along with my hate and anger. No border could contain it, and no wall could insulate my heart from the wrenching pain that refused to go away.

At our Cave Creek house, I set up a little bed in my room for Luis, then got him settled for a nap before I walked out into the warm evening air. The summer weather here wasn't like the cool Montana evenings, but it was more bearable than the constant heat of Sonora. My gaze flickered around the premises, searching for all those signs that immediately indicated management problems. Nothing jumped out to warn me of impending trouble. Raul worked a colt in one of the arenas. It was close to the house, so I sauntered down to watch and talk to him. He saw me before I reached the fence and rode over.

"I thought it was you." He grinned. "What's the occasion?"

"Long story. I'll tell you later. How are things going here?"

"Fine. We sold one of the four-year-olds yesterday. That big bald-faced bay colt of Tia's."

I nodded. "Who bought him?"

"R.J. Branger."

"The team roper?"

"Yeah."

"I hope he likes him. R.J. has been to the National Finals, and him buying one of our colts is good advertising for us." I stepped back and surveyed the jet black filly Raul was riding. "Hey, is that the filly out of Rosita?"

The trim and lithe mare had socks halfway to her knees and a snip in her face that ran halfway to her eyes.

"Yes. She's so big and athletic, and she's only a three-year-old."

I grimaced. Rosita had been one of the mares I'd retrieved from the Garcia Ranch. Raul noticed my immediate disapproval.

"You don't like her?"

"No, it's not that. We've had some trouble at the ranch. Some of the mares ended up missing, and Rosita was one of them. We got them back." I held up a hand. "I'll tell you about it later."

Raul eyed me anxiously, but finally nodded.

I didn't wait for him to ask any more questions. "Anyhow, I entered Payson and Farmington. I hope my horse is in shape."

"Benito? Yeah, Felipe has been exercising him at least three times a week. He should be fine."

"A steady campaigner like him doesn't need much. Has he been ridden today?"

"Not that I know of, but I was in town for a couple of hours. Felipe is in the barn saddling a horse right now. Check with him."

Raul started to ride away.

"Raul, do you think I should take the young horse instead?"

"Cisco?"

"They're not big rodeos. It might be a good place for him to get some experience."

"Your call, but yeah, this might be a good opportunity. If he messes up, it's not going to cost you a fortune."

"I'll ride him this evening. Then, I'll make up my mind."

As I walked back to the house to check on Luis, I thought about Cisco. Was he ready to be pushed that hard? He had a flighty, high-strung personality. If he failed, it would be a spectacular wreck. But he could run like the wind, and I really needed another solid horse. I'd been so lucky with Benito. He was steady and fast. Until now, he'd never had an injury or a bad day, but that wouldn't last forever, and I needed another horse to ride if the worst happened. There was only one way to insure against that event. I needed to start packing

Cisco down the road. He'd never get the experience he needed to become a solid barrel racer if I left him at home.

At Cave Creek, we all ate together. The property had come with a spacious, two story ranch house. The dining room dwarfed our eating quarters at Agua Prieta, so all the crew ate in the main dining room.

After the meal, the crew left, it seemed an opportune time to give Raul an update on what had happened with our mares. What I would never tell him were the events afterward.

Raul's eyes searched my face as I told him how I'd driven the mares back onto our ranch.

"And after you retrieved the mares, you haven't heard from the cartel again?"

I shook my head, knowing that my story had just become larger and more unbelievable. I'd never lied to Raul before. It was not a good feeling, but there was little else I could do. For him to know and do anything about the rape would only place him in danger, and that I could not have.

<u>**Chapter 13**</u>

As quickly as I could, I scooted away from the table to avoid Raul's eyes. He'd known me since the day of my birth, and he had a curious way of seeing right inside me. The guilt written on my face would give me away, so I rushed outside to saddle Cisco as I swallowed the tears that threatened to give me away. I took a deep breath, pushed away my other horrific life issues, and stepped into the saddle.

It wasn't that a last ride would make Cisco any more ready than he already was, but I wanted to lope around the arena and make one run around the barrels, more to give me that last touch of confidence than to do anything for him. He was in top form. I just wasn't sure I was ready to take him to rodeos where the competition would be world-class. And yet, I had to if I was going to discover whether or not he had what it took to be my back-up barrel horse. He had blistering speed, but whether he had the heart and steadiness of a champion was quite another story.

Later that evening, when I unsaddled him and turned him into one of the larger box stalls in the barn, I'd made up my mind. Cisco deserved a chance. He was ready.

After I'd put Cisco away, I moved down the alley to Benito's stall, which was even more luxurious. When he trotted up and stuck his head over the door, I gathered his smooth, silky muzzle into my arms and scratched his ears. He was different than any horse I'd ever had. He seemed nearly able to understand every word I spoke, in Spanish or English. "Benito, my friend, you get to stay home this week. We have to give the kid a chance to learn to play the game, so sometimes you can have a day off. I hope that's all right."

Benito rubbed the side of his head against my arm. I hoped that meant he was okay with my decision, but the next morning when I led Cisco out to the trailer, Benito whinnied, shook his head, then half-heartedly kicked at the back of his stall. I could have sworn he was frustrated and angry at being left behind. Nevertheless, I loaded Cisco into the spacious trailer stall usually occupied by Benito, checked Luis's car seat again to make sure it was fastened correctly, and left the yard. I had a full day's drive ahead of me to Farmington. It was a night performance, so I'd have plenty of time. I might need it. Travelling with a baby was a first, and I had no clue what I would do with Luis. How was I to get Cisco warmed up, and then compete, all while taking care of Luis? While I drove, I stewed over the logistics, but when I arrived at the rodeo grounds, I was no closer to a solution.

Luis was asleep which made it easier to do my usual rodeo routine. I unloaded Cisco and watered him. Later, I saddled up and rode around outside the arena while I kept an eye on the truck and Luis. Cisco, wide-eyed and watchful, seemed to be settling into the fact that though there were lots of strange horses here, he was not allowed to stop and visit with each one. I wished now that I'd at least taken him to one or two smaller jackpot barrel races. However, we'd have to make the best of it. For Cisco, it was like this was his first day in Hollywood. It would take many more trips like this before he settled into the routine.

Cisco was just loosening up from the long trip when my baby started crying. I tied Cisco to the trailer and picked up Luis to nurse him. How was I going to do this? What if he started fussing tonight, just before I was due in the arena? Carefully, I studied the program. It was a seven o'clock performance. The bareback riding was first, followed by the tiedown roping, then the saddle broncs. That should take the performance to about eight, give or take a few minutes. Luis should easily be asleep by then. Then there would be steer wrestling. The barrel racing event would be just before the bull riding. At the earliest, that would be nine o'clock. Luis had never been awake at that time, so there shouldn't be a problem. A number of acquaintances and friends rode by. Several stopped to meet Luis, and for a few moments, I got to do the proud mom act. I had no problem showing off my handsome little boy with his dark face and blondish hair.

Before the rodeo started, I needed to ride Cisco inside, so that when we broke out of the alley and into the lighted arena, everything would be familiar. Rodeos were different than even the largest barrel racing jackpots. There was more noise and action, usually far more people in the stands, which could be a distraction, not to mention the additional pressure from running down that alley into an arena filled with artificial lighting and shadows. It's what every one of my competitors would be doing, showing their horses the routine. I loped Cisco around the perimeter of the arena, just to get him used to the layout.

When I arrived back at my rig, I picked up Luis and tried to get him to nurse again. It wasn't really the right time, and instead of going to sleep, he started fussing. Panicked, I searched the parking lot for help from somebody I knew. Perhaps one of my friends had brought their mom or their favorite aunt along, and they wouldn't mind watching Luis for just a few minutes while I made my run in the arena. There was nobody. Eventually, though the car seat was not his bed, Luis fell into a fitful sleep. It was plain to see that he wasn't at all sure he liked his sleeping arrangement.

I heard the announcer clear the arena. They were setting up the barrels. I was fourth on the list. Panicked, I glanced at Cisco, then Luis. Would I have to leave my little boy unattended in the pickup while I raced? I couldn't do that. I breathed a wild, inarticulate prayer. It was then that I saw Parker Collins trudging across the parking lot, his bronc saddle slung over his shoulder. He was a friend of mine. In different circumstances, we could have . . . well, that didn't matter here.

"Parker," I yelled at the top of my voice.

He changed direction and walked my way.

"Can I ask a huge favor?"

"Anytime."

"Can you watch Luis while I run? I thought . . . I thought I could get somebody —"

Parker grinned as I stepped into the saddle. "You better get with it. And I ain't changin' no diapers, so you better hurry back."

I smiled and blew him a kiss. Right now, I didn't care what he thought. I was just grateful for his being here for me in the nick of time.

I loped through the pickups, trailers, and assorted mobile living quarters until I reached the back of the arena. The second barrel racer, Tracy Adkins, was running the pattern and doing well by the looks of it. I edged as close to the front of the arena as I could. Cisco snorted nervously, and I reached down and patted his neck. I needed to settle him down if I was ever going to get him to make a decent run in there.

I didn't know the next girl. Her horse slipped on the second barrel, and had a difficult time recovering. I studied the ground. The top was too sandy, and the base looked dreadful. I'd better keep Cisco collected. As hard as he turned the barrels, we'd go down in that soft dirt, especially on the second one. He had a tendency to take a wild run at that second barrel and . . . it was our turn. The loudspeaker belted out my name, along with whatever stats the announcer knew, which seemed to be everything in my career. I pulled my hat down and popped Cisco with the bat. Whoops, I shouldn't have done that. It was something I did with Benito. He was always so laid back, it was just the way I told him to wake up, and let's get going. Cisco bunched up, as if asking, "What'd you do that for? What did I do wrong?" I gritted my teeth in anger at myself, but it was too late. We hit the arena running hard. I pointed Cisco at the first barrel, and he never faltered. He dropped his shoulder into the turn and came around it hard. He was powerful, talented. His ears flickered forward, and he found the second barrel. I tried to collect him as he changed leads, and then he slipped. There was no base, and Cisco struggled to keep his feet under him. We lost precious milliseconds, and then I made my second mistake with the bat. I didn't even pop him. I just laid it on his neck. Cisco fell apart. He was a young horse, and the confidence I'd spent months building into him fled. He lost it, and when we rounded the third barrel, it was so far away I don't think I could have even roped it. We still had a respectable time, which told me what I already knew. Cisco had talent, but I would have to figure out how to manage it. I was the one that had to learn—not him.

<u>**Chapter 14**</u>

I hurried back to my truck after my run. In the distance, I could see Parker leaning against the pickup box, his arms crossed in front of him. His worn bronc saddle and gear bag lay at his feet.

He grinned at me as I rode up. "You're just in time. He was fussing. I was dang scared I'd actually have to do something. How'd it go in there?"

I chuckled at his exaggerated fear. "Not good. This is Cisco's first rodeo. We'd have done better, but I messed him up. It wasn't his fault."

"Well, in lieu of a decent babysitting wage, I think you should buy coffee."

"Of course. I'm so grateful for your help." I reached into my jeans and pulled out a five dollar bill. "You go get it while I look after my little guy."

"You're on." He reached for the bill and scissored it out of my hand with two fingers. "Be back in a jiffy."

Ten minutes later, Parker returned, carrying two large cups of coffee. I opened the tailgate of the pickup, and we sat side by side. He handed me a cup, and I pulled the flap on the lid back. "How'd you know I like it black?"

"Oh, I just did."

"Not fair . . . lucky guess?"

His eyes roved over my face, but not in an uncomfortable way. "Not really. I make it my business to know about my friends."

His tone touched a chord I wanted to remain concealed, but the trailer shadowed his face from any of the arena lights, and I could tell nothing. Still, the tone of Parker's voice flashed a warning. I chuckled, but the sound was brittle with my too-recent pain. "Sure you do," I joked. "Are you going to Payson tomorrow?"

"Yep. Got a good one there."

"Which horse?"

"Firewater."

"I remember him from the Circuit Finals. He's hard to ride."

"Can be. But it's the only decent horse I've had in two weeks, so I better cowboy up and get him rode. I need to win some money."

I chuckled softly, suddenly glad to be sitting on a pickup tailgate, just visiting, making small talk with this cowboy. Parker Collins was comfortable to be around. I'd never felt the undercurrent of pressure for a one-night stand, or for that matter, anything else.

We finished our coffee. I held out my hand. "Here, give me your cup. I'll take care of it."

Parker handed the Styrofoam cup to me and picked up his saddle. "Holler if you need me to keep an eye on junior while you make your run tomorrow. I'd be glad to do that for you."

I wished it wouldn't have been dark, so I could have read his eyes. "Hey, thanks. I really appreciate you bailing me out."

His voice floated back to me as his form faded into the gloom. "Anytime. See you at Payson."

I turned back toward the lights of the arena. It was all over. The crowd pushed toward the parking lot, as if to be last was to lose your place in some mythical line. I thought about Parker, and hoped desperately that I'd read too much into what he'd said earlier. The last thing in the world I was looking for was a man, and certainly not one my female colleagues would have derisively referred to as a "catch and release." Maybe someday, it would be different, but that was a long way away. For now, the thought of any man in my life was almost more than I could manage.

We got an early start for Payson, another lesson in motherhood. Luis wanted feeding at his regular time: six in the morning time, and after that, as usual, he wanted to play. I'd fixed a little bed alongside mine in the tack compartment of the trailer. It wasn't great, and I wished I'd taken the big trailer with its more adequate living quarters. We were only spending one night away from home, so I'd thought we could manage, but it had been a mistake. Luis wanted things the same as they were at home, and I was finding out the hard way that if he wasn't happy, nobody else was going to be, either.

I nursed him, then tried to lay him back in his bed. He wanted none of that and fussed until I sat up and held him. I had a snuggly he could ride in, so I dressed and wandered out to check on Cisco. Most babies would have been afraid, but Luis thought it was great fun when Cisco stuck his muzzle next to Luis and tickled his face with his whiskers. By the time Luis finally looked sleepy enough to go to bed, I was more than awake. I loaded Cisco, and we headed down the road to the next rodeo at Payson. Luis slept at least half the way, which meant I only had to stop a couple extra times during the trip to change diapers or feed him. I was beginning to understand that this was a part of my being a mom on the road. Once, I reached over and caressed his fat, little leg. He was a good baby. If we had to stop a few more times, so be it.

I wiggled into a contestant parking spot at the Payson Event Center. After unloading Cisco, I watered him. There were still two hours until the evening performance; so once again, I tried to make Luis as comfortable as possible. Meantime, I kept an eye out for Parker, hoping he wouldn't forget his promise. Cisco appeared to have resigned himself to all the people and noise, which was good. This was even worse than last night for a young horse, so I made a point to ride through the pickups and trailers, all the time in sight of where I'd left Luis. Though this was an outside event, riding in the arena wasn't an option. They had an afternoon and evening performance, and the arena staff was now busy grooming the turf in preparation for tonight.

Once again, the first time Cisco would see the inside of his stage was when the bright lights hit us as we dashed through the gates. I reached down and caressed his neck. "This time, we're going to do good, my friend. You've got worlds of talent, and we're here to show these folks how fast you can run. We're in this together, and tonight, I'm going to help you do your very best."

As I rode back to the trailer, I hoped my pep talk would help both of us, because if we didn't learn to trust each other and work as a team, we'd not have much of a future. I'd seen it often in others. Good rider, great horse, but they couldn't mesh. Tonight was our night.

I stood on the tailgate of the pickup during the bronc riding. I wanted to see Parker ride Firewater. It wouldn't be much of a view from here, but there was little I could do about that. I couldn't leave Luis alone, even if he *was* asleep in the tack compartment.

Parker apparently was the last of the bronc riders, which meant he had the feature horse. If I stood on my tiptoes and leaned far out to the side, I could see the chute where he was carefully slipping his feet into the stirrups. He nodded his head, and when the gate opened and Firewater bailed into the arena, it was apparent to everyone that Parker was at the top of his game. Halfway through the ride, I could no longer see them, but from the sounds of the crowd, Parker had made a good ride. Then there was a big ooh and aah, and I wondered what had happened. It didn't take long to figure out everything had stopped while they packed Parker out on a stretcher. I asked one of the timed-event cowboys who rode by what had happened.

"He did the fancy jump-off right in front of the pickup man and got run over. Broken leg, I think. Anyhow, they packed him out. Those crazy bronc rider guys shouldn't be doing that. It's too dangerous."

I reckoned if those "crazy bronc rider guys" were worried about doing dangerous things, they wouldn't get on bucking horses in the first place, but it didn't seem productive to point that out. My immediate problem was that now I had nobody to watch Luis while I made my run. I peeked inside the tack room. Luis was sleeping quietly. Softly, I closed the door and tightened Cisco's cinch. I'd be gone —what . . . ten minutes? Luis would be fine. I was parked right in the middle of about thirty rigs, all rodeo people, contestants I saw fifty times a year. Even if they weren't all friends, everybody looked out for each other. Not a one of them would leave you stranded on the road with a flat tire. No, Luis would be just fine. Ten minutes—that's all I needed, and then we'd be on our way home.

I mounted up and loped Cisco in a few wide circles, then pulled the bat out of my hip pocket and chucked it at the pickup box. I didn't want him to even see it in my hand. Where he'd picked up his fear of that little piece of leather was beyond me. Actually, I think it just hurt his feelings. Last night, it was like he'd said, "Hey, I'm trying as hard as I know how. Why did you hit me?" I shook my head, again chagrined and embarrassed. I should have known better.

By the time the barrel racing started, Cisco was as calm and collected as he'd probably ever be. I'd stopped him by the trailer one more time and listened for any sounds. There was nothing. Luis was still asleep. I trotted toward the arena. I would be the second-to-last racer tonight. I waited for my turn, walking Cisco back and forth, keeping him quiet, building confidence, letting him know that though there was more noise, this was just like at home.

When our turn came, I trotted him to the gate before I broke him into that long-legged, smooth run he did so well. We hit the first barrel, and he scooted around it fast. At the second barrel, I cringed, hoping he'd be able to power into the turn without remembering our near fall last night. We made it, my inside foot so low to the ground that it scared me, but at the same time, I marveled. What an athletic colt. When he headed toward the third barrel, he was in overdrive. I wanted to check him early. He'd never slow enough to make a decent turn at the speed he was going. Nevertheless, he did, and when we hit the home stretch, he had wings. We went out the gate still flying, and somewhere in the distance, I heard the time. We'd gone to the lead by a wide margin, and it was pretty much a cinch we'd keep it. Several girls rode over and congratulated me while eyeing Cisco covetously. That was good. I wasn't sure he was for sale, but if he was, tonight had escalated his value by at least ten thousand.

We trotted back to the trailer. I jumped off, and before I even haltered Cisco, I tiptoed up to the door of the tackroom and quietly opened the door. The little nest of blankets I'd made was still there, but there was no Luis. My baby was gone.

Chapter 15

I must have screamed, because suddenly there were faces all around me. Some were familiar, though I was too distraught to put a name of any of them. Somebody found a security guy, who called the police. Between sobs, I blurted out the story. I'd left my baby, and now he was gone. My good friend Connie Mack had a spare spot in her trailer, and was headed to Phoenix anyhow, so she offered to drop Cisco off at Cave Creek.

The officer who had responded to the call took me to the police station, where I talked to a detective. He did his best to answer each of my frantic questions. Had they cordoned off the rodeo grounds?

They had.

What about the highways in and out of Payson?

He assured me that every exit in and out of the town had been blocked a half-hour after the call had come in.

That was too late. I knew it. Luis was gone, and at that point, I had to make the phone call I dreaded. Frederick had to know.

Luis was his son as much as mine, and though his reaction would be volcanic when he found out I'd left Luis alone, there was nothing else to do. During a lull in the conversation, I pulled out my cellphone.

Instantly, the detective had his hand out. "No—no phone calls yet."

"Why? I need to let his father know."

"Where is he?"

"He lives in Albuquerque. When we divorced—"

The detective's lips hardened. He leaned forward, his eyes searching my face like he'd stumbled on the Holy Grail. "How long have you been divorced?"

"Six months, a bit more I guess."

"Tell me about the father."

"Listen." I stood, and paced to the far side of the room. "Frederick would not take our child. Our separation, like most, was bitter. But for whatever he lacked as a husband, he is a good and honorable man. He would never in a thousand years take Luis. Besides, what would he feed him? I'm nursing him."

"What is anyone going to feed the boy? Pablum, baby formula, or whatever else you call that stuff? Nutritionally, he will probably survive, though admittedly not as well as if he was with his mother."

I shook my head. "Whatever you think, let me call Frederick. He didn't do it, so let's not waste time and resources there."

He pushed a phone across the table. "Use this one."

"So you can record the call?"

He shrugged. "Our experts will do a voice analysis."

"Whatever." Exasperated, I pulled the phone closer and punched in Frederick's cell number. It was now an hour from midnight. Even Frederick didn't usually work this late. And though he wasn't on speed dial anymore, we had a son together. For the foreseeable future, he would be in my contacts list, and I would know his number. Frederick answered on the first ring. In ten years of marriage, he'd not done that more than twice. Why now?

"Frederick?"

"Of course."

"Yes, well, I just wanted to tell you that . . . that—" Desperately, I tried to choke out the words, but they wouldn't come. All I could do was weep, the fear growing like some monstrous genie let out of a bottle. The detective held out his hand. It wasn't the way I wanted it to be. I should be the one to tell Frederick that our child was gone, but I didn't resist. I handed the phone to him and listened to the one-sided conversation.

"Mr. Roseman? This is Detective Bert Logan with the Payson Police Department. We received a report from your ex-wife tonight that your son is missing."

The detective listened to whatever Frederick was saying. "Yes, it seems he was taken at the fairgrounds on the edge of town."

The detective nodded. "Yes, this is very hard. I've been in this business for thirty years. Some things never get easier."

I watched the detective close his eyes, as if he hated what he was about to say. "No, at this point we have no leads. But we were able to react early. That vastly increases the odds of finding the missing child."

Though I hardly cared, Detective Logan opened his eyes and caught me staring. "Certainly, you are welcome to come, but it may be more productive for you to stay there and—"

Frederick had clearly cut him off. He nodded again, though this time with a hint of frustration. "Oh, I understand completely. Sure, when you arrive, come to police headquarters."

So Frederick was coming here. That wasn't a surprise. We'd sit together in the police station and pretend. No, we wouldn't have to do that. Whatever we'd had died a long time ago. We didn't have to pretend anything. We had a son whom we both loved, and we needed to focus on that. The other baggage didn't matter anymore, and even if it did, I had no intention of dragging it to the surface. I hoped Frederick felt the same.

After the detective hung up the phone, he turned to me. "At the beginning of an investigation, we follow every lead, and certainly estranged spouses are usually at the front of the line. In your case, that doesn't seem likely, but I'm sure you can appreciate the fact that we still need to cover every angle."

I wiped away a few more of the many tears of recrimination and fear that had periodically flooded my face since I'd opened the tack compartment door and found Luis missing. The detective's body language said we were done here. He didn't want or need any more of my input to carry on with the investigation. I tried to understand, but inside, I screamed in anger and fear.

"Where can we reach you?" The detective leaned forward, his pen poised over his yellow scratch pad.

Woodenly, I rattled off my cell phone number and gave him Frederick's as well.

"And where are you staying?"

"For now, can I just sit in your public area? I want to be as near as possible so when they find him, I—"

He nodded before I could finish. "That's fine, though it's not very comfortable. If you leave, let the front desk know where you can be reached." He handed me his business card. "Do you have any friends here —somebody who can stay with you? If we don't find him right away, it could be a long night."

I shook my head and glanced at my watch. "I'll be okay."

Even if I would have had a close friend in the vicinity, I didn't want to share the guilt that fluttered over my head like a flock of screeching, black ravens. This was my fault. I never should have left Luis, not even for five minutes. Frederick would be here in three hours, and I would spend the rest of the night trying to avoid his accusing eyes.

My brain repeatedly lashed me with the evidence. I'd left my baby. I deserved Frederick's condemnation.

How I wished I could go back and do it over. Of course, I couldn't. During those long hours of police department mayhem, I tried to justify my actions. Luis had been asleep in the trailer. What could be safer? Ten minutes. It couldn't have been longer than that, but now he was gone. Never had I been so full of fear, because at the bottom of my heart—I knew who had taken my baby.

Chapter 16

Two and a half hours later, Frederick stalked into the reception area of the Payson Police Department. I sat hunched in a chair against the wall on the far side of the room. When he saw me, our eyes clashed, unhampered by any of the warmth or gladness that had once characterized our meetings. I suppose that's what happens in marriages that go sour. The excitement of seeing each other becomes routine, then mundane, without any of the vestiges of joy that originally defined the relationship. It's all chipped away until all that's left is a frozen core of tolerance. The negative events relentlessly grind away the happiness, eventually destroying the love, until one day there is nothing, not even disdain or scorn. That is now what I felt. The sparks that had once defined our relationship were now only a distant memory.

Frederick walked slowly toward me, his face frozen, devoid of emotion. He stopped. Three feet between us. This would not be a huggy moment. We'd had precious few of those at the best of times, and I doubted either of us in this present circumstance was inclined differently. But tonight, we had a child we both loved who was in great danger, and whatever other problems or trials we had were insignificant compared to that. I waited for the angry accusations that surely must rain down on me.

Eventually, Frederick spoke. "Would it be better if we sat?" He indicated the chair I'd vacated.

"Yes, I suppose it would."

At least if we sat, we didn't have to play pinball with our eyes. We could sit side by side and stare at the far wall while he told me what a crappy mother I was.

Frederick lowered his big frame into the chair one over from where I sat. There would be no accidental touching, and momentarily, I wondered if other divorced couples were as careful as we were about physical contact. My mind drifted through the years. There was a time when we couldn't get enough of that. How had love turned to disgust?

I squeezed my hands together, trying to keep them from trembling. This was not the time for blame or self-recrimination over our marriage. Luis had been kidnapped. I grieved. Frederick did as well. We couldn't solve what had happened if we focused on our own issues. It was important that we talk, so I tried.

"Okay, I guess you want to know what happened."

"That would be a good start." Surprisingly, his voice wasn't sarcastic or accusing.

"I hope you know that despite our differences . . . I know you think—"

"Please." Frederick held up one of his hands. "This is about Luis, not about us or our relationship. Can we agree to keep it to that?"

Anger at his interruption threatened to overcome the sadness and fear in my heart. "Certainly. I couldn't agree more. I was just trying to . . ." Suddenly, the horror of what I'd caused was more than I could cope with, and the tears I'd sworn would never come while Frederick was here rolled down my cheeks.

"Frederick, I'm so sorry. I left him alone for a few minutes. It wasn't supposed to be that way, but I had to be in the arena, and —"

" You don't have to explain or make excuses." He stared at the log beam overhead. "Dina, whatever you are or aren't, I have no doubt you're a good mother. So let's get that out of the way. You made a mistake. We both have plenty of those to our credit. So, let's move on."

I daubed at the tears and nodded without actually looking at him. *If* he was able to move past my leaving Luis unattended, I appreciated it more than he could ever know. But for what I'd done, I could never forgive myself. My little boy was gone, and if the kidnapper ever smuggled him out of the country, I would never see him again. Of that, I was certain.

"I think I know who has him. I never told the police, but I'm quite certain the Jalisco Cartel took him to punish me." Out of the corner of my eye, I watched Frederick lean toward me, and I knew without looking that his piercing, blue eyes were searching my face. He was an intelligence agent. He trusted nobody, including me.

"Why the Jalisco Cartel? There's a bigger story here, isn't there?"

"There is, but I had no idea they would be able to strike here in the United States."

He grimaced. "Any of the larger cartels have the capacity to strike anywhere they want in the world. But here, it is very easy for them. So tell me why you think *they* have our son."

For most of the next hour, I related everything that had happened at the ranch. He listened, asking frequent questions.

"And Raul is still at Cave Creek?" he asked.

"He is."

"So there's nobody at the ranch but a few cowboys and the house staff?"

"Yes, but I'm going back as soon as Luis is found."

"Why?"

"Because it's mine. I need to look after it, which is something you never—"

"Never understood? Really, I don't think it's productive to go there."

I squeezed my hands together, angry at my unfeeling stupidity. "Yes, I didn't mean to bring that up. Forgive me."

Frederick nodded his head. "I do."

There was little I could say after that, and though I wanted to doubt his sincerity, I couldn't. He was right. Our focus needed to be on finding our son.

The space behind the counter at the far end of the room had been empty since Frederick had arrived. A uniformed policeman now appeared behind the probably bullet-proof glass and began to shuffle papers. Once, he glanced at us. His eyes settled on Frederick for a moment. Several times, he picked up a phone and talked, and I wondered whether his calls were related to our dilemma, or if he was just a disinterested dispatcher.

Somewhere past three in the morning, Detective Logan walked into the room. He didn't look like a detective. His iron-gray hair was nearly as rumpled as his short-sleeved shirt, and the trousers he wore had grass and dirt stains on the knees. Wearily, he trudged across the room and held out a hand to Frederick as he introduced himself. Frederick nodded a polite greeting.

I couldn't wait for the detective to speak. "Have you found him?"

He shook his head. I'd hoped the rapid response team would have been in time to apprehend the kidnapper. It didn't happen, and at this point, I need to be completely honest with you. It's been six hours since your baby was taken, and the odds of us finding him have . . . well, it gets more difficult as time passes. There may be contact from the kidnappers for a ransom. Then, of course, everything changes, so we need to keep our hopes up.

"What are the odds of finding him?" Frederick asked.

The detective didn't hesitate. "If this isn't a ransom situation, then not good. Baby-napping is a lucrative business. A quick sale could easily net the kidnapper twenty thousand."

Giant vise grips of fear clutched at my chest. Luis gone forever? That could never be. The thought was too horrible to even contemplate. "You have to find him."

"Ma'am, we're trying. I have every available member of the force—"

"Can't you call the FBI?" I burst out. "Anyone more capable than this backwater bunch of losers? You should have found him by now, and what's more—"

Frederick laid his hand on my shoulder. "Dina, they're trying."

Tears stung my eyes. Somewhere in the back of my mind, I knew I'd lost it, that there was no rational reasoning in my accusations. But now, nothing else mattered. My baby was gone. He was hungry and cold, and maybe afraid, and I couldn't fix it. Nothing in my life had ever ripped at the visceral, innermost part of my soul like this. I jerked away from Frederick's hand and stumbled out the door and into the night with hot tears streaming down my cheeks and clenched fists. I would never see my baby again. In my mother's heart, that was a sentence worse than death.

Chapter 17

Emotionally exhausted and mindless of anything other than my pain, I trod the sidewalk in front of me. Sometime later, I collapsed beside a parapet that in better times had held a fountain. Now, in the drought that gripped all of the southwest, the dry concrete carried no water, not that I cared. Somewhere beyond the limits of my grief and incoherent anger, I knew the odds of finding Luis were now nearly non-existent, but I had to try.

Through every back street and alley, I listened for the cry of my baby—and prayed, though even that was a lie. The words that spewed from my frozen lips were not a prayer. They were a no-holds-barred attempt at a bargain. "God, if you bring Luis back to me, I will . . ." The ante on my end of the deal increased, directly proportional to His silence. As time passed, my belief in God as the author of love faltered. At this, the most traumatic time of my whole life, when I needed Him the most, the God of my childhood, the all-powerful, divine being I'd always believed in, was absent—gone.

I must have slept, because the rough fieldstone wall behind my head had worn raw tracks in the back of my skull. I didn't care. I wished only for death. I strained against the hard surface, my body huddled into the fetal position, and that's where Frederick found me. I didn't want to be discovered, least of all by him, but when he cradled me in his massive arms it felt like I was protected from the worst of the wrenching fear and grief. There was no longer love between us, nothing sexual, and only a distant memory of the comforting, familiar caresses between a husband and wife. Those emotions had long since fled, chased away, pounded to oblivion by the indifference of distance and separation. His embrace was purely platonic, a good man who had gone out of his way to offer aid to a grieving and broken stranger, and I appreciated it. For a long time, I cried. They were frightened, desperate tears, lonely tears. Somewhere in the midst of them, I understood that God did care, but it was a long time before I could put Luis into His loving arms and know that He could and would take care of my baby.

Sometime later, Frederick spoke into my silent, tortured world. What he said seemed like such a man thing. "Would you like to go eat?"

"Eat?" My voice trumpeted the anger and desperation of the long hours since I'd opened that trailer door to discover Luis was missing. Didn't he understand *anything*? Our baby was gone. How could he think about food?

Gently, he pushed me away and stood. "Yes, eat. I'm not hungry, but despite everything that's happened, you need to take care of yourself, because if you don't, you can be of no help to Luis."

"Food is the last thing on my mind."

"I understand, but you need to eat—for him."

My overfull breasts told me that I needed Luis more than I needed food. Nevertheless, I shrugged an unwilling acceptance, and Frederick drove through the breaking dawn to a small corner restaurant a dozen blocks away. We ordered, and when the waitress slid my plate onto the table, it might as well have been sawdust. I pushed the contents around on my plate and tried to take a few bites. What should our next move be?

What if the police didn't find Luis tonight? Suddenly, I could stand it no longer. I shoved the plate away, my hands trembling as I shrugged into my jacket.

"We need to go back to the police station. Maybe they've found something about Luis."

Frederick carefully placed his fork on the side of his plate. "They have my phone number. They have your phone number. If anything—"

"What if they lost them? Maybe a new dispatcher came on shift, and he doesn't know who to contact."

"Dina, they are professionals. That doesn't—"

I didn't hear what else he had to say, nor did I care. I bolted through the door, and with tears sliding down my cheeks, I hurried back to the police station. I had to know what was happening.

Five blocks from police headquarters, Frederick caught up to me in his car. Silently, I slid into the passenger seat, only because I would reach my destination more quickly. Luis would be there, or the police would have found something about the kidnappers so that we could get our baby back. When Frederick pulled into the parking lot, I was out of the car before he'd even properly stopped. I rushed into the station and up to the desk, sure that there would finally be news. The desk sergeant was new, polite, and firm. There were no breaking developments in the case. Luis, my precious baby was still missing.

I turned and stumbled toward the front door before one more gathering storm of tears exploded. How had I thought . . . ? Frederick met me on the steps and guided me toward a park across the street. Picnic tables huddled together in the grassy expanse that butted up to a playground. We sat across from each other, and once more, I could no longer contain the ache in my heart. Later, when it seemed every last tear had been expunged from my body, I wiped at my eyes. There was nothing more I could do. If I could have given my life to bring Luis back, I would have done it in a second, but I couldn't. I rummaged in my purse for more tissues. I'd failed my little boy. Now, I could only wait and pray.

In the meantime, life carried on. Frederick gave me a ride out to the rodeo grounds where I'd left my pickup and empty horse trailer. I glanced across the car. His face, as usual, showed no emotion. He could do that better than any man I'd ever known.

I clenched my hands together, my fingernails biting into my palms, wondering whether my thoughts were fair. Frederick was hurting as much as I was. It's just that he was better at hiding it. I spoke, attempting to keep my emotions in check. "I'm grateful for you coming, for being here." That didn't sound right. Why wouldn't he? He was Luis's father, but I didn't know what else to say.

Frederick cleared his throat, turned, and stared down the street. "I will call every day, and just so you know, the company will put every effort into finding our son. If this is about a drug cartel, we have resources that are unavailable to other agencies. Probably by the end of the day, the FBI will be involved, so we have to be careful. But if the cartel took him across the border into Mexico, we'll have agents on it immediately."

"But Fredrick, who can you trust enough to manage this? If Luis ends up in Mexico, can't you go down there yourself?"

Frederick sighed. Actually, he didn't sigh like most people do. The side of his mouth tightened while he let out his breath, and the moment of common cause and warmth between us instantly vaporized. To me, it was the "you are so dumb" look. There were times when I might have deserved it, but the response always hit my anger button because it was like I was just another one of his agents. I'd never tolerated it well, and it was probably one of the top three issues that led to our divorce.

When he spoke, Frederick's voice was measured and slow. "Dina, there are a number of reasons that one of our hand-picked professionals can do this better than I can, the first one being the color of my skin. Second, as you know, I don't speak the language any better than a low-level tourist, which means I don't have the skill set to survive in that environment. I am very good at hiring agents that have all those attributes, plus a few more. They are men I'd trust with my life—or our son's life."

Frederick stuffed his hands into the pockets of his fake jeans. Anything but a suit on Frederick looked fake. He was not a casual guy—never had been. His shoulders slumped as his eyes battled with enemies I could not see. Seldom had I seen my ex-husband so distraught, which I guess meant he was worried and afraid. So was I, and in a perverse way, it was comforting. It meant he cared deeply, and that what he'd spoken was from his heart. That's what I needed to know, because whatever differences we had, which were many, if Frederick cared that much, he was a force to be reckoned with. Whoever had been foolish enough to take our son had better run far and fast.

Over the years, Frederick had risen to the top of an organization that had gathered immense credibility and power in the intelligence field. They had people and contacts rivaled only by the U.S. Central Intelligence Agency, which meant that whatever other issues I had with my ex-husband, I couldn't ask for a better partner in our present circumstance. If there was any way to get results, Frederick had the tenacity and connections to do it.

I stepped forward, and we hugged, as opposite sex business associates, a big step

down from lovers who had married and
pledged their lives to each other. I tried not to
think about that, and he probably did as well.

<u>Chapter 18</u>

When I pulled into the training facility at Cave Creek, the whole crew, including Raul, was there to meet me. Luis's kidnapping had made the national news, so everyone knew the details, at least those presented by the major networks.

I stepped out of the pickup, hugged each one of my people, and thanked them for their prayers. Frederick, because of his position in Stirling Associates, had over the last twenty-four hours become the dominant parent, and not only on the news. Until I heard from him, there was little more I could do to find our son. All I could hope for was that there would be a ransom note.

Day after agonizing day passed, with no communication from the kidnappers. After the third day, I called Frederick, though I knew if he'd heard anything, he would have notified me immediately. But still, I wondered. Did he actually have people working on the case? And if they were, was that their first priority? There had never been any doubt in my mind that Frederick loved his son, but he'd loved me as well, and too often,

I'd seen his devotion to his agents preempt any of my needs. In his life, I played second base. That had been a bitter pill to swallow. Stirling Associates was his life. Now, I wondered. Did Luis reside in second position as well? I had to presume he did, which meant I had some difficult decisions, ones I didn't want to make.

A week after I'd arrived in Cave Creek, a white, nondescript government car pulled into the yard. It was early morning, and I watched from the sunroom as two men stepped out onto the paved driveway and surveyed their surroundings. They strode up the red brick path to the front door. I didn't need to be told they were intelligence agents. From the time I was a little girl, I'd been around their kind. I could spot them a mile away. It didn't matter whether they were CIA, FBI, or any of a host of other alphabetical agencies that cluttered the border. They reacted the same.

At the official and carefully correct knock, I immediately opened the door. The two mid-twenties crew-cuts on my veranda might have been male clones. Both were well-dressed, medium height, serious demeanor, one my hair color of brown, the other a Nordic blond. With appropriate name tags, they could have passed for Mormon missionaries. I wanted to push them away, refuse to hear their pitch. Instead, I tucked away my distrust, tamped down my anger, and invited them into my house—after they'd showed their badges and introduced themselves. They pulled out stools at the island counter.

"Would you like coffee?" I offered. Both appeared grateful, and nodded. I poured the black liquid into two mugs, refilled mine, and sat on the far side of the counter.

"So, you have news of Luis?" I asked fearfully.

The agent with the light pencil eyebrows answered, "No good news."

"And . . . ?" My voice squeaked downward into silence and dread. I didn't want to hear what they had to say. It couldn't be good, or they wouldn't have started the conversation this way. They would have told me they'd found Luis, that he would be in my arms tonight, or at the latest by tomorrow morning. It wasn't to be, and I knew it.

"We have found no trace of your son, which means the kidnappers may have succeeded in taking him out of the country." The pronouncement came from the shorter of the two, the one I presumed carried Mexican ancestry. He spoke perfect English, with less accent than I had.

I glared at him. "How did that happen? I thought you guys were on it, that you had the border sealed."

The brown-haired clone squeezed his cup with both hands and stared into the black liquid before answering. "Thousands of vehicles cross the border every day. It is logistically impossible to search them all. Besides, the kidnappers may not have crossed at Nogales or Douglas. They could have gone through at any one of a half-dozen other transit points, or they may have just walked across in the desert."

I took a deep breath and tried to rope off the anger that boiled up inside me. Probably, they had tried, at least as much as any government agency tries. At the end of the day, they would go home, leave the office problems behind—while I, and the multitude of others they had failed, wept buckets of tears.

"I can't accept that. You've done nothing to find my son."

Both men leaned forward in their chairs and placed their hands on the table, nearly in unison. I searched their faces, trying desperately to ferret out a fragment of truth.

The Nordic blond spoke. "Miss Rodriguez, that's not true. We have six agents on this case. We've done everything we can do, and have come up empty-handed. Are we frustrated? Better believe it. Every lead we've followed has turned into a dead end."

At that moment, something died inside me, and I refused to listen to the rest of their spiel. If I was to find my son, I could no longer depend on the police or federal agencies. I would have to rescue Luis myself. The last thing in the world I wanted to do was go back home and face the Jalisco Cartel, but if that's what it took to find Luis, I would do it. I would not wait for Frederick or the agents in front of me.

I twined my fingers together and squeezed my hands to keep them from trembling as I spoke. "I do appreciate you keeping me informed. Although the news you've brought is bad, at least it gives me a place to start." I stood and squared my shoulders as I tried to reach my tallest height, which was barely over five feet. "I will find Luis myself."

Both agents appeared suitably disturbed. What I'd said had been spoken to evoke some kind of response. I wanted them to tell me they had agents embedded in the Jalisco Cartel; that if they'd taken my son, these men would know immediately and take action. They said nothing. Their silence permeated the room like invisible poison gas, and I understood more than ever that whatever good intentions they might have had, they were part of an incompetent and broken system that had quit working decades ago.

The two men stood to leave. I ushered them to the door. The one with Mexican ancestry started to warn me of the danger involved in doing anything on my own. My cold stare must have been enough to discourage the speech, because his voice trailed off like a cordless drill with a dying battery. At the door, I thanked them for coming. Both men muttered platitudes that meant nothing before beating a hasty retreat to their car. They'd done their duty. I'm sure they reckoned there was little to be gained in further discussion about the case with a raging, slightly deranged parent.

When the car disappeared, I slumped into one of the deck chairs and wept. I'd hoped for more, and to have them seemingly shrug their shoulders and say that the case was unsolvable because they *thought* Luis was now in Mexico was more than I could bear. They didn't know he was in Mexico. They were only guessing. Besides, if the Jalisco Cartel had been the ones who had kidnapped Luis, why would they take him *there*? Nobody needed more kids in my country. The United States was where people paid big bucks for babies, and it didn't matter whether they were Mexican, Ukrainian, or Italian. The only answer I could come up with was that they had taken Luis for revenge. They had done it to punish me. If that was the case, I was in even more trouble.

<u>**Chapter 19**</u>

Now, it seemed the best chance to find my baby was back in the country of my birth. I bid goodbye to all our people at the Cave Creek Ranch and with much trepidation headed for Douglas and the border. Crossing there was uneventful. I knew most of the personnel on both sides, and, in fact, had gone to school with the agent who checked my passport.

Mid-afternoon tranquility dominated the plaza when I rumbled over the cobbled street on the Mexican side. This was the time of the siesta, when most Mexicans with any sense close their shops and take an afternoon break to escape the heat of the day. By three o'clock, the shops would again be open, and would stay that way until late in the evening, or as long as there were customers to serve.

I hurried through town and took the south road that led to the ranch. Lupita would have stocked up on groceries, or so I hoped. I certainly didn't want to stop in town for food and risk running into any of the recently deceased Carlos's slimy friends. That day might come, but I had no wish to hasten it.

I would turn over every stone in Mexico to find my son. Did that mean I would have to again be in contact with the Jalisco Cartel? I didn't know, but I was glad I didn't have to think about that today.

As I drove the short distance to the ranch, I mentally ticked off my few acquaintances who might have some connection with the cartel. The list was short. We'd made it a policy at the ranch to keep those who had anything to do with any of the cartels at arms-length. The first favor one accepted from any of the cartels was like a slimy, cold tentacle. Too many of our rancher and business friends had discovered that the web of deceit the cartels spun around those they chose to use soon became so strong that death, or a middle-of-the-night flight to the border were the only escape. My experience with their brutality was recent and traumatic, but my heart overruled the screaming voice of caution in my head. I had no choice. I knew I would do whatever it took to have my son back in my arms.

When I pulled into the circular drive at the ranch, Lupita scurried down the steps to meet me. For a long moment, we hugged and she wiped at her tears. I patted her shoulder, trying to comfort my friend, when I had little of that to give. Every tear in my eyes had long ago fallen to the earth. Now, it was as if my emotions were welded into a white-hot triangle of fear, anger, and desperation.

"Is there any news?" Lupita asked.

"Not really. Apparently, the FBI had a trace on the kidnappers, but the trail went cold at the border. They seemed sure that it was one of the cartels that took Luis, and that they crossed into Mexico at Nogales."

"The Jalisco Cartel?"

"They didn't say, but who else? We've always paid our dues to the Sinaloa Cartel, and we've had no run-ins with any of the smaller gangsters. The only group with any reason to take Luis is the Jalisco bunch. This is my fault. I never should have taken the mares back."

Lupita hoisted one of my heavy suitcases onto her ample hip and followed me into the house.

"Dina, you did what you thought was right. Who could have known that even the cartels would stoop this low?"

The lump in my throat kept me from answering as the anger that would never go away welled up inside me. Carlos had violated me in a way that I could never forget. By taking the mares, I'd at least partially taken my revenge. But now, they had hurt me even worse.

Lupita dropped my suitcase on the tile floor at the bottom of the stairs. Momentarily, she turned away and wiped at her eyes. She was strong, but I could see the ache in her heart for Luis, for our family, and for all of our people who would bleed and die in the never-ending battle for drug corridor supremacy that had devastated border towns like ours. And as long as there was the wildly lucrative market for marijuana, fentanyl, and cocaine to the three-hundred-million-plus residents on our northern border, nothing would change.

As I trudged up the stairs to my bedroom, the anger melted into another rising tsunami of fear. I bit my lower lip as a new flood of tears threatened to reduce me to the quivering victim I didn't want to be. This wasn't a time to cry; it was a time to fight. But it had to be like the good book said; with the innocence of a dove, and the wisdom and deadly venom of a serpent. Maybe the Book didn't say that, but if I was going to get Luis back, I reckoned that was how I had to plan my battle campaign. I was a woman, and a pretty small one at that. I wouldn't be punching my way to success, and I had little experience with guns, so an AK-47 in my hands probably wouldn't work either. If I was going to succeed, I had to use what few skills God had given me, which in no way seemed adequate for the task ahead. Cattle and horses were my life—always had been. I walked to the window in my bedroom that looked out over the big coulee and tried to think through some kind of plan. I had a shaky ranch and a fractured marriage, which didn't say much for my business and people skills. So what were these supposed skills that were going to get my baby back? I had a bulldog tenacity, which had often not been an asset. Other than that . . . well, I'd have to think on it.

That resolved, I went down to help Lupita with supper. The few hands left at the ranch now ate in the main house. I saw no reason to change that. In fact, I rather looked forward to the camaraderie at the table. It was much more pleasant than eating alone, and I truly liked each one of the employees who had tied their star to the ranch.

Lupita had most of the meal fixed and ready. She knew better than to count on me for any serious kitchen help, though I did try, and I think she enjoyed having me at least make an effort.

Sometimes, I regretted the way I'd grown up. Though I would have loved to have been able to cook like Lupita, that was one of the many skills I'd never mastered. In the early years of our marriage, Frederick had suffered greatly through my dinner disasters. Eventually, he took over much of the cooking. However, his job didn't lend itself to regular culinary efforts, so we ate out a lot.

When the men trooped in, I greeted each with a warm hug. The four of them found their places at the table, two on each side. Lupita took her usual place at the end closest to the kitchen. There was only one place left, the head of the table, where years ago, my father had sat. After his death, Mama had laid claim to that chair. I'd never sat there. The place at the head of the table had always been left vacant. Now, I slowly pulled out Papa's chair while every freshly washed face watched me, their eyes shining with affirmation. I understood the significance of what I was doing, and what it meant to those at the table. Our people viewed this moment as the "changing of the guard." I wasn't ready for that, but I guess there wasn't a lot of choice. Papa was gone. Mama had passed to her heavenly reward. My older brother, Alejandro, was far away in Washington. There was only me, and though it had been that way for some time, this was the first time I'd consciously taken the place of authority.

I sat in what to me would always be Papa's chair and bowed my head to a greater authority. My people followed suit. Most, though not all, at the table were Catholic. But this was a moment when we put aside whatever faith differences we had. We were a people in need of heavenly protection and help.

There seemed no sense in keeping any of what had transpired over the last week from any of the crew, so while we ate, I brought everyone up to date. They all listened attentively as I related what had happened in Arizona.

Pedro, a family man with six little cherubs of his own, gave me a puzzled look. "So why do the American *federales* think the kidnappers took Luis across the border? In Mexico, stolen babies are worth nothing. Everyone has quite enough of their own."

Despite the ache in my heart, I had to smile. Pedro was so right in his assessment. It was a question I'd grappled with, and I wasn't sure I had the answer, though I'd thought it through from a dozen different angles. Nevertheless, I tried. "Pedro, you're right. From a ransom perspective, kidnapping Luis doesn't make sense. There are Americans who will pay many thousands of dollars for a baby, so why would the kidnappers smuggle Luis back into our country? The only answer I can come up with is that they didn't take him for money—at least, not immediate cash. They want something more important. Either that, or it's simply . . . punishment."

Sandy paused with his fork halfway to his mouth. "Punishment for what?"

I scrubbed my hands together under the table. I'd wanted to avoid this question and where it might lead. No one, not even Lupita, knew what I had suffered at Carlos's hands. That was something I might never be able to talk about. All any of our people knew was that some Jalisco Cartel honcho had been killed in the parking lot at the Bonanza Restaurant. None of them were aware I had been there, or what I had endured in the hours before the assassination. And no matter what else happened, that was something I could never divulge.

From the moment I'd discovered Luis missing from the tack compartment of my trailer, I'd known that the kidnapping of my baby was inextricably tied to Carlos's death. The Jalisco Cartel had spirited Luis into Mexico for a much more important reason than a simple ransom payment. They were businessmen, and in the end, money would be a part of the price. But the pact I would have to agree to would be many times whatever ransom they might ask. The message would come soon. And the price? It didn't matter. I

would pay—and those who had my baby
knew it.

<u>**Chapter 20**</u>

The next morning dawned clear and unseasonably cold. I dug into the back of my closet and found a fleece-lined denim jacket I'd not worn since my Montana days. It served to beat back the chill as I hurried down to the barn. Sandy and Paco both stood inside the door, hunched up and shivering. Neither had clothes suitable for this weather. Riding in the thin jackets they both sported would be miserable.

"Hey, why don't both of you forget about training this morning. Take the blue pickup, drive down to the west pasture, and check on those yearling heifers. If there are any that need doctoring, you can saddle horses and doctor them this afternoon—or tomorrow, if it doesn't warm up."

Both men nodded enthusiastically, glad of the reprieve from saddling cold-backed, humpy horses. Horses are no different than humans. Most will voice their displeasure at frigid saddle blankets and icy bits in their mouths, so I tried to help out both the horses, and the humans whenever possible. Paco and Sandy skedaddled, probably afraid I would change my mind. Actually, there were two blue ranch pickups parked in the bunkhouse parking lot. They took the one that had the best heater. As I watched them drive out of the yard, I wished that my biggest problem was like theirs—trying to stay warm.

My morning routine had always been to stop at every stall, to pet and talk to each horse before moving on. It gave me time to assess their general well-being, because if the young horses in our care were to reach their potential, they had to be healthy and happy. Sandy and Paco made amazing progress with the two-year-old colts who were fortunate enough to fall into their care. My job was to make sure those youngsters were ready for their training classes, no matter the temperature outside.

After I'd reached the last stall, I leaned against the door, turned, and gazed down the alley. The familiar smells of rich alfalfa, horse manure, and leather were the same as they'd been since I was a child. I wished for nothing more, and even on this cold and miserable morning, I thanked the Creator for this, my place on the earth. This ranch was where I belonged, and though the future looked bleak,

I clenched my fists and tried to calm my spirit for what lay ahead. Whatever it took, I would never stop searching for my son. Somehow, I would find him and bring him home. Even the thought of that reunion brought quick tears to my eyes. Afraid that one of the men would walk into the barn, I quickly wiped them away. This was not the time, nor the place, to let my grief show.

Sandy and Paco had apparently taken care of all the feeding before they left, so there were no chores that I could do. I walked back down the alley and opened the door that led into the tiny barn office where we kept performance and training records. I cranked the baseboard heaters up to take off the morning chill, then stuffed my hands into the oversized pockets of my coat. The icy seat of the vinyl office chair was too much to bear. I remained standing as I wiped away the week-old layer of dust on the desk in front of me. Though we'd moved important ranch and employment records to the house, we still used the barn office as a coffee place where we met with employees to plan work schedules, strategize training regimens, and exchange knowledge.

Idly, I traced a series of concentric circles through the dusty sheen of neglect on the top of the desk while I considered the day ahead. Paco and Sandy were off to the south pasture. Pedro and Ernesto, our now skeleton farm and fencing crew, had more than enough work in front of them. The only idle one was me. Was there some ranch chore that needed my attention? Probably, but I couldn't stop my mind from zeroing in on Luis. Where should I start looking for him? What more could I do to find him? I hunched forward, then slid onto the slowly warming chair, determined to concentrate enough to methodically categorize the steps I should take.

An hour later, I was no closer to solving the problem, but the sound of horses chewing their morning ration of hay, the scream of an eagle, and the ever-present cooing of doves had calmed my mind. Any answers for the ranch and the search for Luis were still distant. In a moment of desperation, I reached for the phone.

"Hi, Dina." Call display meant Frederick's response was familiar and guarded, rather than cryptic.

"Have you found anything about Luis?"

"Maybe—not sure yet. What do you know about your old flame?"

He could only mean Eduardo, our ranch neighbor. He'd never been a flame of any kind, and though I'd told my ex-husband that numerous times, he hadn't believed it. I did my best to hold my anger in check. This was about Luis, and I refused to rise to his accusation. Instead, I answered his question as best I could.

"I know nothing about his activities, other than he is involved with the Jalisco Cartel, but that's not exactly classified information."

Frederick took more time in responding than was necessary. "I just wondered. We know Eduardo wasn't personally in Arizona at the time Luis was kidnapped, but two of his close associates were there. Also, his name keeps coming up from agents embedded in the cocaine pipeline. He's developed a working relationship with several Columbians who are of great interest

to our drug enforcement people. I'm
wondering if there's a connection.

The fear I'd carried for too long
exploded. "What do you mean?"

"Our son is possibly in Mexico, but
I'm wondering for how long. There may be
only a narrow window of opportunity to get
him back."

Panic constricted my throat. "What are
you saying?" I choked out. "You mean, they're
trading babies—children to the Columbians
for cocaine?" Suddenly, all the panic of the
last month was nothing compared to what
Frederick had implied. Luis sold to some
Columbian drug lord—then traded to the
highest bidder in that vast South American
continent, where I would never find him? I
couldn't deal with that.

"Yes, that is exactly what I'm saying."

"But why? People don't pay for babies
in South America any more than they do in
Mexico.

"Actually, Dina, there *are* other people
who pay for babies. If our son is traded to the
Columbians, it is only a temporary stop. He

would likely then be sold to either ISIS or al-Qaeda."

"Why?" I didn't want an answer, but some visceral need to know forced me to grind out the question.

"The terrorists fly children they kidnap to camps in Afghanistan or Pakistan. They're indoctrinated from birth to be suicide bombers."

"Why are they using *our* children?" My hands shook, and I gripped the phone with both hands to hold it steady. "Don't they have enough of their own?"

"I can't answer why. All I know is, they are doing this, and it's possible our son may have been kidnapped for that reason."

Long ago, I'd sworn I would never cry in front of Frederick. It had been a promise I'd kept. But now, I couldn't hold back the tears. My son, growing up without love, programmed only to hate, to use the breath that God had given him to kill others. The concept was beyond anything I'd ever imagined possible, and silent tears tracked down my cheeks. Frederick likely carried as much hurt and fear as I did, but our relationship was by now distant enough that support for each other was as likely as consensus on global warming. It wasn't going to happen. We would deal with our son's kidnapping privately—and alone.

When the conversation ended, I hung up the phone, leaned back in my chair, and twined my fingers together in a futile attempt to keep them from trembling. Any prior urgency to find Luis was nothing compared to now, and as much as I tried, I could not process Frederick's sentence of doom. But whatever it took, I would find Luis before the cartel traded him to the worst evil the world had ever seen. I didn't care if it cost me my life. My son would never wear a suicide belt filled with explosives. As long as there was breath in my body, my son would never be indoctrinated with the devil siren of Mohammed.

I pushed the chair back and left the cobwebs and dust of the defunct barn office. As I walked to the house, I considered my options. There weren't many. Each was dangerous, but I was becoming accustomed to danger. Nevertheless, when I thought of what might lay ahead, my insides tumbled into a knot. Dying held no fear for me, but at the hands of any of the cartels, pain was an issue one had to consider. They were experts at torture. With them, the release of death never came quickly.

<u>**Chapter 21**</u>

For the rest of the day, ranch work suffered. I hoped Sandy and Paco were accomplishing something, because I was too distraught to deal with anything as mundane as feed bills and fence repairs. I left the barn, slipped into the house, and ensconced myself in my bedroom. This was not the first time I yearned for the privacy I'd had before I'd married Frederick. I'd rented a basement suite from his grandmother, though that was a fancy name for the dingy quarters she'd provided. Nevertheless, they'd been mine, with no family or employees to barge in at inopportune moments.

Our house in Albuquerque had been almost as good, though there, the phone rang incessantly, mostly for Frederick. Here, there was no place of privacy, not even my bedroom. Between phone calls and interruptions by ranch staff, the office afforded little solitude. If my bedroom door was closed, most of the time I could expect it not to open, unless it was Lupita. She tended to knock, then open the door and stick her head in with a barrage of requests or questions. I hadn't the heart to change anything. She was more like a favorite aunt than an employee. No matter whose name was on the title, the house was hers as much as mine.

By late afternoon, I'd formulated a plan. Frederick had thought that Luis might still be in the country, though that wouldn't last. If I was to find my son, I had to move quickly, and there was only one place I could think of to start. My neighbor, Eduardo, might have the information I needed. Even if he didn't, he would know who to contact, that is if he would tell me.

With great trepidation, I punched in the cell number of the man I'd sworn I would never call. I took a deep breath and bit my lower lip to stop the shaking. If this had any chance of working, I had to sound calm and collected. After the fifth ring, Eduardo's voice mail kicked in. I breathed a sigh of relief. I wouldn't have to talk to him, at least not now. I took a deep breath.

"Hi, Eduardo. This is Dina. I would like to talk to you. Please call me."

Would he actually return my call? As teenagers, we'd been friends, but that was long in the past. Our last meeting had been acrimonious. I now despised the man and everything he stood for. Nevertheless, this was about Luis. Whatever I thought about Eduardo was secondary. I slumped onto the stool by the phone and tried to formulate a coherent case if he actually called back.

For the last ten years, the only reason Eduardo and I had spoken was because we owned neighboring ranches. We had cattle that strayed, fences between us that needed regular maintenance, and a dozen other housekeeping issues that required at least a minimum of communication. It had never been easy, but we'd managed, and Eduardo, to his credit, had done his part. It appeared that his infatuation from our teenage years was long gone, unfortunately replaced by a smoldering anger at my indifference to his advances, which likely meant he wouldn't be inclined to help me find Luis, unless there was a big payoff.

I would probably be spared any proposals for bedroom favors. At least, I hoped that was the case. The recurring nightmare of that evening with Carlos had become a constant reminder of my vulnerability. I hoped time would eventually lessen the psychological damage, but I had no doubt that if there was another shattering, degrading experience like what I'd gone through, I would break into a thousand pieces. That couldn't happen. I had to be strong. I would negotiate some kind of payment to Eduardo for information, and then I would rescue Luis from wherever he'd been taken.

My fingernails dug into my palms. If ever I needed divine help, it was now, but my anguished prayer seemed to stop at the ceiling. After I could no longer endure the crescendo of silence, I raised my head and stared out at the Joshua trees and Grease wood. My feeble attempt to implore the Almighty for help had produced—silence. Where had God's loving kindness and protection been when Luis was kidnapped? Obviously, nowhere close, and like a bubbling vein of lava, anger seeped to the surface of my soul.

It's not as though I'd expected an answer to my petition. Long ago, I'd given up on God. Even if He was real, He'd done nothing for me. My marriage was history, my barrel racing career had hit a brick wall, and now my son had been taken from me in the worst possible way. Faith? Belief in the tenets of Christianity? Those sacred precepts had now been jettisoned to the gutter.

The shrieking phone interrupted my bitter soliloquy. I glanced at the call display—and froze. This was it. My response could determine Luis's future. I stabbed the green icon on my cell.

"Hello?"

"Dina?"

"Yes, Eduardo. Thank you for returning my call. I really appreciate it." It didn't hurt to lay it on a little thick. I needed him and whatever information he might have.

"What do you want?" His words dripped sarcasm.

"Well, I'm sure you know my baby boy has been kidnapped."

"So? Kidnapping is a big income stream. That happens in our country. What do you want me to do about it?"

I gripped the phone and took a deep breath while I tried to formulate an answer that might expedite my son's return. "I'm not

sure what I want. But I think the Jalisco Cartel
has my son."

"Why do you think that? They don't
make a practice of snatching children."

"So, it wasn't them?"

He snickered, but the momentary
silence was telling.

"Why would I tell you? As I
remember, we're not on the best of terms. I
owe you nothing, Dina Rodriguez."

"Eduardo, I realize that, but we were
once friends."

"That was a long time ago."

"So even if you knew who took Luis,
you wouldn't tell me?"

"We are not baby kidnappers. I will tell
you no more than that."

"I guess that has to be enough, and
Eduardo, I accept it. Whatever else I ever
thought about you, you were never a liar."

His laugh was instantaneous and
scornful. "I'm so grateful you at least give me
that much credit."

"We travelled different paths. I don't
know why you chose the cartels . . ." *This was
a bad idea. Moralizing with Eduardo was not*

going to be productive. "I guess is what I'm trying to say is that—"

"Listen, Dina. I got it. You want me to help you, and I probably would. But that doesn't mean I will sit here and listen to your sucky little speech. For the last time. To my knowledge, the Jalisco Cartel does not have your kid."

"So who does?"

"How am I to know? Try some of those thug 'wannabe' gangs that hang around Juarez. How about La Línea or those Barrio Azteca hoods? And I'll tell you something else. There are at least two new players along the border, neither one Mexican. Rumor has it they are a ready market for kidnapped kids."

"What do you mean?"

"Al Qaida types. Over the last few years, we've left them alone because they're no danger to us. They just wanted to get their people across the border. That's no concern of ours. But kidnapping kids is different. When that happens, law enforcement from both sides of the border pile on more agents. That's scrutiny we don't want or need, so we would be more than pleased if the DEA, or any of the other American agencies, sent them packing."

"What are they doing with these kids? Where are they sending them?"

"I don't know, but there appears to be a ready market for as many as they can provide."

Eduardo had just corroborated what Frederick had already told me. I bit my lower lip to keep the rising emotion at bay. "Thank you, Eduardo. I appreciate what you've told me. At least it gives me a place to start looking."

"You're welcome. Send a crew to fix the east end of our boundary fence in payment. There are some rotted and broken posts, and I have bulls in that pasture. I don't want them getting out."

"Consider it done. I will send men over there tomorrow morning."

Eduardo hung up with no further comment, which was fine with me. I'd dreaded the call and what it might mean. At least for now, we were going to enjoy an uneasy truce. That was more than I'd expected, especially after the back-and-forth tug-of-war over the theft of our mares. That said, what should I do? My mind was a complete blank. Al Qaida? Islamic State? The Egyptian Brotherhood? The list of middle-eastern terrorist groups was long. And now they were flooding into our country because of the nearly open border in America? Judging by the amount of foot traffic through the ranch, the border was now more porous than it had ever been, and in the back of my head, I heard my father's stern voice. His whole life had been spent fighting to avoid what was now happening.

I paced around the room as I pictured Papa's face. His grandson kidnapped and in danger? Though inside, Papa would be furious, his features would be unreadable. I leaned back and stared at the ceiling. What would Papa do in my shoes? I held my hands out, palms upward and open, trying to bring my father, and a silent, faraway Heaven down to my level. How I needed my father's wisdom, and God—yes, I needed His as well, but He was just as silent as Papa.

Where did I go from here? I had no contacts who could penetrate either of the Juarez gangs Eduardo had mentioned. Did

Frederick? He might. I picked up the phone and punched his number. He answered immediately, which was unusual.

"Dina?"

"I just talked to Eduardo. He says there are two Juarez gangs that may be kidnapping children and selling them to some al-Qaida-type organizations. Do you have any intelligence on them?"

"Which ones?"

"La Línea and Barrio Azteca."

"We have extensive files on both." Frederick's answer seemed routinely bored.

Frustration, lack of sleep, and too many hours of worry overflowed.

"Just in case you forgot," I yelled, "this is about our son. I want more from you than a file. You have the resources to actually make a difference, yet you do nothing. Why? Don't you care?"

"Dina." His voice sounded tired. "You know that's not true. I have agents in every area of Mexico. All of them are searching for any clue that might lead to Luis's return. So far, there's been nothing, and I'm not at all sure either of those two small-time gangs had anything to do with his kidnapping."

"Eduardo thinks they do."

"Eduardo. You and him are an item now?"

"Give it up, Frederick. You know better, or you ought to. I called him because I thought our long acquaintance would carry some weight."

"Really? Kind of like you naming our son after your lover?"

His sarcastic rejoinder was more than I could handle, and though I knew better, I rose to the occasion. Before I slammed down the phone, we were both shouting. Tears of anger and disappointment filled my eyes. It was my fault. I shouldn't have lost my temper. All I'd done was alienate Frederick more than ever—if that were possible—and I couldn't afford to do that. I needed him.

<u>Chapter 22</u>

My ex-husband was in a better position than anyone in the law enforcement community to find our son. That was a given. Stirling Associates had agents embedded all over Mexico and Latin America, which meant I needed to put my anger and animosity aside. Though we'd never been much of a team, now it was even more important that Frederick and I bury our volcanic past.

I pushed away from the stool I'd perched on and walked over to the open window. My eyes involuntarily followed the contours of the brush-covered pastures that sloped downward toward the big coulee. By American mid-western standards, that land was barely productive and hardly worth owning, but it was my family's, and now mine.

I'd made little progress, and though Eduardo's reception had been cold, he'd at least given me a place to start, which was more than I'd gotten from my ex-husband. Frederick had been no help at all, though if I'd been more diplomatic, we might have at least spent more time talking about the issue. He'd been so typically Frederick. Do nothing—until you have every available scrap of information. In this case, it seemed he was still in the do-nothing mode. I couldn't wait, not if there was a chance of finding Luis before a drug cartel sold him to some wing-nut Muslim jihadists. Whatever I was going to do had to be done immediately. Next week or next month was not an option.

I jammed my hands into the pockets of my jeans. Who could I count on? I stared at the barn and corrals as I ticked off all our people. They were horse trainers, cowboys, cattlemen. They didn't have the experience to handle—hold it! I watched Sandy through the rails of the round pen. His movements were deliberate and slow. Somehow, I'd transcribed his lack of action to what happened inside his head. Sandy's mind was certainly deliberate, but slow? Hardly. The same for Paco. They were valuable men. I needed to use them.

I walked to the back door and grabbed one of my ball caps. I didn't always wear one, but this morning, it seemed appropriate. I marched down to the smaller of the two round pens.

"Sandy?"

"Yeah." His attention remained focused as he picked up a rein and put gentle pressure on the left side of the colt's mouth.

"Could we have a meeting this evening . . . I mean, with everybody?"

"Why, what's happening?"

"Well, it's hard to explain. I need advice, and we have some really good people on the ranch. I want to listen to what *you* have to say about how we should move forward."

Sandy's head swiveled toward me, fast enough that it startled the colt he was riding. The colt immediately tensed, ready to bolt or buck. Sandy spoke to him and stroked his neck, gradually returning him to trust and calmness. As soon as everything was under control, and the colt was quiet, he dismounted and led him over to where I was standing by the fence.

"Okay, say that again."

"I need advice. I have some ideas on how to move forward, but I need to listen to what you and the rest of our people have to offer."

"That's what I thought I heard. Kind of unusual for you. What brought this on?" Sandy's slow grin took any sting out of his blunt assessment of my management style.

"You know about Luis, and that's my focus now. I would just like for all of us to sit down and brainstorm options for finding him."

Sandy's gaze flickered over my face, then swept past the bars of the corral to the far bluff on the other side of the big coulee. He turned back to the colt and loosened the front cinch. "What do you think we can add that we haven't already?"

"I'm not sure. But you are not just an employee. You're a friend with exceptional skills and abilities. Everybody here has experience that goes beyond training horses and moving cattle."

Sandy avoided my eyes, and I wondered what he thought of this new chapter in our relationship.

"I will pass on the information to the rest of the crew. What time do you want to meet?"

"Does five work? Afterward, everybody can stay and eat. Kind of a dinner meeting."

"I'm sure that will be fine."

I trudged back to the house, consumed by doubts. What should I tell the crew? The rape by Carlos was out of the question, which meant I would confine the agenda to Luis's kidnapping and their thoughts on how we could find him. To bring anything else into the discussion would only focus on me, which would be counterproductive. The rape was a raw, festering nightmare that might never go away, but even that didn't compare with the loss of my son. I slumped into my father's office chair and tried to write a point-by-point agenda for the five o'clock meeting. The exercise was futile. All I could come up with was one word—Luis.

The rest of the day was consumed with necessary and sometimes every-day issues. Bills to pay, calls to suppliers, personnel problems, the list was never-ending. Nor was

it new. I paid careful attention to each problem
as I worked through them. Somehow, I made
it to the bottom of the pile.

Precisely at five o'clock, Sandy and
Paco trooped into the dining room. Both sat
down on the back side of the table. Tomás and
Antonio came in next, followed by Lupita. For
a few minutes, we talked over pasture and
cattle problems before I placed my hands on
the table and started with the real agenda.
Though I'd had more than sufficient time to
put together an opening statement, nothing
seemed appropriate, so what I said came from
my heart.

"I think you all know why I've called
this meeting. What has happened with Luis
has affected me more than anything in my
whole life. Yesterday, I talked to Eduardo
Garcia."

Eyebrows raised around the table at
this news.

I held up a hand. "I know, he's not
exactly our friend. Though he didn't betray his
cartel buddies, he did give me some
information. La Linea is kidnapping children.

They trade them to the Colombians, who sell them to either al Qaida or ISIS."

Antonio, a shy introvert, raised his hand. Seldom would he speak at a meeting, so I was surprised when his hand shot up like he had the answer to a question in a third-grade class. I smiled, trying to encourage him. "Antonio, please speak."

"Señora, I am only a simple laborer, and all of my family are laborers, but I have a cousin in Juarez who is a member of that evil bunch of thugs. We are not close, but I can talk to him. Who knows what he might tell me?"

In the next five seconds, a dozen thoughts blew through my mind. How did I handle this unexpected gem of intelligence? My response had to mirror the same transparent honesty this valued employee had displayed.

"Antonio, I appreciate that so much. How soon do you think you can contact him?"

"I will call him tonight."

After my sudden euphoria over a lead that might produce information, Antonio's enthusiastic response worried me. A phone call to his cousin could be dangerous. The last thing we needed was for word to get out that there was an aggressive search for Luis. That might drive the kidnappers underground and cause them to get rid of Luis even faster.

"Be careful, Antonio. We don't want to tip our hand."

"Señora, I understand, truly I do. My cousin has done many bad things, but he is loyal to our family. He will tell me if he has any information about the baby."

"Thank you. Come to the house and tell me as soon as you hear anything, no matter how late it is."

Antonio nodded and immediately retreated into his shell, like he was embarrassed he'd spoken so many words in public. Silence reigned as I scrutinized the other faces at the table.

Lupita spoke next. "Has Frederick been able to find anything?"

My lips tightened. There were so many other issues with my ex-husband, which only added to my anger over his lack of immediate action on a multitude of issues, our son being the most important.

"Nothing." My single-word answer was clipped and angry.

Lupita held up a hand. "Sorry, I just thought he might have uncovered something worthwhile."

"He hasn't, and I doubt he will." That wasn't fair, but it wasn't in me to cut any slack to Luis's father. Frederick's usual snail pace wasn't going to work—at least, not this time.

Lupita rubbed at a spot on the table and refused to meet my eyes, for which I was grateful. She hadn't deserved my curt reply, but the wounds in my soul would brook no other response.

On the far side of the table, Tomás sat silently, his downcast eyes fixed on his clasped hands, the work-thickened fingers worrying each other as he followed the dialogue around him. He was a farm hand. He would never be a leader, nor did he want to be. I'd kept an eye on him throughout the meeting, along with the rest of the crew.

Paco shrugged off any response when my questioning gaze fell on him. Though I knew he liked his job, if the pressure became intolerable, he would move on. Nevertheless, I nodded and smiled at him while I tried to forgive his lukewarm support.

"Tomás." I turned to the man to my immediate right. "What do you think?" I asked.

"I have little experience in these matters, Señora. My family is not from here. They are poor farmers in Michoacán. There, we had to pay tribute to La Familia. All I know is that the cartels have no mercy. They do whatever it takes to maintain power and control over the people. That may be why they kidnapped Luis. If they can make you afraid— they win." He shrugged, and his eyes dropped to his rough, work-worn hands. "All I know, is that's the way it was where I come from."

I studied Tomás's earnest face, well aware that no Spanish blood flowed through his veins. In a culture that too often put a premium on lighter skin, he was looked down on, at least in some circles. He seldom spoke, other than to reply to a direct question.

After a long silence, Tomás raised his dusky eyes toward mine. "Do not be afraid, Señora. We are here, and we will fight. We will not leave you alone. Neither will our God.

I know in my heart that somehow, Luis will be found."

More than I ever had before, I understood and appreciated this itinerant, loyal farmhand. What he'd said had been difficult, but it had come from his heart.

Chapter 23

We ate, and continued to talk—as a family. No subject was off the table, whether it was the added workload or the lack of direction since Raoul's absence. Frequently, the conversation returned to Luis.

I picked at Lupita's spicy rice and bean casserole as I listened and occasionally replied to those around the table, pleased that there were no inhibitions, no lines in the sand. Several times during the evening, a warm sense of success surged up from my heart. This was what Papa had accomplished. He'd been successful as an agent and employer because of the intense loyalty he'd engendered from those who came to our ranch. Tonight, I was reaping the benefits.

Throughout the evening, Sandy had been uncharacteristically quiet. He was never garrulous, but neither was he an introvert like Tomás. Why was he holding back? Did he have something to say that he didn't want to reveal with all the crew at the table?

The evening wound down, and as they rose to leave, I hugged each member of the crew and thanked them for what they'd contributed. Lupita, of course, got an especially long hug. We had always been close, and if I had anything to say about it, we always would be. She was much older, and though our stations in life couldn't have been more different, Lupita was my soul sister. Nothing would ever change that.

One at a time, the crew filed outside. Sandy was the last to leave, and I walked out to the veranda with him. The evening was warm, the air devoid of any breeze, not unusual for our part of the world. Lupita had returned to the kitchen, and the other men had sauntered toward their quarters east of the barns. Tomás and Antonio stood at the fence that separated the yard area from the two training arenas, both with one foot propped on the bottom rail, elbows akimbo on the top rail.

Sandy pulled out a toothpick, placed it in the side of his mouth, and leaned back against the pillar to the right side of the steps.

I waited for whatever he had to say. Over the last year, he'd shown himself to be a steady and dependable leader. He could never replace Raoul, but he'd often shown unusual leadership qualities, and I was grateful for him.

"If you have a few minutes, Señora, I have some knowledge of the cartels and who has taken Luis. I didn't feel it was appropriate to bring that up in front of the others."

"Please tell me what you know."

Sandy paced to the end of the veranda and stared down toward the round pens and barns. His fists remained jammed deep in the pockets of his jeans. It was like he'd not quite made up his mind to tell me whatever difficult thing he had decided to say, which only made me more curious—and nervous. I studied his face, but the deepening shadows effectively masked whatever he was thinking.

When Sandy spoke, his voice was tense. "I love working here. I want you to know that, because what I have to tell you may mean I have to leave forever. However, your little boy is gone, and I believe it is my duty to tell you what I know. Luis was taken by those evil monsters who call themselves La Linea. Nothing else makes sense."

I bit my bottom lip to keep from crying. It's not that I didn't already know, but

Sandy actually saying what I'd already suspected smashed through whatever defenses I had left, and it brought back all the fear that triggered an ongoing torture, worse than I could have ever imagined. My little boy was scared and hurting, and I couldn't be there to protect him? Nothing in my makeup had prepared me to handle anything like that.

I needed to be strong, or at least not dissolve into tears. It didn't work. I leaned back against one of the pine posts on the veranda and silently sobbed. In my head, I knew this would accomplish nothing. Bawling one's eyes out in front of the crew was not what a conscientious ranch owner did. I understood that, but I couldn't help myself. Finally, I was able to dam the flow of tears. I needed to hear what this man had to say.

Sandy pulled his hands out of his pockets, then nervously jammed them back in. "When I hired on here, I did not tell you about my past."

I squared my shoulders and crossed my arms, not at all sure I wanted to hear this sudden intelligence dump. I tried to smile as I spoke.

"After Raoul saw your skill with the colts, he probably didn't care about your past. You have been a valuable employee and a friend. We all have history, and sometimes it's more productive to leave it buried."

"True, Señora, but I think that mine has now become relevant. Many years ago, I was an enforcer for Los Zetas."

My mouth fell open. "A Sicario?"

"Yes. I grew up in the barrios of Monterrey. My family was the poorest of the poor. The only upward mobility available to us was the way of the cartels. Los Zetas offered money, power, and status. They were the ticket that made a rise above the poverty we were born into something we could only dream about."

"It's a long way from the prestige and wealth of a sicario to a horse trainer on the Rodriguez Ranch. What happened?" My tone was more sarcastic than I'd wanted, and I was immediately ashamed.

"I found out the hard way that I was not a killer," he said humbly.

I raised an eyebrow. "I'm listening."

Sandy paced to the far end of the veranda and back again, until he was standing in front of me. "My Los Zetas boss sent me to kill a small-town politician. She was the mayor of a pueblo a few miles outside of the city, one of the few brave souls who had refused to buckle to the demands of the cartel. The memory of that day will never go away. I drove to the woman's house, a typical middle-class Mexican home on a side street in the city. Monterrey is quite cosmopolitan, at least in the downtown area. The village just outside the city where my assignment waited was anything but modern. Streets ran every which way, clotted with cobbled vehicles, skinny dogs, and street urchins, all in ankle-deep dust. My best chance of success was during the day. A woman would never open the door to a stranger at night, and the safest way for me was to quietly kill her inside the house, then make my escape."

"And you did it?"

Sandy's shoulders slumped. "The woman opened the door. She was the mayor. Her job was to talk to people. My plan was to quickly push her back inside and do what I had to do. This was my first killing, and to have any future with the cartel, I had to do it quickly and cleanly."

Sandy's hand trembled as he reached up and dragged his hat off. He ran his fingers through his thick, black hair.

I waited, aghast at what I was hearing. Never could I have imagined that any of our people at the ranch had this kind of history. Sandy's eyes transmitted a level of pain and regret beyond anything I could have imagined.

"The woman stepped out onto the sidewalk. Her eyes reminded me of my mother's, and suddenly, I knew this was a moment that would affect me for the rest of my life. They say when people die that sometimes their whole life flashes in front of their eyes. For me, it was as if I was the one who was going to die, and instead of my past, my whole future was laid out in front of me. I had complete freedom, and the power to kill this lady, but I knew that she would only be the first. Money, women, and power would be mine, but to make that happen, many more people who would have to die at my hand. I could see it all as clearly as if it had already happened, and then I saw my death. I lay on the ground, my blood seeping into the earth, and God was there. Only, I could not bear to look at His face."

"Why?" In spite of my horror, I was intrigued with Sandy's story. "Was He very angry?"

"No, it was not the anger. It was the sadness in His eyes that was too much for me to bear. At that moment in my life, I understood. My sin was my own choice. It was not God who was sending me to Hell. I had chosen my own path."

"So you didn't kill the woman?"

Sandy, shook his head. "Señora, I told the woman I'd come to the wrong house, then turned away. Once, I glanced back. Her smile seemed almost sad as she waved. I've always thought that she knew why I was there."

Sandy's failure meant he was on the run, which went a long way toward explaining his unwillingness to go to town or be around any gathering of people.

"What did you do then? No sicario walks away from one of the cartels."

"You are right, and I'd broken one of their most sacred covenants. Though I had an apartment, I was afraid to go back to it. I left everything. Two days later, I was deep in the Durango mountains. Though my family lived not far from where I hid, I never made any effort to contact them. I was too afraid. If the cartel found me, they would kill not only me but my family as well. That is their way."

I cocked my head, puzzled at what he'd related. "You've always said that Durango was where you learned to train horses."

"That is true. My uncle had a small *rancho* deep in the mountains. You could only get there with a horse, and I thought that would be the safest place for me, so I rode into his remote property. He let me work with his horses and taught me much of what I know."

A growing anger and concern washed over me. "Sandy, we have enough danger with the cartels. You have brought more. You should have told me this long before now."

Sandy's face contorted with anguish. "Señora Rodriguez, I am sorry, and you are right. I shouldn't have kept this to myself. That is why I have chosen to speak with you. I have no contacts within the Jalisco Cartel or La Linea. None of them would know of my history with Los Zetas, and I know how the cartels work. I can find out whether they have Luis much faster than anyone else.”

“You mean infiltrate?”

Sandy shrugged. “More or less.”

“No, that is too dangerous. We will find another way.”

“And what is this *other way*? We have little time. It may already be too late to find your son.”

Unless Frederick had developed a new plan, Sandy’s proposal was all I had. I walked to the far side of the veranda, then turned and faced one of the most conscientious and best trainers we’d ever had, not at all sure what I was going to say. Though I’d come to respect and value Sandy, by deceiving us, he had made our lives infinitely more dangerous.

“Sandy, I need to think about this, but for now, the answer is no. I refuse to put you in that kind of danger. Perhaps Frederick has found another lead.”

“Okay, but if he hasn’t, then I think I should go.”

I pulled out my phone and punched the contact icon beside Frederick's name. He answered immediately.

"Hi. I will call you back in ten minutes." Before I could say anything, he disconnected.

Angrily, I jammed my phone into my back pocket. Why wouldn't he listen to what I had to say? What could be more important than talking about our son?

I'd barely slipped my phone into my back pocket when it rang. Frederick's name marched across the call display.

"I may have a lead." Frederick's voice carried more passion than I'd ever heard before.

"*May?* What does that mean?"

"We have an agent in Juarez who has a meeting next week with an informant."

"Next week? Are you kidding? We don't have until next week!" I stabbed at the red disconnect button and turned to Sandy. "I've changed my mind. Go, and we will all pray for your safety."

"I will leave in the morning." Sandy started toward the bunkhouse.

Quickly, I made another decision.

"Sandy?"

He stopped and faced me.

"I'm going with you."

"You cannot do that, Señora. It is not safe."

If I'd had any misgivings, they were gone now. I treated our employees like family, but still, no one was going to tell me what I could and couldn't do. I scowled at him, which had the desired effect, because it was something I seldom did with any of our people.

"I will decide that. Meet me in front of the house at six in the morning. We will take that gray Dodge." I pointed to the oldest and most decrepit vehicle we owned, then abruptly turned and stalked inside the house. In my bedroom, I threw some clothes and personal items into a bag. Then I trudged down the hall to Lupita's room, but the door was closed, for which I was thankful. I considered knocking. She should know where I was going. No, better if I texted her in the morning when we were well on our way. There was no doubt she'd object to my plan, and though I could

scowl and throw my weight around with
Sandy, Lupita was a whole different story.
Even at my age, I still wasn't sure she couldn't
just say no. And if I protested? Well, she
might just decide to turn me over her knee for
a spanking.

When dawn colored the eastern sky, I
threw my bag into the box of the old Dodge
pickup and waited for Sandy. This pickup was
the one we used to carry fencing materials and
doing other menial jobs out in the coulees and
cactus. There was hardly a square inch from
the taillights to the front bumper that wasn't
either dented or scratched. Some junior ranch
hand whose name I couldn't remember had
slid off the road and caved in the driver's door
against a big rock, Now, it no longer opened
and one had to enter and exit from the
passenger side. One headlight was held in
place with a short piece of baling wire. The
tailgate had been missing for years, and the
back window was held in place with duct tape.
Fortunately, the side mirrors were still intact,
though another length of baling wire fastened
the passenger side mirror to the windshield
wiper. When the wipers were turned on, the
mirror bobbed up and down, but being as how

we seldom got rain, it wasn't usually a problem.

With growing trepidation, I hunched further into my green denim jacket and stuck my hands into the pockets to warm them against the early morning chill. Why was I going through with this hare-brained scheme? It was way too dangerous to just walk into two major cartel's disputed territory, not to mention several smaller ruthless gangs who did their best to bathe the area in further blood and corruption. Sandy might not be known by the cartels, but I was because of my family. For me to venture into that sucking vortex of evil was not only dangerous for me, but it increased the danger for Sandy as well. Nevertheless, I wasn't about to change my mind. Besides, who else would help? Certainly not Frederick. At least Eduardo had provided a little information. My ex-husband? He'd done nothing but give the same noncommittal answers he always had. His career and precious agents were way more important than our son. Sure, what I was doing carried some danger, but if I was to have any hope of finding Luis, I had to act on my own.

When Sandy appeared, I inclined my jaw toward the passenger-side door. "You drive the first stretch."

Sandy threw his backpack in the box beside my bag, then dragged the door open and crawled across the seat to the driver's side. We wobbled out of the yard and headed east to the murder capital of Mexico.

<u>**Chapter 24**</u>

The fifteen-year-old pickup I'd chosen burned gas like it was popcorn, which meant we had to stop at Janos to fuel up. The attendant seemed surprised when I told him to fill the tank, not that I blamed him. Our rig certainly didn't indicate any ability to cover the cost of a full tank of gas. One of the service station staff half-heartedly scrubbed away at the windshield, obviously convinced our decrepit chariot meant we weren't good for much of a tip. The other attendant had declined to even speak to me, obviously saving his efforts for more well-heeled customers.

I placed a generous number of pesos in the hand of the young man who had made the effort to wash the windshield. The incredulous look on his face was priceless. I hoped he would show the money to his snooty *compadre*.

I grimaced as Sandy and I pulled back onto the highway. My tip to the gas station attendant would be my last expression of generosity. As Sandy shifted the old Dodge pickup into the highway gear, I tried to quiet the butterflies, the trembling fear that threatened to reduce me to tears. What lay in front of me would be an experience I'd never had to face. Now, I was not the privileged owner of the ranch my father had simply called "Rodriguez Quarter Horses." I was only a mother in deep pain, desperately trying to find her baby boy. Whatever it cost, I would pay.

Sandy and I would be operating in the toughest part of Juarez, and more than likely, it would be during hours when no sane person would go there. These wheels would attract no attention, and certainly, nobody would steal them. That anonymity was something we would both need, or at least, that's what I reasoned. Really, I had no idea what Sandy would need. From the time we hit the outskirts of Juarez, I resolved to let him call the shots. After all, he would know way better than I what we each needed to do.

I had some vague idea of moving around and meeting people in a desperate attempt to find some back-street king maker who would know what was going down in the local drug cartel world. It would be naïve to think any street-level hood would have the ear of those who made the big decisions, but I knew enough of drug cartels from Frederick to know that there are people on the street who know everything. They call them *halcones*—hawks—the eyes and ears of the cartel. Often, they are teenagers intent on working their way up the chain to become highly paid killer *sicarios*, and they're not always men. Increasingly, young women were taking those positions, and according to Frederick, there was no shortage of willing applicants. I grimaced, not at all sure a woman would be easier to deal with than one of the male *halcones*.

But even if we got the information we so desperately needed, what then? I had to go with Eduardo's assessment, but what did that mean? It would take an experienced agent with the right credentials and iron nerve to infiltrate La Linea or Barrio Azteca? I knew nobody who had ever had anything to do with either of those low-level hoodlums. They were killers—and yes, probably child kidnappers. Most of all, they were dangerous, their only ambition being to climb the ladder high enough to grasp for a piece of that lucrative pot of gold that defined the drug trade. They would do anything to get there, and if they were kidnapping babies, that was only one of many crimes they'd committed.

My stomach did flip-flops with each mile of pavement. The rape flashed before my eyes. I could never place myself in a situation where that could happen again. Never! Except to save my son. Not for the first time, tears welled to the surface, and I blinked them away. This wasn't the time for fear.

It was past midnight when the lights of Juarez showed through the windshield. Sandy pulled the pickup into the parking lot of one of the smaller hotels that littered the west side of the city. My room wasn't great, but I wasn't here as a tourist. With a thousand worries about the days ahead, I mumbled one more of many prayers for the safety of my son, then fell into a fitful sleep.

It was hardly past dawn when a soft knock on the door announced Sandy's presence, not that it mattered. I'd been up and ready for the better part of an hour, and I was glad to leave. We'd discussed a plan as we drove last night, and though I wasn't completely happy with letting Sandy

disappear alone into the bowels of this
seething cesspool of crime, he was adamant. I
finally gave in. I could hardly picture him
having any success in locating Luis, but I had
no other options.

We checked out of the hotel, and
Sandy maneuvered the old pickup to the curb,
close to a roadside *cafecita* for breakfast.
Everything appeared normal on the busy
street. Snarled traffic barely avoided gridlock.
Buses belched noise along with varying
degrees of pollution. People scurried past on
the sidewalk, avoiding eye contact, their faces
devoid of emotion, intent on reaching
whatever employment they'd secured to push
away the cockroaches of poverty that afflicted
so many in our land. Best of all, no gunshots
broke through the cacophony of street sounds
to trigger the underlying tension of Juarez into
a dash for safety. This was the safest time of
the day, if such there was such a thing in this
city of death.

Surreptitiously, I scanned the people
around me, wondering if one of them had
some knowledge of my baby boy. This was by
far the most likely place for the Jalisco Cartel
to have taken him, and if it was actually La

Linea who had Luis, this seemed the best place to search. They wouldn't likely have the resources to keep him anywhere else. Besides, if their plan was to send Luis out of the country, it would be easier to hide him in a large city with a busy airport. This was by far the most obvious exit point.

Sandy pushed the remains of his plate of *huevos rancheros* aside, and was finishing his coffee while I toyed with the eggs and chorizo sausage on my plate. Neither of us seemed able to eat.

"Any change in plans?" I asked.

He shook his head. "No, I think . . ."

My phone beside my plate vibrated. I glanced at the number. The call was from the crew quarters. Quickly, I hit the green button to answer, and tried to change tracks in my mind. Whatever was happening here in Juarez had little to do with cattle, horses, and general ranch problems. As much as I felt ill-equipped to deal with those this morning, it was necessary that I was available. I was the boss. There was no one else.

It was Tomas, and immediately, my heart jumped. Maybe he'd found . . .

"Señora, I called my cousin. I'm sorry I couldn't get hold of him sooner."

"That's alright, Tomas. What did he say?"

For a moment, there was silence. "I only talked to his mother. Last week, my cousin was shot and killed in a gun battle with federal troops."

"Tomas, I'm so sorry."

"I am sorry, as well. He chose to do wrong, and now he has paid with his life. It is hard on all my family."

"Tomas, if you need to take some time off for the funeral and to be with your family, that will be okay. As long as Antonio is there, the ranch will be fine for a few days."

"Thank you, Señora. I will leave tomorrow morning. The funeral is in the afternoon. I might stay one more day, but I will be back by Thursday."

"That will work, and take one of the ranch pickups. We will likely still be here in Juarez, so call me if you need anything." With that, we ended the conversation, and I told Sandy what had happened."

He nodded. Both of us had hoped Tomas might produce information that would speed Luis's return. Now, that appeared unlikely.

"Where are you going to stay tonight?" he asked.

I considered each of the downtown hotels. "Villa del Sol."

His eyebrows shot upward.

I clenched my teeth at his obvious disapproval.

Finally, Sandy shrugged. There were sleazier hotels than what I'd chosen, though you'd have to hunt to find them. I didn't want a quality hotel. What I needed, the Villa del Sol provided.

"Let's go." I gathered my purse and paid the bill for the food we'd barely touched.

At the truck, Sandy pulled his worn backpack out of the box while I stood on the sidewalk and waited. As he brushed past me, I squeezed his arm. "I will say many prayers for you." I reached out a hand and touched his. "Be careful."

His dark eyes held mine in an instant
of deep understanding and connection over
our shared danger.

<u>**Chapter 25**</u>

After Sandy disappeared around the corner, I started the pickup and dived into a gap between cars in the eastbound lane that would take me to the downtown area and my less-than-acceptable hotel. Either of us could be dead by tomorrow morning, but I had no intention of pulling away from the vague plan to which I was committed, despite Sandy's warning. Time was short. If Luis was still in the country, I had to move quickly.

After stopping at the hotel to check in, I drove back and forth through the barrios. There was nothing in my mind other than a vague and useless hope that I would run into someone who knew who, or what gang was kidnapping babies. In the early evening I dined at an absolutely gross restaurant in the worst part of town, and cursed my ex-husband —several times. Why hadn't he taken responsibility for this? I was attempting to accomplish what he did all the time, yet he couldn't seem to make any effort to find our son. The only other restaurant occupants appeared to be weary workers from the nearby Sorianas Supermarket. None of them looked like someone from a drug cartel. So what now?

Wearily I drove street after street. As twilight darkened the sky, I pulled to the curb and hunched down in the seat. Like every other cellphone user in the world, I pretended to check my phone for messages while I thought through what to do next. There were no messages, which meant I might have a serious social problem. At the intersection ahead, a hooker fell into step with a prospective john. He waved her away. She shrugged and returned to her corner, prepared to troll for another customer. I suspected Tuesdays might not be the best night for the girl's business. The street was nearly deserted, and I surreptitiously studied the prostitute. The saggy underarms and spreading hips meant she was past her prime. She appeared to be on the back-side of forty, though that was hard to tell with all the gobbed-on makeup. This was a hard part of town, in a city that was a cesspool of crime and killing. I reckoned this lady would know something about La Linea, and because I didn't have any other place to start, I slipped out the passenger side door and onto the sidewalk.

Though the pickup was several hundred feet from her corner, the lady was sharp-eyed enough to notice I'd crawled out the passenger side. She studied me as I approached her. Maybe she thought I was an aggrieved wife of one of her customers. I suppose that could have been possible, though I'd never suspected my ex-husband of cheating on me. Whatever Frederick's failings, I'd not had reason to think that was one of them.

I walked right up to her. She never stepped back or displayed any fear. I'd have been surprised if she'd done so. When she spoke, her voice was raspy and hard.

"Whaddya' want, lady?"

Right away, I noticed the overlarge pupils. She was high on cocaine or some other drug, which is what she probably had to do to get through a shift on this street. I didn't blame her, nor did I judge her. The Bible says we're not to do that. I couldn't have, anyhow. My whole life had been turned upside down. The rape I'd endured meant that every day, I cried for relief. Drugs—I understood. I longed for something to numb the pain. I was not inclined to judge this woman's addiction.

I stuffed my hands in my coat pockets. "I want nothing except to talk. I promise I won't get in the way if you have a customer come along."

Her eyes conveyed distrust. Few men want to talk to a whore, unless it's about price. Women generally don't want to talk to them at all. In our modern world, there are exceptions to that rule, but Juarez is very much part of the old order. There's little respect or love for prostitutes.

I stood my ground and waited for her to process my strange request. Eventually, she answered.

"I don't talk about customers, so if this is about yer' old man, forget it."

"It's not."

"Then what do you wanna' know?"

It hit me that this lady of the night was speaking Spanish with a slangy Texan accent. Why was she here? What was her story? Like every other trade, wages were considerably higher in El Paso on the Texas side, and the way she spoke indicated she'd not grown up on this side of the border. Though I felt bad about her circumstances, it didn't change what I'd come for. I needed information, and she might be my only chance to get what I needed. "How much do you make in a good night on this corner?"

"What's it to ya'?"

"Nothing, other than I need information, and I'm willing to pay a lot of money to get it. Is that something that would be of interest?"

Her eyes attempted to focus on mine. Focusing is difficult when you're high on drugs. She did her best.

"So . . . I'm all ears. Spill yer guts, baby doll."

There didn't seem any sense in holding back, so I spilled. I told her about my little Luis and how he'd been kidnapped, and why I thought he'd been smuggled across the border into Mexico.

At first, her lips formed a hard line, and her eyes constantly scanned for customers in the sporadic passing of cars. When I finished my story, I pressed my case. "Do you know whether any babies have been kidnapped and brought here?"

Her face had softened, and now it seemed I had her full attention. She was no longer cruising for customers. "What do I get out of this? Talking is dangerous."

Her gaze once again slipped past my face to the street, though this time, I suspected it was for a different purpose. She was afraid, and for good reason. The cartels were not to be trifled with. They had ears everywhere, and anybody who valued their life kept their mouth shut.

"If you can give me information about my baby, I will give you a thousand American dollars."

"What do you want to know?"

"The answer to three questions. Which cartel kidnapped him? Why did they do it? And, three . . . where are they selling babies?"

She hesitated a moment too long before answering. "That's more than I know."

"Maybe, but I'm betting you can find the answers."

Once more, the oversized pupils tried to focus on mine. "What makes you think you can get him back?"

There was no way I could explain the fierce love I had for my son to this broken, bitter woman. How could I relate to her that my life was nothing without Luis, and that I would do anything to hold him in my arms again? I simply shrugged, "I'm not sure I can, but I have to try."

Her voice hardened. "Mind you, I'm not saying they have him, but La Linea is where I'd start, and you didn't hear it from me. They work with some middle-Eastern Muslim outfit."

"Muslims? Who?"

"I don't know. If you want to know more, go there." She pointed down the street to a garish, neon sign advertising the Seven Jokers Strip Club. "Talk to Delora Rivera."

I did my best to maintain a friendly and expressionless smile, but my head was churning with possibilities.

"Thank you so much. What is your name?"

"Never mind . . . well, probably it doesn't matter. My street name is Esmerelda." She glanced furtively over my shoulder. "You didn't talk to me." Her eyes softened enough that I forgot about her disorientation and dilated pupils. "I had a baby once. I don't know where she is. I hope she's in Heaven."

I reached across the chasm between us and patted her arm. "Esmerelda, I firmly believe that all babies go to heaven when they die. I will say a prayer for you . . . and thank you." I slipped a wad of American dollars into her hand, then turned and hurried toward the strip club she'd indicated.

The Seven Jokers, one of at least a dozen Juarez brothels, advertised their wares with a half-dozen scantily-clad girlie signs plastered across the front of the building. I had no desire to know what the place was like, but no matter what happened, I had to go inside. As incongruous as it might seem, I had an old acquaintance there. It was time to renew my acquaintance with Delora Rivera.

My hand shook as I tugged at the ornately carved double doors. Inside, a long bar with upholstered stools ran nearly to the far wall on my left. Ahead of me, a scuffed dance floor shared space with several pool tables, I suppose placed there for the clientele while they waited for other more passionate pursuits. I scowled. Passionate? Hardly. What happened here was a consensual coupling for money—nothing more. The thought turned my insides into a quivering jelly of fear. I could barely control the sudden impulse to turn and run.

The madam . . . is that what one calls them? Honestly, I didn't know, but whatever her title, a heavyset, aging woman walked toward the spot where I stood glued just inside the door. Her hair, dyed a streaky platinum blond, was piled on top of her head. Heavy mascara and eyeliner disguised any hint of her age. Her eyes, calculating and hard, measured me.

"You're looking for a job, honey?"

"Yes, I might be. But first, I would like to talk to an old friend of mine who works here. Is Delora available?"

The woman's now skeptical eyes roved over my face. I should have known better than to try to pass off that 'looking for a job' line, but there was no going back.

"Any experience?"

I averted my eyes and pretended to survey the room. "Not really. I know I have to learn, but I need to get through college, so—I'm looking for work."

"Well, aren't you the practical sort." One side of the woman's mouth turned up slightly.

My face flushed, and the dusky interior did little to hide my consternation. "Hey, it's a job."

"That it is sweetie, and for you, it could work well. You'd draw 'em through the door like flies."

I couldn't stand any more, and my face fell. "Could you tell me where I can find Delora? Does she live upstairs?"

Though the lady's powder and paint did a passable job of covering her wrinkles and age, her disgust burned through to the surface. "You're a real babe. First, we rarely have customers this early in the day. And second, our girls don't live upstairs. They have houses and apartments, and they work regular shifts. Delora doesn't start until seven."

"Oh . . . I didn't know that. I just thought—never mind. Could you tell me where she lives? I would really like to see her."

"So would lots of people. And no, I don't give out phone numbers, and certainly not addresses of any of our employees. But good try, honey boobs. Better luck next time." The woman turned away, my interview at an end.

"How about the job?"

"No."

"But I thought—"

She turned toward me, her voice tight with anger. "You thought what . . . that I'd believe your phony college story? You're good looking enough, but you're thirty if you're a day. This isn't a good trade to learn when you're nearing the backside of the hill. Go find a sugar daddy and milk him for whatever you can get."

My crimson face heated further, if that were possible, my humiliation now complete. "And Delora?"

"Come back at seven. If she wants to see you, fine. If she doesn't, or if you give her any trouble, Gustavo will escort you out the hard way, which means the way to the street leads through one of the bedrooms, so mind your manners. I won't put up with any nonsense."

There seemed little more to say. I nodded politely and stumbled through the double doors that led to the street. The gaseous smog enveloped me, but after the potent fumes of alcohol and cheap perfume inside the brothel, the street smelled as pure as the breeze off the tallest peaks of the Sierra Madre.

<u>**Chapter 26**</u>

My hands were still trembling when I reached the pickup. The worst part was that in an hour, I had to again force myself to go back inside that den of iniquity, simply because the woman I sought might know something of my son. And there was no guarantee of success.

Contrary to what I'd told the madam in the Seven Jokers, Delora Rivera was not my friend. We were acquaintance with an old— and at one point, bitter—history. Her father owned a small grocery store in a middle-class area in our town of Agua Prieta. Her family was not rich, but neither were they poor. They lived in a single-level house next to the store, and our teenage social scene consisted of the following: Through the last couple years of high school, Delora had a crush on our ranch neighbor, Eduardo Garcia. He ignored her. For some reason, he had decided to turn his affections on me. I'd always viewed Eduardo as simply a good friend. Our common socio-economic strata meant we were often thrown together. I couldn't say I was completely oblivious to Eduardo's affections or Delora's jealousy, but at the time, the seriousness of it certainly didn't register in my teenage horsy existence. My world was barrel racing. Love or marriage to Eduardo—or any other man—was the last thing on my mind. Nevertheless, Eduardo's infatuation—and later, his supposed love for me escalated Delora's antagonism to full-fledged animosity. In a perverse way I never fully understood, my spurning his love turned the animosity into full-fledged hatred.

Later, after I'd made it clear to Eduardo that he and I were never going to be an item, he did turn his physical affections toward Delora. They even lived together, though it didn't last long. Her parents, like mine, were strict Catholic, and living together without the sacrament of marriage was frowned on. Eduardo had no intention of marrying her, and eventually they split, but by this time, her parents disapproval was the least of their problems. Eduardo had become firmly entrenched in the Jalisco Cartel hierarchy. With the contacts he'd developed on both sides of the border, he became a fast-rising star. Money, cocaine, and women were the fruits of his new status. He was no longer content with one middle-class girl from the barrios, and he soon left Delora for other, more glamorous bed partners. Delora, already hooked on cocaine, didn't do well with the split. For her, it was a steep and precipitous drug and alcohol-fueled slope that had deposited her at The Seven Jokers in Juarez. The curious part was that Eduardo never completely broke the ties he'd had with Delora. Whether it was actual love or something more sinister, Delora still held a part of him. His occasional visits to The Seven Jokers were well-known, which meant that Delora was at least an option in the search for Luis. All I could hope for was that our common past counted for enough goodwill to have a conversation.

I drove the few blocks to the hotel and lugged my bag up the worn tiles to my threadbare room on the third floor. Mentally exhausted, I slipped out of my scuffed tennis shoes and flopped onto the bed. Though I considered calling Frederick to see if he'd found out anything, the exercise didn't seem productive. He'd give me the same run-around as usual. I didn't need that. I closed my eyes. A nap would have made the time pass more quickly, and though it would have been a welcome reprieve from the confused mental gyrations in my head, sleep refused to come. What if Delora didn't know anything? Were she and Eduardo still seeing each other? Not for the first time, I wondered what hold Delora had over him. By all reports, she was still a drug-addicted prostitute. Eduardo, on the other hand, had all the money and power any criminal could want. What attraction still held him?

I tried to remember the last time I'd seen Delora. It had been at least two years ago. Frederick and I had been at Los Arcos, one of Juarez's nicer restaurants. We'd just finished our meal and were about to leave when a waiter had escorted Delora and a man to a table on the other side of the restaurant. Painted and blinged from head to toe, she looked nothing like the girl I'd known back home in Agua Prieta. Her flinty face had hardened, the first turkey tracks of age starting to radiate from her eyes. A dark maroon slash defined her lips, one more garish detail in her heavily painted face. Frederick and I slipped out of the restaurant without her seeing us. I could only imagine what she looked like after several more years of the hard life she'd chosen. I doubted her girlhood dream had been to be a stripper at The Seven Jokers. Whatever had happened back then was something I'd likely never had to face. Anyway, it wasn't my place to judge her. This afternoon, it would be best to mind the old saying: "Except for the grace of God, there go I."

With that decision, I did drift off for a few minutes. When I awoke, I showered and made a cup of coffee with the two-cup unit in the room. Eating until this was over was out of the question. My insides were already knotting with dread. Food would not better the situation. Besides, it was time to go. It would be best to be at The Seven Jokers before Delora started her shift. I certainly didn't want to wait one minute more than I had to in that sleazy place while she did whatever was required of her on the stage or with a customer in one of the back rooms. Best to be there when she walked in the door.

It was 6:45 when I pushed through the doors of The Seven Jokers. I'd not gone ten feet toward the bar when an inebriated customer threw his arms around me. I fought to escape with little success until the madam happened to notice. She strode over and pulled the guy off me. Anger collided with fear as I stammered my thanks.

"You're still wanting to see Delora?"

"Please. I wanted to be here early so I didn't take any time from her shift."

"Tell you what, honey. Go around and wait at the back entrance. She should arrive shortly."

Grateful for her rescue, I stepped closer. "Thank you . . . I didn't properly introduce myself when I was here this morning. I'm Dina."

She eyed me coolly. "Just tell the first girl that shows up that Consuela sent you around to the back, and to let you in. Wait inside until Delora shows."

My head bobbed up and down, double-timing the love ballad wailing in the background. Relief washed over me. In different circumstances, I might have cried. There had been too much emotional upheaval, and whatever toughness or resilience I might have once had was long gone. I stumbled for the doors that led to the street and made my way around the side of the building to the back entrance. Several late-model cars were scattered around the small parking lot. I glanced at the steel door at the back of The Seven Jokers and made an instant decision. No, I would not go inside that building again, not if I could avoid it. I leaned back against the rough adobe wall. I would wait right here for Delora.

Several cars pulled into the lot. All of the vehicles carried single occupants, ladies of varying ages and build, some pretty, some not so much. What they had in common were their eyes. I want to say they were hard, which they were, but that doesn't really do them justice. Each one stared suspiciously at me as they used their keys to let themselves into the building. After the fourth girl had passed, I nailed the common factor. None of their eyes were a window to their true self. To survive in this profession, they had erected an impermeable wall between their body and soul. As I watched them pass, their eyes seemed to carry a message. "For the right amount of money, you can ravish my body, but you will never reach the real me." Again, I wondered what drew Eduardo to Delora.

At five minutes after four, a red Ford Fusion screeched into one of the parking stalls. Delora drove like she was late, and my heart sank when she jumped out, slammed the car door, and scurried for the entrance. As she fumbled the key into the lock, I spoke.

"Delora?"

Her head swiveled toward me as she turned the knob. She immediately recognized me, because she slowly let the knob go and withdrew her key. "Hi, Dina." She backed away from the door and faced me. As she did, suspicion hardened her features. "What do you want? Why are you here?"

I stepped forward and touched her arm. It seemed an evening of pressing flesh I didn't want to touch, but I didn't know any other way of connecting. Hugging would be phony, not at all appropriate. "Can we talk?"

Delora glanced at her watch. "I'm late for work. It has to be fast."

"Oh, I already talked to Consuela. It will be okay." That wasn't strictly true, but at this point, I was willing to bend the truth.

Suddenly, I had an idea. "Maybe we could go inside and talk while you're getting ready."

Delora eyed me through the same impenetrable barrier I'd seen in the other women. "All right. Come on." Her voice said she would listen to whatever I had to say, but as she opened the door, her hard eyes indicated something completely different, and the message was clear. My time was limited. I would have one chance to state my case.

<u>Chapter 27</u>

I followed Delora inside the building and down a carpeted hallway. At the far end, she unlocked a door on the left. A king-sized bed dominated the room, and if I'd had any doubt about what my school friend did for a living, it was now settled. However, this was not the time to dwell on that sad fact of life.

"Sit there." Delora pointed toward a chair on the far side of the bed. "Sorry, I have to be on the floor in ten minutes, so if you have a speech, get on with it."

"My baby boy was kidnapped. The La Linea gang may have him, though it may have been the Jalisco Cartel who abducted him."

Delora's head turned from the mirror, where she was expertly applying eyeliner. "What makes you think that?"

"I talked to Eduardo, and though he denied any involvement, I think he was lying."

Makeup complete, Delora pulled a purple stocking over her right leg as she searched my face. I should have left Eduardo out of it. It was clear she thought I had an interest in him.

"Delora, I know—everybody knows what Eduardo does. We dislike each other intensely, but he is my neighbor. We share many miles of fence line, so we have to get along. And once in a while, we have to talk to each other." I held up a hand. "There is nothing else there. I thought he might tell me something helpful, so I called him the other night." My voice trembled and I bit my lower lip while I gained control. "I just want my baby back. I hoped Eduardo might have told you something, or that you might know where I could start searching."

The other stocking slid over Delora's long, but thickening leg. We were no longer school classmates. We were both barely thirty, but for her, time and gravity had already started its relentless march. I couldn't help wondering how a good Catholic girl like Delora ended up here. I didn't have time for an answer—if there was one. I needed to focus on whatever Delora could tell me.

She pulled a dress out of the closet. It wasn't much more than a long, skinny shirt, but she managed to wiggle into it.

I waited. The closet produced a pair of stiletto boots, which covered more leg than the dress did.

"Okay, time's up. I'm out of here," Delora announced.

"Please, Delora. I'm begging you. If you know anything—"

"I don't, at least not much. Eduardo and the Jalisco Cartel may not be lily white, but they don't kidnap babies."

"La Linea?"

"That's different. They're just hoods, and they'll do anything for a buck." She eyed me. "Dina, I always hated your guts because I thought you were sleeping with Eduardo. Now I know you weren't, so I kind of owe you. One of my occasional customers is a street *halcone* for La Linea. He likes to think he's more important than he is. I don't know why men talk more when they have their pants off, but he does, and I listen. A girl never knows when information might come in handy. Anyhow, if they have your baby, this is where he will be."

She rattled off an address, and I reached in my purse for a pen.

"No." Her voice was hard. "Memorize it. Do not write that on anything."

I dropped the pen back in my purse. "Absolutely. I understand, and Delora, I'm so grateful."

"Don't be. If you go there, they will kill you, and that will be the best part of what will happen. By the time they finish with you, death will be welcome."

I shivered at her words. The rape spread like a black Satanic cloud of fear over my head. I could never go anywhere where that might happen again. And yet, I was here —here in a . . . okay . . . a whorehouse, at least, that's what the men at the ranch called places like this.

Delora's lips were flat, her obsidian eyes liquid with fear. She'd stepped way out on a limb for me, and we both knew it. Only God above could have given me the courage to walk into this place, and I figured it was only Him who could have prompted Delora to give me that address. What she'd done was dangerous, but she'd tossed me a lifeline. I would never betray her.

Delora held the door open. Before I walked past her into the hallway, I reached over and gave her a hug. She obviously hadn't expected that, and for a moment, I thought her eyes had filled with tears, and there was probably little in her life that prompted that kind of emotion. To survive, she had to be tough as rawhide. She turned away and shook her head. I didn't ask why. There wasn't time. I padded down the hallway and softly closed the outside door behind me.

The afternoon had turned into early evening. I recited the address over and over in my head as I made my way out to the street and my junky, old pickup. What should I do now? Though Delora had given me the information I'd hoped for, she'd also warned me. To go to that address would expose me to more danger than I was capable of handling. But what if Luis was there? The address pulled me like a magnet. I started the pickup and pulled out into the street. Carefully, I navigated several side streets on the east side of the city until I'd found *Calle* Valenzuela.

The area wasn't poor, but neither was it Loma Arroyo, one of the tony residential areas where businessmen and cartel goons lived in sprawling ranch houses with maids, butlers, and bodyguards.

Some houses had numbers. Others might have, but they weren't visible from the street. Finally, I saw the house I was looking for. Two-forty-five. I tried to memorize every detail of the yard and outside façade as I drove past. At the next block, I pulled to the curb. My hands trembled as I drove past the house. Was my son behind one of those windows? In my mind, I picked through every detail of the house. Magenta adobe. No contrasting trim on the windows. Every piece of glass I could see, barred, and probably all were wired with the best burglar alarms money could buy. That wasn't unusual, not in our country. I peered over my shoulder at the three windows I could see above the wall on the east side of the house. And why was there a third floor of rooms on a middle-class street like this one? The other houses were either one story or, at most two, with a flat roof that was most often used for hanging laundry or growing salsa vegetables. It didn't take long for the answer to come. This location had been hand-picked, but like any gang clubhouse, they needed rooms for a multitude of nefarious activities.

I slumped over the wheel. So, I'd found what might be the house where La Linea was holding my son. What now? Sandy had decided not to carry his phone. He'd left it in the truck, so I couldn't call him for help. And though we still had lots of payphones in our country, it wasn't likely he'd use one. And what about Frederick? I grabbed at my phone. My thumb hovered over his name. The least he could do is offer advice. If he had any credibility, he would immediately send a squad of undercover agents to search the premises of the house beside me, and possibly blow a few low-level La Linea gangbangers into the next life. If Luis was in there, Frederick could send in a commando unit by helicopter. He'd once done it for an agent. Why not our son? Luis would be back in the United States of America within the hour. So why was I hesitating? Frederick should be involved, even if up to now he'd not pulled his share of the load. Several times, I started to push the icon beside his name, but for some crazy reason which I didn't understand, I couldn't make the call, at least not yet.

After driving around the block another couple times, which was dumb, I pulled to the side of the street. There was no better way to advertise my undying interest in the house across the street than to make sure that whoever was in there would be able to recognize my pickup. Not that it would have been hard. I'd chosen this vehicle so I didn't attract any undue attention. However, there was a small hole in the muffler, which gave out a distinct growl. I should have chosen one of our newer trucks. No one would fail to recognize this pickup by its sound or its beauty.

I slipped out of the truck and walked down the sidewalk to the street corner, staying well away from the property, wishing Sandy would call. And what if Frederick called? I would have to tell him what was going on. If I'd actually thought he could or would be a help in getting our son back, I would have called him in a flash. But more than anything, I was afraid he would just complicate the situation? Rather than come, he might decide to bring in the Juarez police. And who knew where that would end? Their first priority would be to get the bad guys. But what if there was a gun battle and something happened to Luis? I could never live with myself if that happened.

I strolled up the street toward the house, trying desperately to look like one of the neighbors out for a stroll. The concrete block wall topped by barbed wire and broken glass advertised better than any sign that trespassers were frowned on. At the midpoint in the six-foot-high wall, wide, black, slatted gates allowed little or no view inside. At the man gate in the middle, a surly teenager slouched against the frame. His eyes flickered downward from my face.

I smiled seductively and gave him my sunniest come-on smile. "*Hola*. I am new in the neighborhood. I have rented a house over on *Calle Gomez*. I didn't know there were any houses as nice as this one. Is it for sale?"

The kid leered at me. "No, lady, but if you'd like to have a look, I could give you a tour."

Inside, I trembled, and my heart sank even further toward my shoes. It was more than obvious what he had in mind. I could never go inside that gate. But I did, because I had to.

When he laid a hand on my arm, my face hardened. "I'm looking for real estate, not . . ." I waved my hand in a sign of dismissal. I didn't have to finish the sentence. The disappointed look on his face told me he knew exactly what I meant.

The young Lothario shrugged. "What are you looking for?"

"Something similar to this. I just noticed it from the street, and thought it might be perfect, so I texted the address to my husband and one of our business managers in El Paso. Even if we couldn't buy this one, I really like the lines of the house. Perhaps we will have to buy property in this area and build something similar."

The boy's eyes narrowed at my mention of, 'a business manager'. In his eyes, that meant substantial wealth. The inference that I had business interests in the United States clinched it. I'd just been elevated from bedroom material to his superior, even if I was a woman. At least, that's what I hoped as I stepped through the gate.

My new acquaintance signaled to another sullen young tough who sat in the shade of the wall, his cellphone in his hand. "Emilio, I'm going to show this lady around a bit."

Emilio eyed me, then scowled at his companion. "It's your neck."

"Never mind. I'll let you know when I need advice."

O—kay, these two weren't great buddies. I strolled ahead of my Lothario tour guide, surveying the roof line and upper windows. When he caught up, I introduced myself. "I'm Dina. And your name is—?"

"Martin. I can't take you inside, but we can walk around the outside."

"That would be wonderful. Do you mind if I take a few pictures?"

The boy glanced back toward the gate. "I suppose not. Just be discreet about it, and if anybody comes, make sure they don't see you. Esteban wouldn't like it if he found you here."

"Esteban?"

Martin flinched. "You don't want to know. He's the boss."

"You mean, he owns the house?"

"Yeah—sort of."

"Immediately, I turned as if to go back
to the gate. "I'm so sorry. I thought you owned
the house." I touched his arm with the tips of
my fingers. "You seemed like a man with
authority. I would not want to get you in
trouble. Perhaps I should call and talk to
Esteban."

"No, it is fine." He waved off my
concern and stuck his chest out. "It will be my
pleasure to show such a beautiful lady around
the property, a little secret between us."

I flashed my most radiant smile,
hoping the fluttering fear in my chest didn't
show on my face. "If you're sure?"

He cupped my elbow in his hand.
"Absolutely. Come, I will show you the back
of the house."

As we strolled toward the back yard, I
continued to feign whatever interest I could
muster in the architecture and lines. All the
while, I scanned the windows. Who was
inside? Was Luis still here, separated from me
only by a wall? That thought was nearly more
than I could stand.

We followed the brick walkway that appeared to run around both sides of the house. At the back, Martin stopped as I exclaimed over the greenery. The problem was, I knew little about plants other than what grew on our arid range back home. Several transplanted palms rose out of the unidentifiable fronds and bushes, which provided shade to the area next to the double garage on my right. The ornate walkway scribed a half circle that ended at a massive veranda on my left. I gushed over the beauty and how it added such character to the house while my heart sank farther toward my feet. How would I ever find out whether Luis was here?

Martin seemed nervous. Clearly, he'd overstepped his authority by giving me a tour of the grounds, but I wasn't leaving yet, not unless there was no other option.

"Martin, this is so wonderful. Are you sure the owners wouldn't sell it? I don't even have to talk to my husband or any of our business people. This is exactly what we're looking for."

Martin fidgeted from one foot to the other. "No, pretty lady. At least, not that I know of."

I slipped my hand under his arm. My behavior was so brazen, I had to make a conscious effort to keep from blushing. I didn't. This was about my baby. "Martin, would it be possible to take a quick peek inside—I mean, not upstairs, of course. Just the layout of the main floor."

His eyes flickered from my face toward the gate at the front of the house, clearly torn with the danger of taking me inside the house versus the possible reward. His eyes flickered downward toward my breasts. I did nothing to change his mind. He was a cartel goon, and suddenly, I knew beyond any doubt that the organization this man represented had kidnapped my son. If it came down to his life over Luis's, I would slip a knife between this young man's ribs. The problem was, not only did I have a moral distaste for killing a man, I didn't have the knife to do it. Once more, I gave him the best "come on" smile I could muster. It wasn't a look I'd had much practice with, seeing as how, until recently, I'd been a reasonably happy married woman.

Martin's eyes seemed to have stuck in the middle of my bosom. At least, that's what I thought until the sound of a vehicle slowing in the street brought panic to his beguiled features.

He whirled and sprinted as fast as his legs could carry him to the corner of the house. Instantly, he froze. He backed away from the corner and whirled toward me. Whatever he'd seen had drained the last bit of blood from his panicked face.

Chapter 28

My teenage guide turned terror-stricken eyes toward me. In three paces, he was back in front of me. "If Esteban finds me here with you in the yard, he will kill me. Lady, please help me. I promise, you won't be sorry."

Instantly, I understood. This boy had played the big shot, but he had no authority to tour anyone through the property, and it would be especially frowned on if there were contraband, drugs, guns, or perhaps a kidnapped baby inside.

I squared my shoulders and stepped back. "Excuse me? I have done nothing wrong. I think I will leave now." I went to step around him.

"Lady—Dina, please, it is just a small favor. Let me quickly hide you in a safe place for just a few minutes, until Esteban leaves, and then we can carry on with our tour of the property."

I pouted. "No, I think I would like to leave." I backed away.

His face showed even more panic, if that were possible. "He may very well kill both of us."

My chin jutted forward in anger. "Why? I did nothing wrong."

The boy stepped forward faster than I'd have thought possible. He grabbed both of my arms, the fear growing in his eyes with each passing moment. The growling sound coming from the street could only be the gate rolling back, which was followed by an accelerating vehicle pulling into the driveway.

I searched Martin's eyes, hesitated, then shrugged. "Very well."

Car doors opened and slammed shut.

"I will do as you say, but no—"

"You won't regret it. I promise." His head swiveled one way, then the other before going back toward the corner of the house. It could only be seconds before this Esteban and whoever was with him appeared, and I had little doubt that if Martin died, I would as well. The cartel would not leave me as a witness.

"Hurry." The boy grabbed my hand and dragged me toward the veranda. Then he shoved open the back door and pushed me inside. "Go up the stairs to the third floor. A door leads outside to the rooftop. They never go up there. When it is safe, I will come for you."

I scowled at him.

"I'm sorry," he whispered.

The door hadn't completely closed behind me when we both heard the steps rounding the corner of the house next to the veranda.

"Martin!" The voice cracked through the heat like a small-caliber bullet. "What are you doing here?"

I tiptoed away from the veranda door. The voices faded, but not before I heard Martin's answer. He was clearly going for broke, presuming his gate guard buddy hadn't ratted him out.

"I heard a noise, and I thought I should come to investigate," Martin stuttered.

I had no intention of staying long enough to hear the conclusion to their conversation as I took the stairs two at a time to the second story. There were no gunshots, so I guessed that, at least for now, the leering cartel boy had survived. In between panting breaths, I said a prayer of thanks. Only God in Heaven could have got me into this house. But what was I to do from here?

Downstairs, another door opened. Voices drifted up to the landing, as I frantically scanned the layout around me. The house was built like a small hotel, and perhaps that had been the original use. A short vestibule and hallway ended at the front of the building, with rooms on both sides. A quick glance showed two open doors. Three or four others were closed. All was quiet.

I tiptoed up to the third floor. Same layout. To my left, the stairway led upward, presumably to the door that led out to the roof, where I was to hide. Voices rose and fell from a door at the far end of the hallway. Once, a child whimpered, and my heart went to my knees. It had only lasted a second, but instantly I knew that Luis had made that sound. Rapidly ascending footsteps from the staircase gave me no opportunity to investigate. I scuttled around the corner and up the remaining stairs to the roof. Fortunately, the door opened silently. I slipped through and closed it softly behind me.

The flat roof, cluttered with broken furniture, a monstrous black water tank, and several air conditioning units provided a multitude of places to hide. Unless there was a concerted effort to find me, I would be reasonably safe here.

When there appeared to be no immediate effort to hunt me down, I crept back to the door and opened it an inch. I could hear no sound of pursuit, so I propped the door open with a broken table leg and slipped far enough down the stairs to hear the voices below me. There were two. A male, who I presumed must be the feared Esteban, was giving instructions to a woman. She had questions, and although I couldn't hear what she asked, it was obvious from the high-pitched tone of her voice that she wasn't happy. I crept lower. The sharp retort of a hand against flesh silenced the woman's voice. A child cried. I needed no more proof. That child was my baby. Luis was thirty feet away. Just down the hallway. But I could no more reach him than I could move the chasm between heaven and hell.

Hidden in the stairwell, I watched as a heavy, middle-aged woman with my baby in her arms appeared behind the man. My heart raced. Luis appeared to have been well cared for. His face was still chubby, and the clothes he was wearing seemed clean and quite new. I had only one glimpse, and then my baby was gone. I couldn't stand it any longer. I slumped forward, my face in my hands. How could this have happened? God above had provided a miracle to get me into this house, only to have to watch my son disappear—perhaps forever?

I texted Frederick. Then, as I heard the car drive away with my son, I wept.

Chapter 29

When Martin, the cartel boy, tiptoed up the stairs and found me, I'd not moved. I still sat dejectedly on the top step, my tear-streaked face and tousled hair quite a different sight than when he'd let me into the house. He stopped at the landing below me and stared.

"Lady, what happened?"

I didn't smile, nor did I answer. Recriminations haunted me. Why hadn't I stopped the man? Would he have shot me? Did I care? Death could be no worse than this ripping, visceral pain. I stumbled to my feet. The boy turned, and I followed him down the stairs to the back door. Before he opened it, he turned to me. "I'm sorry you were so afraid, but I do thank you for letting me hide you. You may have saved my life. Esteban is not a forgiving man."

"Can I ask you a question?"

He nodded.

"Who is this Esteban, and where was he taking the baby?"

His eyes grew wary, and they slid away from mine. "I don't think I should . . .

look lady, why don't you just leave? You didn't really want to see this house, did you?"

"No, Martin. That baby is mine."

The boy pulled the door open. "You need to leave. I don't know anything. I'm just a—"

"I saved your life. I'm not asking for anything that will ever come back to bite you." My eyes never left his face, and I tried to telegraph my commitment to keeping his indiscretion between the two of us.

He fidgeted from one foot to the other, clearly weighing his fear against his debt to me. "Alright, but I do not know where they took the baby. One of the men said they had to be at the airport by three. That's all I know. Listen, lady, I need to get back to the gate. I appreciate you helping me, but I shouldn't have let you in. And there's nothing more I can tell you."

"And Esteban? Who is he? Just tell me that, and I will go."

"Okay, but no more. Esteban is *el jefe*, the leader of all our Sicarios in the Jalisco Cartel. He is in charge of all executions."

"But the baby?" Fear raced through my veins faster than blood could ever take it.

He shrugged. "I know nothing more. Now go, or we will have to make a different deal."

This arrogant kid was again becoming dangerous. It was time for me to take his advice and get out of here before . . . before . . . I was about to round the corner of the house when the now familiar sound of the gate reached us. Once more, a vehicle pulled up toward the front of the house.

Martin cursed. "Go back upstairs. I don't know what this is about, but it shouldn't be long before we can get you out of here."

I glared at him. "I will do this one more time to save you. Perhaps this time, you will not forget your debt."

"I am sorry. I owe you. Please, do not betray me. I will repay you well."

Once more, I went inside the house and scampered up the stairs, each step hammering a new level of fear into my chest. Now familiar with the layout, I moved closer to the heavy banister on the second landing, and peered between two of the ornate rails. I could reach the roof quickly and silently, if it became necessary. Several men strode through the entry. One held the door back while another pushed a bloodied, stumbling form in front of him. The man's face was beat to a pulp, barely recognizable, but the long, curly hair gave him away. Sandy had found La Linea. Apparently, it hadn't gone well.

Voices drifted to the landing. "Move, traitor."

Traitor? What was this about? And then I remembered our conversation after I'd met with the ranch crew. Twenty years ago, Sandy had been an enforcer, a sicario for Los Zetas. He'd escaped—until now. How had this happened? Juarez was a long way from Monterrey and Los Zetas territory, but then, the little I knew about the eastern cartels started making sense. Los Zetas and the Sinaloa Cartel had always been deadly enemies, both fighting for the same border corridors into the United States, and especially this one. Whether it was corruption, incompetence by American authorities, or simply that there was such a huge volume of drugs being pumped through the Juarez to El

Paso pipeline, this was a prized artery. And because the Jalisco Cartel and their enforcers, La Linea, were at war with Chapo Guzman's Sinaloa Cartel, that automatically made them allies with Los Zetas. It was all a tangled and shifting web of allies that could change at any moment. Apparently, someone had known Sandy in years past.

I shuddered and pushed away from the banister. It was then that my cellphone fell out of my pocket. It hit the marble stair beside me. When plastic hits marble, the sound carries like a dinner gong. Every man at the bottom of the staircase looked up, and it didn't take more than about three seconds for one of those goons to reach the top. His hand closed over my throat, and he smashed the back of my head against the floor before I even knew what was happening.

"Who are you?" The words were guttural and tense.

I choked, unable to answer, even if I'd wanted to. He took his hand away from my throat, though he still held me down.

"I am the new housekeeper." I had to try something, though I doubted what I'd said

would get past first base. It didn't. His hand
rocketed off the side of my face.

"Lie to me again, and I'll cut your
throat right here."

Suddenly, anger beyond any I'd ever
known sent a torrent of resentment through
every capillary in my body. These people had
violated me and my family in every possible
way. Because of them, I, along with millions
of others, lived a nightmare.

"I am Dina Rodriguez, just one more
person in our country who you have abused
and violated. You kidnapped my little boy, and
I came to find him. That man you call a traitor
might have once been a part of your evil
empire. He isn't now, nor has he been for at
least twenty years. All we want is to live our
lives and to be left alone, free from your
depravity." I screamed the last sentence in his
hideous, twisted face, even though his hand
still gripped my throat.

For a while, he simply pinned me to
the floor, I suppose deciding whether or not to
kill me. I doubt any of my words meant
anything. Most of these people have no
recognizable conscience or soul. Although

God placed a sense of right and wrong into every human to balance the evil we're prone to, these cartel thugs had long ago seared that sense into unrecognizable carbon. Nevertheless, for better or worse, I'd said my piece.

If I thought my outburst would make a difference, I was wrong. The man jerked me to my feet, slammed me against the wall, and frisked me. He couldn't have been more efficient, and for once, there was nothing sexual about it. His sole purpose was discovering hidden weapons. Unfortunately, I had none. How I wished I had. I'd have killed every one of them. Sandy and I would walk out of here, and then find Luis.

The man grabbed a fistful of my hair and marched me down the stairs. At the bottom, Sandy painfully raised his head. Close up, his face looked even more of a mess than it had from upstairs.

"Señora, I am sorry. I didn't intend—"

"Sandy, I know." I reached out to hug him, but the goon who held my hair in his fist jerked me back.

One of them shoved Sandy into a room which appeared to be some kind of parlor or lounge. It sported a card table. Cane-back chairs littered the outside of the room. I'd told Martin that I wanted to see the downstairs room lay out. I was now getting my tour, though not how I'd wanted.

At the back of the room, one of the men opened a steel door, painted white. Our escorts shoved Sandy inside, then me. A stairway to the basement stretched down into the gloom. I glanced back at a west window that let in a good portion of the afternoon sun. I doubted either of us would ever glimpse that again—not in this life.

<u>**Chapter 30**</u>

At the bottom of the stairs, the short hallway stopped at two steel doors doors. The man in front of me unlocked the door on the left, flipped a light switch. The goon behind me shoved both of us inside. My gaze darted from one end of the room to the other. Though the lighting was dim, it illuminated more than I wanted to see. My future didn't look good. The unpainted concrete floor sloped toward a drain in the middle of the room, like any mechanical shop, though I doubted this wastepipe was used for oil or grease. The walls were covered with a dark, seamless sheeting, with iron rings fastened at six-foot intervals on two sides. There were more rings attached to the ceiling. Three oversized, wooden chairs, placed near the wall on one side of the room, faced us. When they pushed me into the far one on the right, I saw they were bolted to the concrete floor. It was then that I noticed the stench that seemed to be emanating from the blue, plastic barrels across the room from the chairs. I'd been in an abattoir a few times back when Papa was alive, and this place looked eerily similar. I tried to swallow the fear that threatened to sweep away what little self-control I had left. The man who had slammed me against the wall upstairs and frisked me scooped my cellphone off the floor where it had fallen. The phone was password protected, so he'd not likely be able to access any texts or information from it, not that it mattered. Frederick probably hadn't even received my earlier short text after I'd seen Luis. The last thing I'd needed at that point was the phone making any sound to betray my presence, so I'd turned it off.

They blindfolded me, and then somebody grabbed my wrists and handcuffed them behind me, though they left my legs loose. I swallowed the panic building inside me and clenched my hands into fists to stop the trembling. This would be painful, and would not end well for either of us.

Our captors never spoke while they worked. Footsteps then faded toward the door. Silence. I held my breath, trying desperately to hear any sound that would betray our fate.

"Sandy?"

There was no answer.

"Sandy, are you there?" I spoke louder this time. A sense of dread trickled through my chest and down my arms. Had he passed out? He'd been badly beaten, but he had seemed coherent and alert, so that didn't seem likely. Had they silently killed him? How could they have done that without making a sound? I was seated barely six feet away from him. That wasn't possible, was it? I should have heard some indication of a struggle. The only other option was they had taken him with them. But why? Then I remembered the other door at the bottom of the basement stairs. It was identical to the one that led into this room, and I suspected the room behind it was a mirror image of this one. Either way, there would be no escape. Sandy was dead. I would be next.

Delora had given me good information, but I doubted she or anyone outside of the La Linea hierarchy knew what really happened here. However, her nervous glances toward the door were enough for me to know that she was afraid, and rightfully so. The stories were whispered rumors, tales of what happened to the bodies of those unfortunate enough to run afoul of the cartels.

What was in those barrels across the room was a potent mixture of sodium hydroxide, drain cleaner, and body parts. Or maybe not body parts. Sandy and I would provide those, and I had no doubt the torture would soon begin. The waiting and the silence was the first part of the procedure. The pain would come later. I would break. I knew that. They would start my discovery of pain with medical precision, until I was ready to say or do whatever they wished.

All I wanted was my baby back. I knew nothing that could be of any use to them, and had never had anything to do with any of the cartels. But that wouldn't matter. I was now an inconvenient witness to the kidnapping. And those who walked down the stairs to the basement in this house, were never heard from again. To return from here was impossible.

I strained to hear a sound—anything. There was nothing, and I knew this underground death chamber had broken, then silenced the screams of a multitude of victims. A torrent of tears soaked the blindfold in front of my eyes. The thought of death terrified me, but even more so was the fear of the slow and painful journey to get there. And now Sandy had died as well. I shouldn't have let any of the ranch crew get involved, even if it had been Sandy's idea. The cartels were too powerful, their level of intelligence equal to some sovereign states. Why had I agreed to Sandy's proposal? Why had he thought he could infiltrate one of these deadly organizations, especially in the short time we had to be successful?

Time passed, with only the beating of my heart for sound. I wanted to scream, to plead for mercy, but there was no one to hear my agony. I didn't know if it was an hour or three, but suddenly, the deep silence was broken. I strained to hear. The door knob turned and a hinge squeaked. Soft footfalls approached. I tried to place them—count them. One person? Two? Were these my last moments? My shoulders involuntarily hunched forward. Would they just shoot me in the back of the head? Or would I hear a club whistling through the air before it smashed into my skull? Either option would be preferable to hours of torture. What information would they want that I could tell them? I clenched my teeth, preparing for the worst. Their evil knew no bounds. For them, to torture and kill was an orgasmic high, completely attuned to their father, Satan.

The footsteps halted in front of me. I felt rather than heard another person behind me. I wanted the terror to end, and I braced for the first blow. Hurry! Do what you're going to do. Maybe it would be a bullet, or worse, the cold steel of a knife as it sliced into the tender skin and cartilage in my neck. Get it over with. I wanted desperately to scream, but nothing happened. Seconds passed, each one a minute long. Hands gripped the metal cuffs on my wrists. I felt the release of the pressure as the unknown person unfastened them from the chair. What did this mean? Had they killed Sandy and dismembered his body in the next room? That was it. This room was just a holding cell. The butchery happened behind the other door.

I couldn't stop my weakness from showing. More tears wet the blindfold. My thoughts focused on eternity. Maybe I deserved this. For so long, I'd been angry with God. I'd blamed him for taking my parents, for my broken marriage, for my lack of success in the rodeo arena. Through it all, I'd abandoned the church and my salvation. Now, facing eternity, I wanted to repent, to do it all over again. Most of all, I wanted the security of the Savior. As the men marched me out of the room, I prayed for forgiveness, for absolution. The stark reality of death was imminent, and before that happened, there would be pain and degradation beyond anything I'd ever thought possible. I can't say my prayer for forgiveness brought any peace. But it did quiet my fear. God would supply enough strength—for whatever lay ahead.

The man who had jerked me out of the chair and guided me toward the door had his fingers curled around my neck. I didn't resist. I was beyond that, even if it would have made a difference. I so wished I could have hugged Sandy and apologized for letting him come with me to Juarez. In my heart, I knew I would never see him again. And Frederick? We shared a child. We always would. I'd learned that about divorce. You might not sleep with the partner you'd sworn to love and honor, but you couldn't just walk away when two had become three. There was the unspoken commitment to the child you'd created. It was too late to change what we'd done, but as I stumbled out of the room I said a prayer for my son. I would never see him again, but I prayed that our Lord and Father would watch over him, that He would be a mother and father to him in place of the earthly ones he would never have. And most of all, I prayed that Luis would come to know and trust the Savior I'd so foolishly abandoned.

After they pushed me through the door of the holding room, I expected to make a hard left toward the room where they'd taken Sandy. But much to my surprise, the hand pushed me toward the stairs. A momentary wave of optimism trickled upward to my brain. Maybe—no, I shouldn't get my hopes up. Nevertheless, it didn't appear I was going to die, or even be tortured, at least not in the next few minutes, and for that, I was grateful.

At the top of the stairs, the hand directed me to the left, which I remembered led to the outside door at the back of the property. I stumbled forward. It would have been easier if they'd removed the blindfold, but apparently, that wasn't going to happen. At the end of the veranda, I stumbled down the two steps that led to the walkway. The hand jerked me upright, then directed me toward what I assumed was the driveway that ran along the east side of the house. I didn't even consider trying to escape. Even if they were still going to kill me, I'd rather die by a bullet out in the desert than in a dark, evil basement. For one millisecond, a niggling, infinitesimal ray of hope flared in my mind. Reality washed the hope away long before it took hold. There was no way they would turn me loose. I knew too much, which meant wherever they were taking me had only one ending.

<u>**Chapter 31**</u>

The fingers that bit into my neck were unrelenting. The man shoved me into a vehicle and down onto what I presumed was the back seat floor. They'd not removed the blindfold, so I buried my nose in the carpet and prayed as the vehicle accelerated out of the yard.

Once, one of the men seated up front spoke. His voice, lazy and slow, had a familiar accent. His diction was foreign, and yet it wasn't. There was the odd misplaced word, but still, he spoke like a native. Suddenly it dawned on me. He was Chicano. He'd grown up on the American side of the border, and I'd bet heavily that like my brother and I, he'd learned English as a child at the same time he was taught Spanish. It was a voice I would remember, not that I expected that exercise to be of any value. Though the man spoke softly, I caught most of what he was saying. He seemed to be the one giving orders.

"They will be on the same flight."

Another voice from the front seat replied, "You don't think that will be a problem?"

I strained to hear the reply, but there was nothing audible. After that conversation, there was only the droning whine of the tires on the pavement as the car picked up speed on its way through town. Sometime in the next few hours, I would die. I needed to focus on that, not obsess over some miracle escape that would never happen. I thought of my parents, both gone. And Frederick? It wasn't likely he would be of any help, at least none that would be on time, not even for Luis. His priorities lay elsewhere. Long ago, I'd come to terms with that.

The vehicle slowed, the sound becoming hollow, as if we were in a large building. As I was pulled from the vehicle, the droning rumble of a departing jet jogged my memory. What had the Chicano man said? Something about people on the same flight? If this was the airport, maybe that meant I wasn't going to die, at least not today. And hadn't Martin said they had taken Luis to an airport? The brief moment of hope lasted only until I realized that whatever my destination might be, the end result would be death.

My stomach flip-flopped in time with my steps as I was roughly guided forward. After about a hundred feet, I was wrenched to a halt and spun me around. I didn't care, because at that moment, a baby started to fuss, and every nerve ending in my body froze. Just like in the house where I'd thought I was going to die, nobody needed to tell me about that cry. It came from Luis.

I stumbled forward, desperately trying to scrape the blindfold from my eyes with my manacled wrists.

"Stand still!" He backhanded me and I tasted blood. "You want to see your kid, you do exactly what I say." Fingers were at the back of my neck again.

My head bobbed up and down. To see Luis one more time, I would have agreed to anything.

"You're going for a little plane ride. Any trouble, and the kid goes out the door. You understand?"

A sudden calm that emanated from somewhere outside myself quieted my pounding heart. "You will have no trouble. I will do whatever you want." My voice carried neither despair nor belligerence because I felt neither. This could hardly have a happy ending, but the debilitating fear inside me had stilled. Maybe it had been that desperate prayer when my face was jammed into the floor of that SUV. I'd placed my son's life in God's hands, and my own as well. It hadn't been a hard thing to do. Giving the small part of my life that was left to God was like giving somebody a used-up saddle with a broken tree and the horn pulled off. It wasn't a gift—it was a surrender. I had no doubt my life was over. And Luis? I didn't have the courage to even think about what they had in store for him.

Fingers suddenly worked at the blindfold at the back of my head. When it was pulled off, I blinked, trying to get used to the light, searching for my baby. We were in a large hangar. Off to the left, several men scurried back and forth around a mid-sized corporate jet. The stairs were down, and instantly I knew. That's where Luis's cry had come from. One of the men pushed me forward to the steps.

"Get in."

He didn't have to tell me twice. Inside the jet, the same middle-aged, chunky woman I'd seen at the house scowled at me as she left the plane. Three seats at the front of the plane faced toward the rear. My precious boy was laying across two of them, greedily sucking at a bottle while he waved one leg in the air. His cheeks were tear-stained, though he appeared to have had reasonable care. I knelt down and touched his damp cheek. His little face whipped toward me. He whimpered, then dropped the bottle and snuggled into my arms. I guess he wasn't that hungry, because the plane had long been in the air before I picked up the bottle to resume feeding him. He'd drink for a while, then suddenly look up, I think to see if I was actually there. I tried to understand what must be going through his downy little head. His mom had abandoned him, and now that she was here, he was afraid she would leave again. The thought brought tears I couldn't hold back, because I knew beyond any doubt that our reunion was only a short-term arrangement. Whatever evil La Linea had planned would not include me taking care of my little boy. As I gazed down into his now sleepy eyes, I bit back the tears of desperation that threatened to sweep away any reserve I might have still possessed. Luis would be torn from me again, probably within hours.

As the plane reached cruising altitude, I surreptitiously glanced toward the other two cabin occupants. They sat across from each other, conversing quietly at the back of the back of the plane. Luis and I seemed to be of little interest to them, though I was well aware that were there any trouble, that would instantly change.

From the position of the setting sun on the right side of the plane, I knew our direction was south. Luis slept, and despite my resolve not to miss one minute of gazing at my little boy, I dozed off. When I awoke, a diaper bag on the floor caught my attention. I rummaged through the contents, careful not to disturb my sleeping baby. It was adequately stocked with formula, diapers, a change of clothes for Luis, a few protein bars, and a bottle of water. We needed nothing else.

Sometime during the night, the plane stopped to refuel, then immediately took off again. Wherever we were, Mexico was now far to the north, and I thought back to what Eduardo had told me:*"They trade the children to the Colombians, who then sell them to al Qaida or ISIS. They're indoctrinated from babies to be suicide bombers."*

My throat tightened, and at that moment, when we were probably somewhere over Costa Rica or Panama, I made a vow. If I had to die and take my son with me, I would do that. Luis would never be indoctrinated with the suicidal propaganda of radical Islam. If I could not raise him to love and honor our Savior, then we would walk into the next life together.

I stared at the exit door to the left of my seat. The instructions on the label were clear. Lift the arm, push . . . and then jump into eternity. I shuddered. Could I do it?

For a long time, I stared at that door. Despite the misgivings I had about suicide, I might have done it, but I knew I could never pull it off. With Luis in my arms, I could never open that door, which meant I'd have to lay him on the seat, open the door, then go back and pick him up so we could do the big jump. With those two eagle-eyed goons a few steps away, I doubted that would work. Besides, I was pretty sure airplane doors were nearly impossible to open in flight. I flushed with shame at my sudden intense relief. My terror of falling through space was much greater than any fear of instant death.

I had no way to tell the time other than the level of blackness outside the windows, but it was close to dawn when the pitch of the engines changed, which meant we were descending to land. A new fear paralyzed me. I hugged Luis tighter, which only served to wake him. When he started to fuss, I rocked him gently. Though my heart pounded like a bongo drum, he quieted immediately. This was it. What would happen now? I wasn't ready. My earlier resolutions were laughable. I would die trying to keep them from taking my son, but what could I possibly do to prevent it? The two men at the back of the plane had well above average physiques. They'd have no trouble ripping Luis out of my arms.

Though I'd hoped it would never happen, the plane eventually taxied to a stop. I glanced nervously out both side windows. To my left, the dark jungle rose on the far side of the runway. On the right, a few dim lights flickered fitfully outside a nearby building, dismal failures if their role was to roll back the night. The two goons behind me with whom I'd shared the flight stepped past me. One of them spoke with the pilot who stayed in the cockpit. His job was apparently to watch me while they went about whatever they intended to do. For the moment, I was ignored. How I wished that would last forever.

I watched as both men walked down the stairs and onto the tarmac. It was then that I saw the black SUV with the tinted windows. I'd lived on the border. No, I was born on the border. My friends and everyone I associated with knew about the drug cartels. This was a cartel car. It might not be Mexican, but it was still cartel. Three men stepped out of the car.

Everybody shook hands, all very business-
like. Then, they all walked into the building
that sported the dim lighting. So . . . this was
the end. After they'd done their deal, they'd rip
Luis from my arms, and my son would be
gone forever. As long as I lived, I would exist
in endless torment, my whole life a
continuation of the hell of the last month of
desperate searching for my son. Years down
the road, I would sit over every newscast that
featured some crazy, deranged suicide
bomber, and I would wonder if the one that
had detonated the bomb and been blown to
smithereens had been my baby, my Luis. I
couldn't live with that. My life would mean
nothing. The ranch, my barrel racing career,
everything would be but ashes compared to
the loss of Luis.

I don't know how long I sat there, but
it probably only a few minutes. The pilots up
front were doing what all pilots do—filling
out paperwork. They ignored me. I doubted
guard duty was part of their job description.
The only stake they had in this was to fly the
plane. I had no idea why the two guards who
had exited the plane thought I'd sit here and
wait for their return. I had no place to run to,

especially with a baby in my arms, so it likely never occurred to them that I would leave. It should have—because I did. I gathered up the diaper bag and walked down the steps to the pitted concrete. Though I had no idea where I was going, or what I would do to escape, I started running. As long as I breathed, they would not take my baby.

It wasn't that I didn't know that they would find me. We were obviously in some kind of an airport, which meant it was probably fenced. Fencing means chain link, which is a standard for airports the world over. It keeps terrorists, elephants, and most mischief-makers at bay. This one wouldn't be any different, which meant it would easily keep a woman with a baby in her arms from escaping. In my heart, I knew all that, but I still hitched my sleeping baby higher on my shoulder and headed north, which was the direction where there had been no lights. A small bank of clouds had covered the quarter moon. I placed one foot in front of the other, hardly able to see the ground, though I reckoned that was in my favor. Even wearing a yellow blouse, a hundred yards from the plane, I would be out of sight.

A few feet on the other side of the runway, I hit tall grass—and no fence. I shrugged. So, I'd been wrong. This wasn't the time to complain about the lack of airport security. I crossed into the long grass next to the jungle and hurried forward into the comforting darkness, a new surge of optimism radiating through my chest. Whatever danger lay in front of me could be no worse than what I'd escaped. I peered ahead, trying to pierce the gloom for danger, then glanced up at the sky. The night was clear, and I scanned the stars. Nothing was familiar. I had a general awareness of where the Big Dipper was, and probably could find the North Star. After that, my knowledge of the heavens was sketchy. Astrology had never been necessary for me to find my way around the ranch or into a rodeo arena. But nothing in this sky appeared even vaguely familiar.

I glanced behind me. On the other side of the airport, occasional lights flickered in the night. Farther south, a small cluster of pinpoints indicated what might be a town, though it didn't look to be a large one. Ahead of me, there was only black night. Was it jungle? I didn't know, but there could only be more danger for me that way. If Luis and I were to survive, we desperately needed help.

I hitched Luis higher in my arms and ran along the edge of the jungle. By the time I made a wide circle around the end of the runway and reached the distant town, the sky would probably begin to lighten, which would only increase the danger. But there didn't seem to be any other good options.

I guess God hadn't intended for us to die, at least not immediately. I tramped through the tall grass while I tried not to obsess about snakes and whatever other deadly predators there might be. I had no idea what country we were in, never mind what the town ahead of us might hold. By keeping to the higher ground, I was able to avoid the worst of the jungle. And far to the east of the airport I was able to climb even higher toward a small hill, which gave me a bird's-eye view of the plane and airport. There didn't seem to be any activity around the plane, but vehicle lights flickered back and forth around what must be the outside edges of the runway. I sat on a stump near the top of the hill and watched the scene below as I once again fed my growing son. The cartel guards on the plane had no chance of finding us in the dark. They wouldn't have to. All they'd need to do was wait for daylight. I was a foreigner with a baby, in a strange country with no money or documents. We wouldn't get far.

<u>**Chapter 33**</u>

After I'd rested as long as I dared, I noted the general direction of the village and picked my way down the far side of the hill. The quarter moon was far away in the western sky, but it gave enough light for me to avoid the roughest terrain. Mostly, it was light jungle, with little undergrowth, which made passage easier. Luis didn't fuss or squirm. He seemed content just to be next to me, and I wondered what psychological damage there would be . . . no, I shook my head. We had more immediate issues to worry about. If we had a future, there would be plenty of time later to deal with whatever problems the kidnapping had created. It was more likely we wouldn't be together for long. Now, escape and food were paramount.

When we'd walked away from the plane, I'd had the presence of mind to grab the diaper bag. Now, I took a moment to rummage through it. Along with a few diapers, there was still an assortment of baby formula packs. Luis would be okay for awhile. I would lose some weight, which was the least of my worries. And after I ran out of baby formula? Then what? Even if I'd had a few Mexican pesos, no one would likely take them here. I had no purse, which meant I had no credit cards or identification of any sort. My pockets were empty.

Not far from the bottom of the hill, a faint trail led in the general direction of the village. The eastern sky showed a faint tinge of light. I reckoned we were close enough to the equator it would be dawn within minutes, which would serve to make my escape short-lived. On the other hand, daylight would give me some idea of where I was going. Once, I heard a far-off car engine. Off in the direction where the moon had now disappeared, the strobe lights of a descending plane flashed in the murky dawn. Birds I couldn't identify screeched and squawked in the jungle along the trail, all seeming to mock my feeble efforts. Once, I stopped to rest, then trudged further down the trail, which soon widened into a dusty road. On the left, a faded blue, single-story house appeared. Chickens scratched for the first bugs of the morning in the bare yard. An emaciated, black cow chewed her cud in the middle of a corral constructed with skinny bamboo-like stalks woven through barbed wire. A dog trotted out from the house and stared at me. Thankfully, he decided I was of no consequence and hardly worth his attention.

After another hour, my arms felt like they'd give out. Now, there were more houses. I must be close to the town, though I'd met no other people on the road. I didn't want to see anybody, at least not yet. What would I say? Could I beg for help? I doubted that would get me far. Though I didn't know what country we were in, this *was* Latin America. Everybody needed help, and those who didn't were well used to turning a cold shoulder. Poverty was something I understood, at least, I thought I did. Though we'd never been poor, we'd always done everything we could to alleviate hardship amongst those who God placed around us. I slipped my hand down toward the left pocket of my jeans. I knew I had no money. The movement was involuntary, almost beyond my control. God knows our family had problems, but money had never been an issue. If the cash machine didn't work, I could always put a purchase on one of several high-balance credit cards. But that wouldn't help me now. I had no cash, credit, or bank cards, so what would I say to anyone willing to listen? "Um, actually, my family is wealthy, so could you loan me a couple thousand pesos? And, of course, I have no cell phone, cash, or identification." I hitched Luis higher on my shoulder. I was rapidly beginning to see that understanding and being sympathetic to those who lived in poverty was completely different than the hopelessness of living with poverty.

The first buildings of the town appeared ahead. Now, I was in dangerous territory. I searched for road signs as I hit the first sidewalk, looking for anything that would give me a clue as to what town this might be. A middle-aged man wearing a dark suit and a Panama straw hat strode toward me, his immaculate attire advertising his importance.

"Excuse me, sir." My face instantly flushed with embarrassment. "Could you perhaps tell me the name of this town, and whether there is a payphone nearby?"

He eyed me with immediate distrust. "How did you get here if you don't even know the name of the town?" He switched his briefcase to his other hand as he edged away. "Santa Maria. And there's a payphone around the corner at the end of the block." He glanced at his watch, impatience clouding his features.

"Oh, thank you so much." I smiled as brightly as I could. "I'm kind of in a fix. My baby needs food. Could you perhaps loan me a few . . .." I had no doubt my formerly flushed features were now the brightest scarlet in the universe.

The man scowled, and hurried away before I'd even finished my embarrassing request for money.

I backed against the stone wall of the building behind me. Even if I'd been successful, what good would it have done if he'd given me a few pesos? I needed a lot more money than that if Luis and I were to have any chance of escape. Great breaths of air shuddered through my lips. If I could have borrowed a few coins, I could have called Frederick for help. Well, all was not lost. The stingy businessman wasn't the only person living in this town. There had to be some kind soul who would help a mother and her child.

I repositioned Luis in my aching arms and plodded forward. A plaza to my right with high-backed benches appeared inviting, though I didn't have time to stop. If my captors weren't already here in this town looking for me, they'd be here soon. But I had no choice. Luis was starting to fuss. He was hungry.

Toward the center of the plaza, several benches were placed with nearly complete privacy, undoubtedly a popular spot with young lovers. I needed one for less steamy pursuits. I sank onto the seat and prepared a bottle for Luis. He sucked greedily. I knew it wasn't enough to fill his little tummy, but I had little of the formula left. What little I had would need to be rationed carefully.

When Luis finished the bottle, I hitched him into my arms and hit the street. Time was passing, and I'd have little of that before the cartel men found me.

An older woman in a light-colored pantsuit turned the corner and clacked toward me, her expensive heels beating steady time on the concrete. When she was nearly in front of me, I smiled at her. She averted her eyes.

"Excuse me. Could you perhaps help me?"

Her burgundy lips disappeared in a flat line of white.

"Señora, I wonder if you could perhaps spare a few pesos." Once again, my face turned crimson. "I've had some trouble, and I would gladly pay you back if you could only . . . you see, my baby . . . I have no money . . . ." I wasn't doing this well. I guess she didn't think so, either. The flat line of her lips disappeared completely. She didn't say a word. She didn't have to. Her face spoke volumes as she strode down the street. She was immune to poverty, inoculated by the vast hordes of clamoring hands. A vast chasm stood between us. It reminded me of the Bible story of the rich man and Lazarus. I was Lazarus, and this woman would not sully herself with the likes of me.

I swallowed. I couldn't do this. It wasn't working, anyhow. My shoulders slumped in despair, and my gaze dropped to my stained blouse and dirty jeans. I didn't blame that woman. I *didn't* look like somebody who could or would repay a loan.

Besides, I'm sure my face and accent betrayed me as a total stranger.

A tan Ford Expedition with tinted windows slowed in the street. Quickly, I turned and hurried down the sidewalk, not even daring to glance behind me. The car kept pace with me. A pathway led between two houses. I ducked into it and walked through the first open door. It was somebody's home. Pounding feet ran past the house, and out of the corner of my eye, I glimpsed a man's face. It was one of the cartel men. They'd found us. Though he obviously hadn't seen me step through the door of the house, it would only be a matter of minutes before he figured out what I'd done. He'd be back, and I'd best be gone.

An old woman stepped out of a room. "Who are you?"

I held up a hand. "I'm so sorry. I am lost, and I must have walked into the wrong house."

The wide, toothless grin in her wrinkled face disarmed me completely.

"Actually, that is not true. There are some bad men chasing me, and I ducked into your doorway to escape." Nervously, I glanced over my shoulder at the still open door. "Do you have another entrance to the house, so I can leave?"

The big smile left the old woman's face. She reminded me of my grandmother.

"Come with me." She beckoned me forward. I followed her through a small kitchen and out into a courtyard at the back of the house. She unlocked a solid iron door in one corner. A shout at the front of the house told me that I didn't have much time. I touched her arm, trying to relay the gratefulness I felt, then slipped through the opening. When she locked the gate behind me, my heart sank. I leaned back against the wall. I'd prolonged the hunt, but the end was inevitable. They would find us, simply because I had no resources available to escape.

There was little future in standing here. Crying would solve nothing, though that's what I wanted to do. I kissed my sleeping little angel on the forehead and scurried down the short alley that led to a back street. I'd nearly reached the end when a slight

young man maneuvered a three-wheeled
bicycle taxi around the corner. I judged him to
be in his mid-twenties. His light, sunglasses
framed quizzical, intelligent eyes. His face
still held a vestige of youthful innocence. He
stopped and pulled his bicycle to the side so I
could pass on the narrow path. His T-shirt had
a stenciled reproduction of the Colombian
flag. Was that the country we were in? The
first man I'd met had told me I was in Santa
Maria. Whoopee. Even in my country, there
were probably a half dozen towns named after
the blessed virgin. The man had told me
nothing, but this flagged T-shirt might be the
key. The young man eyed me as I trudged
toward him.

"*Hola,*" he said cheerfully.

I returned the greeting. We were in an
awkward, narrow place and had to sidle past
each other to avoid a collision.

"Do you need a ride somewhere?"

"I would love to have a ride." I
adjusted Luis higher in my deadened arms,
and shrugged. "But I have no money."

The young man eyed me, his
enthusiasm waning rapidly. I wasn't a

customer, at least not one that had any money.
"Where do you need to go?"

I didn't know what to say. Where I
needed to go was about a thousand miles away
from here. Of course, I couldn't say that, so I
just said what came to mind. "Across town.
Actually, I don't know the address."

He chewed at his lower lip while his
eyes searched my face. It didn't seem he'd
made a decision until his eyes fell to the baby
I held tightly to my breast. "Get in. I will take
you."

I was exhausted. My arms felt like lead
weights after carrying my son, and what this
young man offered was a lot faster than
walking if I was going to escape the area. I
slumped onto the padded, red seat of the
three-wheeled taxi. As he maneuvered the
bicycle back to the street, I thought I'd better
be sure he'd understood what I'd said. "I can't
pay, you know. I have no money."

All he did was wave a hand back at me
as he accelerated down the street. The other
side of the town proved to be mostly downhill,
for which I was thankful. I didn't want my
rescuer to have to work any harder than

necessary to get me out of our disastrous situation—if he was, in fact, my rescuer. As we travelled along the streets, I tried to formulate a plan. God had provided an escape—at least for now. But how was I to feed my son? There was still the baby formula, but that would be gone soon. Then what? And if we could avoid the La Linea Cartel, how were we to get home to Mexico and the ranch?

Chapter 34

Before we'd reached the lower part of the town, our driver glanced back and introduced himself. "I am Ernesto."

Though Ernesto might be a lookout for the cartel I'd escaped from, I saw little sense in making up a story. I had little choice but to gamble and tell him the truth. "My name is Dina. This is Luis." I inclined my chin toward the now squirming bundle in my arms.

"Pleased to meet you." He nodded his head toward us while still keeping an eye on the road. "You are not from here. What brings you to Santa Maria?"

I hesitated. Twice this morning, I'd been rebuffed and humiliated. I wasn't sure I could stand one more time. Even if he was just a poor taxi driver, he'd already done more than the other two much wealthier people I'd met this morning. Out of desperation, and because I had no other answers, I just blurted out the facts. "Ernesto, I will be completely honest with you. My baby was kidnapped by a Mexican drug cartel. I found him, but they forced us to come here so they could trade him for cocaine. Apparently, the Colombians then trade the children for cash to Muslim terrorists."

"And what were they going to do with you?" He glanced back, his eyes flickering over my face.

His question stabbed at the reality I'd refused to face." I—I'm not sure what they were going to do with me. Anyhow, it doesn't matter now. I escaped from the plane, but I have no money or way to find my way back home."

Ernesto's hands tightened on the handlebar grips of the bicycle. Then he stopped the bike and looked back at me. "So you have no money and no place to go? I would say you haven't escaped at all."

There was no answer I could give to his reasoning because he was right. I didn't know how to escape completely, and as long as we remained in this town, Luis and I were in danger. If I didn't find food, shelter, and a phone, Luis and I were finished, even if we were fortunate enough to avoid immediate capture.

Ernesto zigzagged the bicycle through back alleys and winding, narrow streets. Several times, he stopped to answer calls on his cellphone. Another time, he dialed a number. There was no answer, so he left a message and carried on. We were now in one of the barrios, and it wasn't a good one. The faded, paint-peeled adobe houses on both sides of the narrow, potholed street had been constructed long before I was born. Dejected, sullen young men monitored the world from crumbling steps. A woman in a micro-skirt and see-through blouse leaned against a once ornate lamp post and followed us with hard, knowing eyes. Though Ernesto had given me no reason to be afraid, a momentary panic enveloped me. Where was he taking us?

Frequently, I peered at the street behind us. So far, the Ford with the tinted windows hadn't reappeared. A minute later, Ernesto pulled the bike over and stepped onto the pitted and cracked sidewalk. "Wait for me. I won't be long." He disappeared through a doorway. I rocked Luis back and forth. He was fussing because he was hungry, and for the first time in my life, I understood the desperate helplessness of having a hungry child in my arms with no food, and no way to obtain any. How many mothers in countries not much different than this one faced this situation every day?

Minutes later, Ernesto reappeared. "Come with me."

I stepped to the ground and followed him toward the narrow doorway. At that moment, I spotted the Ford Expedition at the end of the street. I scuttled through the doorway as quickly as I could. Had they seen me?

Inside the building, a worn, wooden staircase led to the next floor. Ernesto beckoned me to follow him. I hesitated. I would have no chance of escape if I went up those stairs. Reluctantly, I followed him to the first landing. A large window looked out onto the street. The Expedition was now parked in front of the building. Maybe they were looking for someone else, and their being in this area was just a coincidence, but I couldn't even sell myself on that theory. Too many voices inside my head shouted differently.

The whole setup seemed like a trap. If those men in that vehicle had seen me enter the building, I would have no chance of escape. All they had to do was block the entrance and mount a room-by-room search of the building. But I had to trust this young man. Maybe here I had a chance. To go back out onto the street would only lead to disaster.

My legs trembled with the panic that suddenly coursed through my body. This building was the same as the box canyon we had at home on the ranch. Once you entered, there was no escape. Nevertheless, I followed Ernesto up the stairs. No alarm clanged inside me that said I shouldn't trust him. Besides, Luis was really kicking up a fuss now. He was truly hungry, and I knew that any minute now, he'd really let the world know he needed to be fed.

At the second floor, Ernesto did a hard left down the hallway to a door on the back side of the building that had probably the cheapest lock in the history of the world. He knocked on it once, then pulled a clasp knife out of his pocket that must have been bought at the same store as the rickety door lock. Within ten seconds, the lock gave way.

My protector stuck his head into the room. Conchita? Are you home? She obviously wasn't, so Ernesto shoved the door back and beckoned me to follow.

Inside the room, the ancient tile floor in the short hallway led to a neat, but small living room. Closed doors to the right indicated possible bedrooms or a bathroom. Beyond that, I presumed there was also a kitchen. Though this apartment was on the back side off the building, a quick peek out the living room window showed no indication of a fire escape.

Ernesto led the way into the kitchen. He pulled milk out of the ancient refrigerator and inclined his head toward Luis. "What else does he need?"

I scanned the shelves. Some leftover mixed vegetables caught my eye. A banana on the counter caught my eye. I pointed at both. "Would it be okay if I took those for him?"

Ernesto grinned, shrugged his shoulders, and set them both in front of me. "Nobody is here to say no."

"But whose place is this?"

"It belongs to my sister, Conchita. Sometimes I stay here as well. She won't mind."

"Well, I am very grateful." I found a bowl and spoon and mashed the vegetables and banana together along with a little of the milk to thin it down. It wasn't what Luis liked best, but it was a meal. More important, it would save the tiny bit of formula I had left in the diaper bag. Whatever lay ahead, I would need that if we were to survive.

While I sat at the small dining room table and fed Luis, Ernesto paced around the room. Once, he left the apartment. When he slipped out, he quietly closed the door and turned the lock, for whatever good that would do. After I'd finished with Luis, I tiptoed into the next room. A saggy couch beckoned me, and I laid him down with his head touching my leg so he'd know I was still here. I guess we must have both dozed off, because when I awoke, Ernesto stood in front of me.

"Lady, I have to ask you. Do you know the men who are looking for you?"

"Not really. One of them on the plane was a tall man with long shaggy hair and a mustache."

"Did he have a scar on the side of his face?"

"I'm not sure—yeah, I think he did. Why?" My heart sank. I wiped my instantly sweaty palms on my pants and tried to stop the trembling in my arms.

"They are in the street. They may have seen my bicycle near where they last saw you. I don't know. All I know is there are three men below. One of them I know."

"Who is he?"

"On the street he is called El Barney. He is a renegade from the old Medellin Cartel. What you say now makes sense. His people are involved in prostitution and it has been rumored that they deal in children as well. They are very powerful here in Santa Maria."

"But don't the police do anything?"

Ernesto grimaced. "The police refuse to get involved because they are either paid off, or they are afraid. Even though the old Medellin Cartel has been brought to heel, there are other offshoots that are very powerful, and if a policeman won't cooperate, their family are soon able to plan a funeral. There's nothing the people can do. Here in Santa Maria, the police are not trustworthy. I would never have taken you to them for protection."

I nodded, because I well understood. "In my country, we have our own problems with police corruption."

A sudden knock on the door skyrocketed my fear to outright panic. "Ernesto, I need a phone. I can get help if I can just—"

"Here, use mine. I will see who is at the door. It's probably just one of Conchita's friends.

I grabbed the phone out of his hand and rapidly dialed Frederick's cell number as Ernesto hurried back through the kitchen. A man's voice answered, one I didn't recognize. Wrong number. Frustrated, I tried again. Frederick was on speed dial on my phone. Always had been. It was a number I'd never had to memorize. This time, I got it right.

"Dina?" he shouted the one word, worry and relief crystal clear in his voice.

I didn't know what was happening at the door, but there was lots of noise. I ducked my head and plugged one ear as I tried to talk

through the bad connection. "I'm in Santa Ma
—"

At that moment, everything went black, but not before I glimpsed the familiar face from the plane, and the fist that hurtled toward my face.

<u>**Chapter 35**</u>

Ernesto's phone, the one I needed so badly to save my baby's life skittered across the room. I wasn't to know where, because when I woke up, I was again on an airplane, a different one than I'd left less than twenty-four hours ago. This time, the big man with the mustache and scar on his jaw had been replaced with an overweight, middle aged man in a sport jacket. He sat in the seat next to me reading a well-known South American girlie magazine.

I looked around wildly. "Where's my baby?"

He didn't even look at me. "You don't have one anymore. Or at least you won't soon." I tried to stand, but someone had fastened a seatbelt around me. I clawed at the clasp until it gave way, then stood and surveyed the narrow fuselage. At the back, two men played cards. Both looked up, then laid down their cards as I stood. Between us, a small bed had been made up. Luis slept peacefully. I stepped past the man in the seat beside me and tiptoed back to Luis. I knelt

beside him. He appeared to be fine, which was
more than I could say for me. I touched the
left side of my throbbing face. It was tender
and swollen. The man who had rushed toward
me in the apartment when I'd been on the
phone to Frederick must have whacked me
good. At least they hadn't hurt Luis, and praise
be to God, we were still together, though that
didn't sound like it would last much longer if
they had their way.

The evening sun was on the right side
of the plane which meant we were again
flying south. Where to? With my limited
geographical knowledge, I tried to place the
countries that might be our destination. Peru,
Bolivia, Paraguay? Maybe even Argentina?
An article I'd read about Paraguay in the El
Paso Times came back to haunt me. It had
been all about human trafficking, not only
babies, but also women to eastern Europe.
Was that our fate? My son would be sold to al
Qaida or ISIS? I would be sent to some
brothel halfway across the world? The too
recent rape slammed me back against the
plastic coated aluminum skin that separated
my baby and I from eternity. At that moment,
if there had been any way to choose eternity, I

would have gladly taken it. That route
provided dignity and closure. Where we were
going would only bring ripping, cerebral pain
that would, like the torments of hell, never
cease.

Eventually, I was able to regain some
level of calm. Now, Frederick was my only
hope, and as much as I'd often disparaged his
level of commitment to our marriage, he did
love his son. And for whatever Frederick
lacked as a husband, as an intelligence agent,
he had few equals. If there was any way to
find us, he would do it. The problem was, he
hardly knew where to start. I tried to
remember what I'd been able to communicate
to him before the man at the back of the plane
had knocked the phone out of my hand. Had I
told him I was in Santa Maria? I doubted I'd
got that much out, but even if I had, what
would that mean to him—or anybody? Santa
Maria? There were probably twenty towns
with the name of the sainted mother of Jesus
on the north side of the Panama Canal, and
even more in the southern continent. Where
would he even start?

I sat on the floor and stroked Luis'
forehead, then leaned back against the

fuselage as I tried to think like my ex-husband. He would have immediately taken steps to triangulate the call. Did he have the means to do that? How I hoped he'd been successful. Then reality hit. It wouldn't matter. His triangulation would mean nothing, because Luis and I were no longer there. I knew Frederick would try. He would use every Stirling agent, he would call in favors, and bully the whole alphabet of U.S. agencies who had intelligence assets in Latin and South America. But all that would take time. Before they came close to finding us, Luis would be lost to me, and I would be in some eastern European country where every day I would count the minutes until I could die. I'm not sure at what point I'd made my decision, but at some point I'd resolved in my heart that even death was preferable to that. If that were to happen, it had to be by my own hands, the ones that now twisted and worried at each other, in between stroking my son's little form.

Sometime during the flight, I grappled with murder, with the death of my son and myself, inflicted by my own hand. Would killing Luis and myself be a mortal sin against

God. Would He send me to Hell? As jaded as I'd become with my faith and the church, I still cared deeply as to whether what I'd planned was right. The problem was I didn't know the answer. I'd abandoned my faith in God, and it seemed at this moment when I needed him most, He was silent. My pain was deep and wrenching enough, but how could I simply throw myself on God's mercy. He seemed more distant than ever, and I had little doubt, my options to escape would now be non-existent.

I glanced at the man in the seat beside the one I'd left. He'd thrown the girlie magazine aside and was half asleep. A few feet farther back, the other two men slouched in their seats. In between stroking my son's sleeping form, I studied them. They were armed, but neither had shoulder holsters. They weren't the type to wear sport jackets or anything similar to cover up that kind of rig. If they carried guns, they would be tucked in a jacket pocket, or more likely stuffed in a waistband or belt. I stood and stretched. The bathroom? I pointed toward the back of the plane.

The one nearest to me leered and nodded.

As I stepped past them, I got a closer look and my heart raced. Carrying a pistol in your belt in the small of your back, or for that matter anywhere is all fine if you are walking down the street. Sitting, with the butt jammed into your back is a whole different matter, especially for long periods of time. Both had tucked their guns into the custom made magazine rack built into the fuselage in front of their seats. A nice perk on a private jet, I thought. If I could only reach one of them. But as I closed the door to the bathroom at the back, I knew, those guns might as well have been a thousand miles away. I'd have to reach across or distract both men in order to have any chance at reaching one of their sidearms. Besides, even if I did manage to make that happen, then what would I do? Was there a bullet in the chamber? Did I just push the safety off and shoot? Right, and where was the safety? More likely, I would have to chamber a bullet and slip the safety off with my thumb in order to be armed. I stared at the haggard face, the haunted eyes that stared back at me from the tiny mirror over the sink.

Frederick had taken me to a shooting range a couple of times. If either of the guns in the magazine rack were one of the two I'd fired, I might be able to find the safety and chamber a shell quickly, but there was no guarantee. My interests had always been horses, rodeo, and ranching, not guns. I knew little about how to kill people, and for the first time in my life, I wished I did.

When I stepped out of the bathroom cubicle, I ignored the two men at the back. If there was going to be a chance to resist, it would have to be later. Nevertheless, it wouldn't hurt to start preparing for whatever opportunity might present itself. I surveyed the storage area next to the bathroom for something I could use as a weapon. Nothing, not even a simple coat hanger. My eyes flickered over the spacious cabin as I latched the bathroom door. The two bodyguards were still awake, their guns in the same place in the magazine rack. Toward the front of the plane, the middle aged sex magazine voyeur slumped in his seat. Farther forward, the door leading to the cockpit remained open as it had the whole trip. This was a private plane. Terrorists were not an issue. I cocked my head so I could see into the cockpit. Two pilots, probably standard with small jets. Not even these scum were prepared to crash because one of the flyboys had an inflight health issue.

I sank to the floor beside Luis and checked his diaper. He was still dry, which was a blessing. As I tucked the blanket around him, I tried desperately to plan an escape, but nothing came to mind. Three men, all armed? Any chance of escape appeared hopeless. Once more, I glanced at the seat I'd left when I regained consciousness. The guy who'd sat beside me seemed to be the man in charge. Certainly, he was the best dressed. If he had a gun, where was it? I studied his shoulders and the back of his head, because of course that's all I could see. Despite my misgivings at being anywhere near him, he might provide more of an opportunity than the two wary eyed dudes at the back.

After I'd pulled the blanket up around Luis' shoulders, I made my way forward to my seat. I still had a world class headache, and my jaw throbbed with pain. It didn't feel broken, but I had a couple chipped teeth, not that it mattered. Where they were taking me, imperfect teeth would be the least of my problems. My seatmate eyed me as I sat, then immediately rose and made his way toward the back of the plane and the bathroom. I craned my head toward the magazine rack beside his seat. It was identical to the one at the back. A thrill shot through my chest. A semi-automatic nine millimeter rested between two magazines, though I had to read that information on the side of the barrel to know for sure that was the caliber. I leaned over and slipped it out of the rack, hoping my movement wouldn't attract any undue attention from the two in the back. Quickly, I fumbled the slide back far enough to see that there was a shell in the chamber, then clicked the safety off and back on again. That's all I had time for. I shoved the gun under my leg as the man slumped back into his seat. His hand fumbled at the magazine rack, then froze. Instantly, I grabbed at the gun, bailed out of the seat and backed toward the cockpit. The barrel was now centered on his third shirt button, as steady as I could hold it. The man's eyes narrowed, and for a second I thought he was going to lunge for the gun. I clicked off the safety which I should have done when I stood. I'd forgotten. It would be best I didn't forget anything else. At the back, the two men sat straighter in their seats. The one next to the fuselage and magazine rack couldn't help himself. His eyes slid to the guns they'd carelessly stowed in the rack. I swiveled the gun toward them, holding it with both hands to steady it.

"Get on the floor—now!" I screamed.

Both eyed me. They were tough, and they weren't afraid. I raised the gun higher. "Now!"

Both slid off the seats and onto the floor, obviously unprepared to bet on the reactions of a crazy woman.

"Face down—hands stretched over your heads!

They complied readily enough. I turned the gun back on the man in front of me. "You too."

A noise behind me warned I had more trouble. Fear washed over me as I whirled and backed a step toward the fuselage. One of the pilots stood hunched at the open cockpit door. I turned the gun toward him. Get back in there. If you come out, you get a bullet."

He was young, probably mid-twenties with short-cropped black hair, dressed in typical professional pilot garb, slacks with a white shirt and dark tie. "He nodded and backed away.

"Close the door."

He reached back and pulled the door shut.

Three men back here plus the two pilots behind me? I could never watch them all, but hopefully the pilots would just stay where they were and fly the plane.

I turned my attention back to the other three just in time to see one of the men in the back lunge toward Luis. He was still asleep on the other side and a little ahead of where they were spread-eagled on the floor. I'd never in my life thought I would kill anybody. To do that was against everything I believed in. Also, an airplane is not a good place to start spraying lead. Any reasonable person knows that. Bullets can destroy sensitive and integral parts needed to keep the plane in the air. I didn't think about that, and if I would have, the sudden fear for Luis would have cancelled any rational thought I might have had. I fired. With his hand inches away from my baby, he crumpled. Blood colored his blue shirt, the spreading stain a mute testimony of what I'd done. I trained the pistol on the sex voyeur. "Get back there with the others."

He scrambled out of his seat as Luis, startled by the roar of the gun in the confined cabin proceeded to howl. I didn't blame him. My eardrums were ringing loud enough I could hear little of the plane's engine noise.

"Get on the floor. Same thing—hands above your head." I hoped he didn't notice how unsteady my hands were on the gun. The horror of what I'd just done was starting to wash over me, destroying the little confidence I'd had. I'd killed a man, or had I?

The man I'd shot, twitched and groaned, which meant he wasn't dead, at least not yet. I couldn't find it in my heart to wish it so. His blood stained the carpet and trickled back toward the rear of the plane.

Behind me, the cockpit door opened a crack. A different face peered at me. "Please, we will get the plane on the ground as soon as we can get to a runway long enough to handle a Citation Don't shoot any more, please." The pilot's twisted face was almost comical. He was so worried, and rightfully so. If my shot had been anywhere near an engine or fuel line, we would have instantly been blown out of the sky.

I nodded. "I might or I might not shoot. I have nothing to lose, and I would much rather die than allow this scum to carry out their plan. Turn the plane around."

The pilot's head bobbed up and down. "Where do you want to go?"

Never mind for now. Just make sure you're headed north toward Mexico City." That was an instant decision, but it seemed the right one as I flipped through the several bad options I had for escape. Should I force the pilots to fly back to Santa Maria? Why? To presume that Frederick's agents would have been able to trace a fifteen second phone call from a strange phone was too much to count on. Besides, fuel would be a limiting factor, no matter what I decided. What worried me most was that even with the gun, the odds of keeping everything under control with a screaming baby to take care of were slim to none.

Chapter 36

The man I'd shot was the closest to Luis. I made the sex voyeur lay down next to the wall. I wanted him as far away as possible. Even though he hadn't the physique of the other two, an inner warning told me he was the most dangerous. I moved to Luis' side of the plane and with great care reached down and pulled him to the front of the plane next to me. He protested mightily over being dragged across the floor by one leg. I didn't blame him. He'd come to expect gentler handling from his mother, and I tried to soothe him while I kept the gun centered on the two who still didn't have bullet holes in them. The man I'd shot didn't seem to be doing well. I'd asked whether either of the other two were familiar with first aid. Neither seemed capable in that discipline, which was no surprise. Their type were more versed in snuffing out lives than saving them.

Luis still howled. I'm not sure who it bothered more, the goons at the back, or me. My raging headache was getting worse, and my little boy's screeching was rapidly depleting the little patience I had left. It didn't matter. If Luis and I could escape, it would all be worth whatever we had to endure.

I tapped on the cockpit door with the barrel of the gun. The older man who I presumed was the captain opened the door almost immediately.

"Where are we?" I snapped. This wasn't the time for propriety or small talk. I leaned against the bulkhead while I continued to wave the gun in the direction of my captives. Occasionally, one of them would slide their jaw forward on the floor, enough to peek in my direction. I wanted to give them no reason to risk anything further.

"We are . . .," he stared back into the cockpit at one of their multitude of instruments. ". . . about a hundred miles south of Santa Maria—our departure airport."

How long will it take to get to Mexico City?" I glanced back at my captives, then my son who seemed to be out of tears, at least for the present. Despite my shooting, the captives were restless, and I had no doubt that if I dropped my guard for one second, they would be in control, and I would be dead.

"About four hours."

"Okay. How much fuel do you have?"

The pilot turned and studied whatever instruments were applicable to my question, did some calculation, then answered. "Another two hours, and that is absolutely the maximum."

"If we continue our present course, where would that put us?" I asked.

The pilot's jaw muscles flickered back and forth in the dim light. "Maybe Panama City, but to reach that we'd have to throttle back to a slower speed, and we would have to presume no headwind. A nearer airport would be safer."

I didn't argue. Crashing in the ocean held more appeal than where we'd been headed, but I didn't want any of us to die because of the drug cartel goons who had kidnapped my son. This plane was probably a charter aircraft, and the pilots were mostly innocent. However, I figured that whoever owned this plane would have had a pretty good idea who they were leasing to, so I didn't feel too sorry for them. The bodyguard goon at the back moved his arms from straight over his head. I trained my gun on him.

"Go ahead if you want to join your friend. I nodded at the bleeding, and now unconscious man next to him. I couldn't imagine pulling the trigger again, especially when Luis was not at risk, but the goon didn't know that. My earlier resolve to die with my son had weakened with our improved circumstances. Now, whatever it took, Luis and I were going home. The man quickly stretched his arms out over his head, but his narrowed obsidian eyes never left my face. I squeezed the gun butt with both hands, trying to stop the trembling that started right in my belly and ran through my whole upper body. I stared at the rippling smooth muscles in the man's shoulders and forearms. If I let my guard down for even a second, it would all be over.

I turned back to the pilot. Though he'd backed into the cockpit, he still stood, I guess waiting for whatever instructions I had to give.

"What's south of Panama City? Is there some place you can land and refuel?"

"Yes." He turned, reached into a pocket by his seat and pulled out a folder. "Here." I leaned into the cockpit to see the route map he was referring to. "Here is where we're at." He pointed to a point on the five by eight sheet of paper, then flipped to the next page. Here to the north in Panama is the small airport at Garachino. It would be safer if we refueled there.

"Garachino will be fine. If you fill the tanks, how far will that take us?"

"About three thousand miles, a bit more if there are no headwinds."

"Then fill . . ." Out of the corner of my eye, I saw movement. My head swiveled toward the back of the plane in time to see the chunky muscle man as he pulled the trigger. I should have gone back and removed those guns from the magazine rack. Now, it seemed so stupid. Why hadn't I done that?

Perhaps the goon momentarily hesitated at the thought of spraying lead toward the cockpit controls. I dived backward into the cockpit, smashing into the pilot behind me which spilled us both over the control panel and onto the floor of the empty left-hand seat. As if in another world, I sensed the young pilot frantically attempting to fight our tangled bodies away from the rudder pedals and controls. The engines stopped making their usual noise. The pilot who had been standing behind me was now under me, jammed between the seat and the floor. I felt him struggle. We'd have to get untangled and get out of the way if the plane was going to be able to fly, but the steep pitch toward the earth below made it impossible. Somewhere in the back of my mind, I knew it was over. I'd failed. Luis and I would not be going home. Frederick hadn't been able to save us, though in my heart, I knew he'd tried, and that's the last conscious thought I had.

<u>**Chapter 37**</u>

My eyes opened, and I'd not expected that to happen, at least not in this life. All I could see was a palm tree that blocked out most of the stars, though not all of them. I listened for sounds—anything. Waves surged and broke onto a shore nearby. Maybe I'd been wrong and this was heaven, though I couldn't remember anything in the Bible about tropical beaches. But—it could be.

When I tried to move, I instantly discovered that the heaven idea was a mirage because now the only part of my body that didn't hurt were my eyes. There was way too much pain for me to be anywhere close to paradise. I tried to swipe my hair away from my face. The attempted movement brought excruciating pain. I moved my head. No problems there. I flexed the other arm. That only produced normal pain. My left leg seemed okay, but my right calf had a bloody gash in it. Once more I listened. Behind me, someone moaned. I moved my head again. What had happened? The plane had crashed. I knew that, which meant this was unbelievable. Before that, the man had shot me? No, he hadn't. A stroke of luck? He could have easily done so. A nine millimeter pistol at close range in the hands of an expert? Try two strokes of luck? Everything in my life was now a huge question mark. What I couldn't explain away was the fact that I'd survived. Why? Divine intervention was the only explanation that made sense, which meant this was something far more significant than just luck. A frozen tumor of bitterness inside my chest started to dissolve. If this wasn't God, what else could it be?

I reached toward my chest with the arm that hurt the least. Though my left side was sticky with blood, at least it hadn't come from a bullet. My ribs throbbed, but it was nothing compared to the pain in my right arm and left leg. Trapped between the bulkhead and the console, I wriggled backward enough to see the senior pilot's body underneath me. He appeared to be dead. On the right side of the cockpit, the younger pilot slumped over the controls.

Then, it was as if I'd touched an electric wire. LUIS! Where was my baby? I had to find him. I fumbled at the floor, hoping to find some handhold to help me rise enough to peer into the cabin stretching like a tunnel behind me. I tried to concentrate, to remember what had happened before I'd passed out. Luis had been . . . yes, I'd left him snuggled against the bulkhead between the cabin and the cockpit. I'd been giving instructions to the pilot, not paying attention . . . completely oblivious to the guns that were still in the magazine rack. Frederick would never have done something that dumb. Again, I bit back the pain and tried to roll toward the broken seat. Though I bit my lip until I tasted blood and dug my fingernails into my palms, it didn't work. The pain was too much, and despite my determination, the darkness won.

The sound of pounding surf accompanied my return to consciousness. This time, I knew immediately where I was and what had happened. Didn't all these planes have emergency transmitters of some sort? Why weren't there rescuers? I didn't know the answer to either question, but no other sound interrupted the rhythm of the waves pounding against the sand. Somehow, in my unconscious state, I'd turned onto my back, though my lower torso was still twisted to the left. Tears leaked from the corners of my eyes and down the sides of my face. Normally, they would have tickled enough that I'd have scrubbed them away. Now, there was only pain. My little boy. Had he survived? I strained to hear a sound, some indication that he might be alive, but there was nothing. Nevertheless, I had to find him. I had to know.

I knew if I made a sudden move, or tried to extricate myself without a lot of planning, my body would rebel and I would just pass out again. I needed to avoid that if I were to survive. And even if I wasn't sure I wanted to live, if Luis was alive, then my survival was necessary. He would need me.

I lifted my head off the floor and surveyed the cockpit. In the seat on the right, the young pilot still slumped forward over the instrument panel. It took little imagination to know what had happened. After the shot had sprawled the senior pilot and me into the cockpit, the younger pilot had managed to push both of our bodies off the center console. Perhaps our collective weight had disabled some of the integral systems needed to keep the plane in the air. Whatever had happened, the second pilot must have somehow avoided a headfirst dive into the ground. I could think of no other explanation for my being alive.

Painfully, I turned my head toward the cabin. There had been a groan back there when I first woke up, which meant someone else still breathed as well, but I'd heard nothing since. I struggled to get a better view of the situation. Halfway to a sitting position, I leaned back on my right elbow and panted with the exertion. Now, I was able to get a better look back into the cabin. The two goons who had been in the back of the plane were now piled up against the bulkhead. I was no expert on death, but they were definitely dead bodies, which meant that the groaning had come from my seatmate. He had either left the plane, or he was now against the bulkhead where I couldn't see him. I took a couple deep breaths. Luis should be on the other side of the wall that separated the cockpit from the cabin, only a few feet from where I struggled to rise. If my seatmate was still alive, he might be there as well, only inches from my baby. With my bruised left arm, I managed to inch myself toward the bulkhead door so I could see around it.

For a long time, I sat still while I tried to figure out how to extricate my mangled leg from the cockpit debris trapping it. I had to make a move. No matter how much it hurt, I had to make a move. I leaned forward to see what had pinned my leg. A heavy briefcase had jammed my leg against several shards of aluminum sheeting, all of it sharp. I needed to remove the briefcase so I could ascertain whether I could crawl out without ripping my leg to shreds. I reached forward with my good hand and grabbed at the case, one of those black carry-ons that you see pilots wheeling behind them in every airport in the world. I tried to drag it off my leg, which was a mistake. It must have weighed forty pounds, and was dead-center over the lower part of my leg. I'd no more than touched it before shooting, wild pain told me I would never be able to move it. I stared at the case.

It was then my gaze fell on a long rod in the closet beside me. The closet was obviously a place for the pilots to hang their coats or whatever other outerwear they wanted to stow away while they attended to their duties. The rod appeared to be a collapsible clothes hangar, and I grabbed for it with my right hand. That was all fine until it put pressure on my left leg, the one pinned by the heavy case. Just that small movement caused pain to knife through every sinew of my broken body. I writhed, praying for relief. Possibly, I passed out again, but that I can't say for sure. I gritted my teeth. On my second try, I was more careful. Rather than trying to twist around so I could reach the rod as I'd done before, I carefully lay back against the floor and reached over my head with my right arm. My fingers touched the rod, but that wasn't good enough. I stretched further, groaning as I fought off the pain. Finally, my fingers closed around the rod, and I dragged it toward me. This would be my only chance to escape, and if this didn't work, there was no future.

I inspected the collapsible rod, extending it to its full length. Then I studied the area around my trapped leg. If I used the rod as a lever, I might be able to free my leg. Carefully, I threaded the end of the rod through the handle on the heavy briefcase. Then I stretched my left arm out to position the end of the rod over the top of the seat pocket behind the pilot's seat. I thanked God for the lack of aircraft ingenuity. What good was a pocket in the back of a seat? A pilot would be hard-pressed to reach any maps or other relevant information without leaving his seat. I levered the pole upward with my good arm, enough that the briefcase rose off my mangled leg. The relief was intense, but it also opened up the gash on my lower calf. I lowered the valise between my legs and tried to slide backward. That produced more agony, which was no surprise. I gritted my teeth and fought through the excruciating pain. Somewhere in the process, I managed to scoot back far enough that I was able to see into the cabin. The two bodies still lay crumpled against the right hand bulkhead, though it appeared at least one of them might be alive. Up against the wall on the left, Luis lay in a crumpled heap. My chest contracted with fear. Despite the extreme agony, I scooted backward far enough to gently gather Luis into my arms. He had a deep gash in front of his left ear that dripped blood onto my hand when I picked him off the floor. His pulse was fluttery and erratic, and I held him tightly against my breast, frantic with worry. All the fear and grief since Luis had been kidnapped coalesced into that one spot in time. It was all over. My baby would die. Everything I'd lived for was gone, and the pain in my heart was worse than anything I'd ever imagined possible. I gently rocked my unresponsive son and wept, the tears bitter with loss and disillusionment. Where was God when I needed him to save my little boy? Obviously, he was busy elsewhere. So be it. Let him stay there.

<u>**Chapter 38**</u>

I don't know how long I sat with Luis. I drifted in and out of consciousness, or I was in some kind of catatonic state, probably from the loss of blood. At one point, stopping the bleeding in my leg registered as important if I was to survive, but I couldn't seem to translate that thought into action. Or maybe it was just that it didn't matter compared to the loss of my baby. Meanwhile, I ripped a strip off my blouse and used it as a compress over the bloody wound on the side of Luis's head, though I doubted it would do any good.

Time passed. Now, at least two of the other occupants were groaning, which I suppose was a good sign. I'd suspected the young pilot was still alive, along with the goon in the back of the plane, the one I hadn't shot. Even if the authorities didn't have our location, one of these men would surely be able to call for help if there was any cell service, though the odds of that weren't great.

A whimper from the bundle in my arms riveted my attention and sent a thrill right to my fingertips.

"Luis baby?" I crooned to him.
"Mama's here. You're going to be alright."

His eyes opened halfway, then closed again. I wanted to stroke his forehead, but I didn't dare take the pressure off the compress. Nor did I want to put him down to tend to my bleeding leg, especially since the flow of blood seemed to have slowed.

On the other side of the aisle, one of the men pulled himself out of the heap of broken seats, magazines, and various items of luggage piled against the wall. He glared blearily at me, as if the crash was my fault—and maybe it was. He crawled forward on his hands and knees. I clutched Luis closer, but at least for the present, the cartel goon seemed to have lost interest in me. Hopefully, he was just happy to be alive.

Another groan riveted my attention. This one definitely came from the cockpit. It was clear the goon had heard it as well. He peered into the cockpit, then crawled forward. A hot breeze wafted through the cabin, which made me remember that at least one of the plexiglass side windows had been missing. That would have been a good place to exit the plane, though I supposed if anything was going to catch on fire, it would have done so before now.

Within the next two minutes, I realized how fallacious that premise had been. Smoke wafted forward from the back of the passenger cabin, fanned by the breeze coming from a gash along the right side of the fuselage.

Up in the cockpit, I heard the cartel goon rummaging around. What was he doing? Frantically, I glanced back at the smoke. There might be only seconds to get out of the plane before the fire reached a fuel line. Only one option seemed feasible—the big main door behind my head. But how was I to force it open when I couldn't even get on my feet? Panic enveloped me. I tried to stand with Luis still in my arms. I dared not put him down. I would never be able to pick him up, not with a leg that refused to hold any weight.

Halfway to my feet, I collapsed, unable to pull myself up any further. Meanwhile, the smoke was getting thicker, now with a chemical smell of burnt plastic and polymer. Luis fussed and rubbed at his face. We were both having trouble breathing. My heart raced. Think! I needed to think calmly if Luis and I were to survive. Frantically, I tried to pull myself to my feet again. It was useless. Once again, I slumped to the floor. I peered through the gathering smoke toward the back of the plane, but there was nothing back there that would help me. Unless I could get to my feet and open the cabin door, we would die.

A face appeared in the smoke. "Give me the baby." It was the goon.

"No." I squeezed Luis and twisted away from the man's hands. Luis started to cry.

The man grabbed my shoulder and spun me around so that I had to look at him. He was older than I'd thought. A cultivated mat of gray stubble covered his jaw. His skin was lighter than mine, his eyes a dark gray, which I suppose meant he had parentage different than most Latino's.

In one quick glance, I made my decision. I had no other choice. No matter the promises I'd previously made about dying with my son rather than letting him be raised to be a suicide bomber by al Qaida or ISIS, when it came to actually jumping off that cliff with Luis in my arms, I couldn't do it. If there was a chance for him to live, I had to take it. I held him out. The man cradled him and crawled back into the cockpit. I tried to bite back the tears, but between the smoke and my own fear, they came anyway. Nevertheless, I wasn't going to sit here. Once more, I gritted my teeth. Without Luis in my arms, I was able to struggle to my knees and reach the door. A red handle provided the necessary leverage to pull myself upward. I gathered what little strength I had and tugged on the red handle. The door tipped out and toward the ground, or it would have if there hadn't been a big rock in the way. For a fleeting moment, I realized how different the crash landing would have been if the plane had clipped that boulder.

I pushed harder at the door, but it did no good. I was able to grab a few mouthfuls of air before I had to turn back into the smoke. A hand on my shoulder startled me. It was the gray-eyed man.

"Come on. I'll help you." He nearly picked me up as he helped me toward the cockpit. Inside, the younger pilot was gone, and there was no sign of Luis, so I presumed they'd both exited through the broken and missing windshield. I peered outside as the man helped me as best he could over the controls. The edges were sharp. The smoke now boiled out of the floor below us which encouraged me to move quickly.

"Crawl out on the nose." His voice was sharp with worry, and I wondered why he'd come back for me.

I did my best, and it wasn't hard to slither from the nose to the ground. The front wheel had either collapsed or was so buried that the nose itself was half buried in the sand. Once more, my leg was pumping blood in a slow but steady stream, but there was no time to worry about that. Frantically, I looked around for Luis. A hundred feet to the left, surging waves crashed onto a mostly rocky shore. To the right, a sandy expanse ran toward a line of jungle. The man beside me said nothing as he helped me up the beach to where the pilot lay back against a log. Beside him, a small bundle squirmed. Luis was okay, and I started to sink down beside him.

"No." The gray-eyed man pulled me back up. "When that fire reaches the fuel tanks, she's going to blow. We need to move farther away."

Again, he practically carried me for another hundred yards, then stumbled back and brought Luis over to where I lay. Unlike my leg, Luis's head wound had stopped bleeding. The man returned with the pilot and lowered him against the base of a palm tree, then slumped to the ground. The pilot appeared to have some kind of internal injuries, which was no wonder. I tried to imagine what it had been like for him, fighting to keep the nose of the plane up as he powered into the deep sand. The g-force would have been off the charts. No wonder he had internal damage. Once, the pilot vomited what appeared to be blood. The gray-eyed man squinted at him, scowled, then shook his head.

He crawled over to me. "Lay down. Here." He grabbed a piece of driftwood and placed it under my leg. "You need a tourniquet, or something. Let's try this." He pulled out a handkerchief that looked anything but clean and bound it tightly around the gaping wound. He shrugged at my disdain of his compress. "It's all I've got."

I nodded dreamily. Icy fingers ran down my arms, and I felt faint. He was right,

of course. That bleeding leg did need some
attention, but maybe it no longer mattered. I
laid my head back on the ground. Even though
I'd escaped the crash, if I didn't quit bleeding,
I might still die. As much as I fought it, the
dark demon I'd resisted slipped a black hood
over my eyes. But before the night carried me
away, I wondered about the schizophrenic
God I'd always believed was real. He'd let my
son be kidnapped—bad. He'd allowed me to
find him—good. Then, He let the plane crash.
Real bad. But miraculously, He'd saved Luis
and me from death. Why? What was next? I
wasn't sure I was up to knowing the answer to
that. At least for the moment, I didn't have to
be.

Chapter 39

When I woke again, daylight streaked the eastern horizon with the purple and mauve of early dawn. In different circumstances, it would have been a gorgeous tropical morning. Just beyond where I lay, a macaw squawked about affairs of the jungle. Deeper in the labyrinth of soaring trees and tangled vines, a troop of monkeys squabbled over matters of import known only to them. I lay still and listened. One more sunrise, and I'd not died. I tried to raise my head to examine my throbbing leg. It was no longer bleeding, thanks to the gray-eyed cartel guy. Beside me, the diaper bag lay against the log, and someone had wrapped Luis in an old jacket, then tucked him close beside me. I tried to remember whether either the pilot or the cartel guy had worn a jacket. I didn't think so, which meant my cartel savior had gone back inside that smoldering plane to find something to cover my son—and bring out the diaper bag. Why? I doubted he'd suddenly turned benevolent. It likely had more to do with the fact that Luis and I were worth a few bucks if he could carry on with the original plan and get us to a buyer.

My eyes shifted to where the pilot had been propped against the palm tree. He was still there, with the gray-eyed man kneeling in the sand in front of him. They talked, the pilot obviously in great pain, their voices so low that I could hardly make out what they were saying. Neither had noticed that I was awake. I studied the cartel goon. I wasn't even close to trusting him. Nevertheless, if it hadn't been for him, I doubted any of the rest of us would be here today. Was I right? Had he helped us out of the plane only because Luis and I were assets—collateral that could be cashed out in the near future? What about the pilot? He was hurt so badly, he was only a liability. Time would tell, but for now, I had no answer.

From the few words I overheard, it seemed Gray Eyes was trying to ascertain from the pilot what our location might be. Ah, that was it. The pilot would know our location and the best way to get help. However, from what I could hear, he seemed to be having trouble communicating because of the pain. Sweat dripped off his fevered cheeks as he writhed and groaned. Once, Gray Eyes glanced my way. He nodded toward me, then quickly wound up his conversation with the pilot, rose, and walked over to where I struggled to a sitting position.

"Good morning." He peered at my leg. "You are lucky not to have died. But then, I guess we all are lucky, thanks to him." He cocked his head toward the pilot.

"How bad is he hurt?" I asked.

"I'm not a paramedic, but I know enough to say his chances of survival are not good unless we can get him to a hospital within the next few hours."

"It's that bad?"

He nodded. "And you?"

"I didn't die, so I guess I have nothing to complain about. I am also thankful to that man for what must have been a heroic effort to get us on the ground." The pilot now had his head resting against the tree, panting, his eyes shut tight against the pain in his body. "Do you know where we're at?"

"Apparently, we're about thirty miles from Puerto Bianca, which means nothing to me."

"Panama?"

"I think so."

"That's the only Puerto Bianca I know. My husband and I once did a short vacation here. If we're north of Puerto Bianca, then we're in what's mostly an uninhabited wilderness."

I stared off into the jungle while I tried to process what he'd said. Thirty miles from a town? With no food for my baby? We adults would manage for a few days, even with our collective injuries, but Luis could not. He could never survive long enough for us to reach help.

My mind ricocheted through a half-dozen possibilities, but none of them seemed very good. Gray Eyes still squatted next to me, also surveying the jungle.

"What is your name?"

"Chano."

"I'm Dina, which I guess you already know," I said with a hint of sarcasm, which may not have been wise. This man was our only chance to survive. I leaned toward him, trying to mitigate whatever damage I'd done with my sarcasm. "Why did you drag us out of the plane?"

His jaw clenched, and he refused to meet my eyes, which reiterated what I'd already suspected. There was nothing humanitarian in his actions. His motive was strictly about protecting assets. He immediately rose to his feet and stalked up the beach.

At least now, I had no illusions. On the plus side, Chano would take care of Luis and me to the best of his ability until we, like any livestock, could be sold to the highest bidder. But regardless of the reason, this man *had* saved my life and the life of my son. He might possibly be the most perverted kidnapper and killer in Mexico, but he was our only hope for continued survival. It would be wise not to anger him.

I struggled to my feet and tried to walk. It was hopeless. The thirty miles between us and the nearest town might just as well have been thirty thousand. I would never make it, especially not packing Luis. I sunk back to the ground and turned to my son. Though he still slept, I knew it would be less than an hour before he awoke. He would be hungry, and I had nothing to feed him. Frantically, I peered at the broken hulk of metal that had once been a sleek bird of the skies, then I surveyed the jungle in front of me. There must be something I could feed Luis. If my son were to survive, I had to find it. Besides, I had no wish to subject Chano to the continual wailing of a hungry baby. A few hours of that would dramatically change his attitude and lessen whatever goodwill he presently possessed.

Against the base of the palm tree, the pilot still moaned in pain. I rolled onto my knees, then scuttled over the sand until I sat beside him. It wasn't what I wanted to do. I didn't know what to say, or how to help him. I just felt a deep tug in my heart to do whatever I could for this dying man, so I sat beside him and held his hand. Later, in between fits of intense pain I held the pilot's head against my breast like he was a child as he fought the creeping fingers of death. At one point, the pain must have lessened. He sat up straight, and his fingers clenched my arm.

"Promise me something."

Without thinking, I answered, "I will."

"Go to Creel and tell my wife Carmen what happened here, and that I loved her very much."

I put both arms around him. "You are not going to die. We will do whatever it takes to get you medical help."

"No." His fingers now squeezed my arm like bands of steel. "I have had all night to think about this. It would be wonderful if I could live, but we are too far away from the kind of help I need, so promise me you will do that."

I pulled his head onto my shoulder. "Your heroic landing saved our lives. I will do whatever you wish."

The sun was well into the sky when the pilot died, but I still held him while I murmured a repeat of the promise I'd made to him. No matter what, if God saw fit to get us out of this alive, I would go to the little mountain town of Creel and do what I'd promised. I laid the pilot's body down and crabbed back to my son who had still not awakened. Possibly, it had to do with the gash on the side of his head. Whatever it was, I was thankful that he'd slept through the intimate moments I'd spent with the pilot. I'd not want a crying baby to mar my last moments on this earth, and I was thankful to the God I'd abandoned that my son had not disturbed the pilot's last hour.

As I sat in the hot sun, I reflected on the pilot's request. Creel was a hotspot of drug cultivation. Its position on the rim of the vast Barranca del Cobre, the canyon that dwarfed even America's Grand Canyon, made it a frequent target for federal troops. Chapo Guzman and the Sinaloa Cartel held it with an iron hand, and there was no indication they would give it up. The canyon's vast reaches were immensely important to the drug trade, simply because of their inaccessibility. Hundreds of acres of marijuana or heroin poppies could be cultivated with little worry of discovery. For the indigenous Tarahumera who inhabited the canyon bottoms, drug cultivation and the affluence that it brought had rapidly become a way of life.

None of that was of any importance, other than I wondered about the pilot's story. It was now one I would never know, at least not from his lips. But whatever I had to do to find the pilot's family, I would do. Someday, they would know that a brave husband, father, and pilot, on a remote Panama beach, had died after doing the impossible. Then again, they might never find that out, because it was far from certain I would survive.

<u>**Chapter 40**</u>

Sometime after Luis awoke and announced to the world, perhaps as far as Mongolia, that he was hungry. Chano strode up the beach. He stopped and dropped to his knees beside the dead pilot. Once, his hands went to the man's face. I didn't know whether he was checking to see whether the pilot had a pulse, or whether he was just touching him one last time. Whatever, it was respectful, and my estimation of the man rose a little higher. He looked my way.

"I'm sorry for what I said," I apologized.

"What?"

He hadn't heard me, but that was no surprise. With Luis yelling like it was the second coming of our Lord, nobody could have heard anything. I tried to shush him, but he was hungry, and until he got fed, his little lungs were going to do their best to protest the injustices of a situation he didn't understand.

I spoke louder, nearly yelling. "I'm sorry I said what I did. You didn't deserve that. Sometimes I speak before I think."

find the pilot's family, I would do. Someday, they would know that a brave husband, father, and pilot, on a remote Panama beach, had died after doing the impossible. Then again, they might never find that out, because it was far from certain I would survive.

<u>Chapter 40</u>

Sometime after Luis awoke and announced to the world, perhaps as far as Mongolia, that he was hungry. Chano strode up the beach. He stopped and dropped to his knees beside the dead pilot. Once, his hands went to the man's face. I didn't know whether he was checking to see whether the pilot had a pulse, or whether he was just touching him one last time. Whatever, it was respectful, and my estimation of the man rose a little higher. He looked my way.

"I'm sorry for what I said," I apologized.

"What?"

He hadn't heard me, but that was no surprise. With Luis yelling like it was the second coming of our Lord, nobody could have heard anything. I tried to shush him, but he was hungry, and until he got fed, his little lungs were going to do their best to protest the injustices of a situation he didn't understand.

I spoke louder, nearly yelling. "I'm sorry I said what I did. You didn't deserve that. Sometimes I speak before I think."

He waved a hand my way. "I understand. No problem."

Nevertheless, he again refused to meet my eyes, and I knew what I'd said was still an issue, a big one. Icy tentacles of fear trickled through my arteries as I watched his response. What a fool I'd been. I needed this man if we had any chance of survival. My big mouth and over-sensitized understanding of right and wrong may have skewered any chance of continued help.

After Chano had paid his last respects to the pilot, he rose and glared over at my howling baby. Nothing had changed. Luis was still adamant that he had to be fed if the earth was going to continue on its axis. By now, I would have sold the whole United States of Mexico to feed him. However, I didn't have that option, so Luis kept bawling.

"What's wrong with your kid?"

I shrugged. "He's a baby. He's hungry."

"You have nothing to feed him?"

I glared at him. "No, of course not. Can I ask you something?"

He shrugged.

"Did your people kill Sandy?"

"Your friend at the house?"

I nodded, afraid, not wanting to hear the answer, but I needed to know.

He paced back and forth while he alternated between staring out at the rolling breakers that crashed with monotonous regularity onto the rocky beach and the dark jungle behind us. Several times, when Luis's volume became nearly unbearable, he grimaced, his lips flat against his teeth. "He deserved to die, but no, we did not kill him. Let Los Zetas take care of their own traitors. Wait here. I will be back soon."

As if I had a choice.

Chano wordlessly strode past me and into an opening in the jungle. I had little hope he would return with anything that would quiet a baby's hunger. Nevertheless, gratefulness for Sandy's life momentarily usurped my own fear and pain.

The minutes ticked by. Fear and desperation drove me to my feet. Luis still wailed, and my heart broke for him—and for me. I needed to do something. Never in my wildest imagination would I have thought there would be a situation where I could not provide for my baby, and not for the first time, I realized how sheltered by money and prestige my life had been. Now, none of that protected me, and I had nothing to fall back on. The only bulwark between us and death was a drug cartel goon who might take care of us because we had monetary value. I stared down at my leg, the one that wouldn't even hold me up, never mind the weight of my baby. How could I find help in these circumstances?

I cradled Luis in my arms, trying to understand my schizophrenic God that had allowed this horrible situation to happen. I cringed at the thought. I'd accused God of malfeasance, not once, but at least a half dozen times. Would He strike me with lightning? Turn my sharp tongue to stone? Maybe He would just abandon a faithless Christian like me. Or had He already done that? Questions ricocheted inside my head like a hive of African killer bees, and in the end—I had no answers.

But the strangest thing happened, something I wouldn't expect even my closest friends to believe. All the anger I'd carried ever since Luis's kidnapping drained away, and I had total peace. Marooned on the edge of a vast jungle, with my hungry baby squalling at the top of his lungs, a dead body not thirty feet from where I lay, and a perverted drug cartel goon my only hope of rescue, I had peace. If that isn't crazy, I don't know what is.

As the sun heated the sand around me, flies started to buzz around my face. Something had to be done with the pilot's body. Nothing lasted long in this tropical heat. I glanced over at him and frowned. He lay semi-prone in the sand, his young face devoid of wrinkles or concern. His visage communicated only contentment, and I bit back a surge of emotion I'd not expected, especially for a stranger I hardly knew.

Something inside me beckoned me toward the pilot. Was it to pay my last respects? I didn't know. But I had to drag myself over to him. I knew I didn't have the strength to bury him, not in the physical condition I was in. Still, I had to pay my last respects. I laid Luis down and painfully scuttled over the sand like an injured crab until I was in front of him. Hesitantly, I reached out to straighten his tie. Then I buttoned the top button of his jacket. After all, he was a pilot. He would want to be buried looking as respectable as when he'd strode up to the plane that was to take him to his death. As I fumbled with the top button of his jacket, I felt a hard lump inside the breast pocket of his shirt. Whatever it was, it might be something of value to his wife and child in Creel. I reached inside his pocket, and immediately knew what he'd put there: his cell phone. I dragged it out and punched at buttons, hoping to turn it on. That was relatively easy. The next part wasn't. The phone was password protected. The odds were more than even that there was cell service, even here. Panama wasn't the only Central American country that boasted countrywide cellular towers. But that would do me little good if I had no password and couldn't even open the phone. I looked at the top of the screen, searching for the little icon that said

there was cell service. None. No bars.
Nothing. Maybe I could text. However, even
to do that I needed to get into the phone.

I leaned back against the sandy wall
beside the pilot. Men! What do they use for
passwords? What would Frederick use? I
rolled my eyes, again trying to shut out the
wailing of our hungry son. He used his son's
name, or on some accounts, mine—well, not
anymore. I doubted my name was used for a
password, but I'd almost bet on "Luis,"
possibly with a couple numbers attached.
After I thought for awhile, I decided he
wouldn't use numbers if a shorter password
was allowed. At the core of his man-being,
Frederick was lazy, and I doubted he was
much different than other men. At work,
everything was triple protected, but messages
to his wife about when he expected to be
home for supper did not need cyber security.

A twinge of regret and nostalgia rose
to the surface. In those early years, there had
been those other messages, the ones I'd not
have wanted anyone else to read, steamy
words between lovers. That was a long time
ago. For a brief moment, the phone in my
hand was forgotten as I remembered a past

that had been uncomplicated by the growing separation that affected every area of our lives. Eventually, the little that remained was easily given up, maybe by both of us.

I shook my head, again focused on the phone I held in my hand. Frederick had a part of his life that needed to be behind a cyber-wall, which perhaps made him even more determined to keep his personal life simple. I hoped the young pilot, like Frederick, had gone to great lengths to keep his personal life separate and simple.

So . . . what would the pilot have used for a password? I would have three guesses before the phone locked me out of his account. My guesses had better be good. My index finger hovered over the keys. What would he have used? His wife—up in the Sierra Madre at Creel. He'd loved her dearly. The odds were good that his password would have contained either the name of his wife or his child. He'd not told me the name of his child, so I made a wild guess and typed in "Carmen1."

INCORRECT PASSWORD. I don't know what I'd expected, but those capital letters seemed a fitting epitaph. I slumped forward, defeated and broken by what seemed a whole string of failures in my life. was stuck on a deserted beach with a hungry baby. The only possibility of survival lay with a man who had every intention of selling both my baby and me into a living hell, and I was too injured to walk away. So what could I do? I didn't know, but as I stared bleakly at the phone screen, I knew I had two more chances to get the password right. I didn't intend to squander them.

Chapter 41

Chano still hadn't returned, so I scrubbed at my forehead and desperately tried to come up with another password. There were few options. If what the pilot had chosen didn't include his wife's name, I was finished. All I could do was include some random numbers at the end of "Carmen." If that didn't work . . . well, I would face that if I had to. I tried to think the way the pilot might have. Was he like Frederick? Suddenly, I knew. The screen had said, 'Backup Password.' If that meant what I thought it did . . . all I could do was hope.

I limped painfully over to the dead pilot. The temperature was fast approaching ninety degrees. Flies buzzed around the man's body. We needed to bury him, and fast, though I suspected that might not be a high priority with Chano. I knelt beside the body and picked up one of his cold hands, grasped the index finger and swiped it over the small, oblong button at the bottom of the phone. "No Match." The sudden dejection of failure coursed through me. I'd been so sure I was right.

Then, it was as if a lightning bolt hit me. What about the other hand? The gathering horde of flies made me too queasy to reach across the body, so I rose and hobbled around to the left side. If the pilot had been left-handed . . . that made sense, at least I hoped it did. Once more, I reached for his hand and pulled his index finger across the screen. Instantly, the display changed to the home screen, complete with the icon I needed most: Messages. After breathing a huge sigh of relief, I opened the pilot's messages and typed a text to Frederick, a brief message that included my best guess at our location. Once, I glanced up, worried that Chano might return. Then I tapped a quick update to Frederick on how we'd arrived here. That seemed important. Frederick needed to know what had happened so there was no misunderstanding on our location. When I'd finished, I quickly read over what I'd written. It seemed clear. He should be able to find the plane, and if he found the plane, he'd find us.

I never saw it coming, and I should have. My finger was hovering over the send button when a man's hand closed over the phone. I suppose it was the rising wind and pounding surf that had muffled the sound of his approach. Chano stood behind me, the pilot's cell phone now in his hand. He didn't even look at me as he read what I'd written. He didn't delete it. He just slid off the back cover, pulled out the battery, and flung it into the ocean. Then he squeezed what was left of the phone into a "V" and threw it into my lap. "Carry on." His laugh was low in his throat, demonic, a sound that drove despair into the deepest recesses of my being. How could this happen? It was like a replay at the apartment in Santa Maria. I'd been so close to summoning help, and once again, it hadn't worked. The disappointment was almost more than I could stand. That phone had been my last and only hope.

As if to punctuate my own sorrow, Luis let out another howl, this time an octave higher. I rose to my feet and limped over to him. Chano watched as I knelt beside my son. It was then that I saw the bananas. They were so overripe, they were almost black. Luis wouldn't care. In fact, they were perfect. He loved bananas—pureed, of course.

"Thank you."

Chano turned away, the pouty anger I'd seen before clear on his face. I ripped off one of the bananas and kneaded it between my fingers. I couldn't even imagine what bacteria my hands had been exposed to. I didn't care. My little boy needed food.

With most of Luis's hunger assuaged, I laid him down and limped over to the water to wash the gooey mess off my hands. Chano sat on a piece of driftwood and stared out over the waves. He never looked at me as I knelt at the edge and rinsed my hands in the salty water.

"You don't need to worry, you know. They will come to rescue us," he said.

I dried my hands on my pants. "Who will?"

He shrugged. "I don't know. The people who always come when there's a plane crash."

"Well, how will they know?"

His pained expression told me what he thought of my intelligence level, not that I cared. He pointed at the fire-scarred metal hulk a hundred yards to the south. "It has a transponder, a black box. Actually, I think most jets have two of them. Plus, the pilots would have had to file a flight plan. When they failed to arrive, it triggers a search. The problem is, their flight plan was filed for Ascuncion, Paraguay. That of course is nowhere near here. But still—there are the flight recorders and the ELT."

"What's that?"

"The Emergency Locator Transmitter. It puts out a signal if there's a crash. But our flyboy may have done too good a job in landing. It may not have activated."

"How soon will we know?"

"About two hours ago, which means it either didn't activate, or this being the armpit of the world, it just might take a rescue team this long to rally."

I turned away so he wouldn't see the disgust and disappointment I felt. Why had he destroyed the cellphone? That might have been our only chance for rescue if his ELT thing hadn't deployed. And if it had? What then? I didn't have long to wonder. Chano rose and walked toward me. I backed away, but he didn't touch me.

"If the government search and rescue folks come waltzing in to take us back to civilization, we need to come to an understanding."

"Meaning?"

"You, my little dove, are my wife." He scowled over at Luis. "That little bundle of joy is our son."

"And if I don't agree?"

"Oh, that is quite simple." A pistol appeared from under his shirt. He didn't point it at me. All he did was caress it as he talked. "Although I have gone to much work to keep you marketable, make no mistake. With little regret, I would cut my losses and start over."

I understood. Though I knew little of planes and emergency locator thingies, I was well acquainted with guns and drug cartel goons. I'd hoped he'd not made it off the plane with one of the guns. Obviously, he had, so I nodded my agreement because there was no other choice. But it didn't stop the sour wine of bitterness that welled in my stomach.

Where was God? Wasn't He supposed to be there when a person needed Him? All of my life, I'd been a devout believer in His omniscience, his benevolence. And now, when I needed Him more than at any other time in my life, He seemed non-existent.

A voice inside me whispered accusation I could not answer. "The plane crashed, and against all odds, you are alive. Why?"

I stared out at the waves, ignoring Chano's vengeful hand. The gun didn't worry me, at least not now. Later, that might change. But for the present, as long as I didn't anger him, our monetary value would keep us safe.

The rescue never came. Luis and I spent the second night huddled together. I hadn't enough clothes or blankets for him, so I made a nest in the sand and kept him cupped into the hollow of my body. Mostly, it worked. When he woke before dawn, I mushed up more banana in my hands and fed it to him. I was thankful that Chano had found them, and I wished I'd communicated that. Whatever other mortal issues we had, he'd protected my baby from hunger. To any mother, that is huge, and I appreciated it.

After Luis again slept, I rose and hobbled down to the sea to wash the banana off my sticky hands. When I returned, I snuggled beside my son and tried to lure the land of Nod. It didn't work, at least not as fast as I wanted. My mind flipped through every scenario that might happen in the coming days. None worked in my favor, and all had an unhappy ending. There would be no rescue, and as much as I wished it were different, there was no way I could hike across thirty miles of sand to reach the nearest settlement. That was my last thought as sleep spirited me away to places I didn't want to go.

Chapter 42

There's little in life that equates with the chagrin of failure, and my inability to rescue my son from what lay ahead weighed heavily in the early dawn. Though I was grateful and in need of Chano's help, as soon as we were able to reach civilization, the tables would tilt toward the same danger my son and I had faced in the first place. Chano would do everything in his power to shuffle both Luis and me off to the highest bidder. Just because a couple of the cartel goons had died in the plane crash didn't mean anything had changed. What Chano had planned could still happen, and the same anger and determination I'd had before the plane went down suddenly came roaring back. I would die before I'd let Chano's plan come to fruition.

Last night, Chano had taken away any doubt I might have had. Whatever the danger, I had to escape with my son. We must take our chances in the jungle. Anything that happened there would be preferable to what Chano had in mind.

I stood and craned my neck, trying to pinpoint where Chano had bedded down. I couldn't see him anywhere, which was good. He'd wanted privacy, probably to get away from the crying baby. He could have it.

I shouldered the diaper bag, picked up my son, and stumbled past the dead pilot. It seemed only fitting to stop and say a prayer after all he'd done for us. I freed one arm and made the sign of the cross, then stumbled through the only prayer I could remember. It may have been said at my grandmother's funeral. I wasn't sure, but I did my best.

"In sure and certain hope of the
resurrection to eternal life
through Our Lord Jesus Christ,
we commend to the Father above, this
man.
And God, I'm sorry because I don't
even know his name,
but we commit his body to the earth:
ashes to ashes,
dust to dust.
Lord, bless this husband and father,
keep him, and give him peace.
Amen."

It wasn't a prayer out of the Bible, but it was the best I could come up with.

I hitched Luis higher in my arms and struggled up the sandy break, heading for the jungle. I would have loved to just walk along the tree line until we were out of sight, but I didn't for a couple of reasons. One, I might walk right into wherever Chano had bedded down for the night; and two, I couldn't walk more than a few yards before I had to rest. It would be best if I had cover, and even more important, left no tracks. The jungle would provide a more secure place to rest when my injured leg gave out, and the leafy soil would do a reasonable job of covering my trail. Once, I turned and scrutinized the sign I was leaving. My shoulders slumped with discouragement. A seasoned tracker would follow it at a trot. But as I stared at the obvious signs of my passing, I thought about who Chano was. He was a drug cartel city boy. He knew about guns, smuggling drugs, and killing. But the odds were high that he knew little about the jungle or how to follow the faint smudges and indentations that made up the trail of a fleeing person. At least, that's what I hoped. I couldn't be sure, so I did everything I could do to make sure I left little evidence of my passing. Mostly, that pursuit was an abject failure. I had a baby in my arms, and most of that weight fell on my good leg, which left plenty of evidence for anyone behind me to see.

As I hobbled through the trees, I tried to plan ahead. First, my destination. I only knew of one. Before he'd died, the pilot had said we'd passed over a town just before we'd crashed, so I struck out in a generally southwesterly direction toward where I thought the town might be. The pilot had indicated it was about thirty miles away, but before I'd traveled a mile, I knew thirty was impossible. My leg was better than it had been when the plane crashed, but that distance was not going to happen.

Luis was now awake and squirming. He wasn't hungry yet, but he was already tired of this whole "let's get up at dawn and stumble through the jungle" routine. I sang softly to him as I limped along, which was hard. The pain from my mangled leg and the exertion of packing a twenty pound baby made each step excruciating, but each time I tried to stop and rest, Luis would start to fuss. The last thing I needed was for him to start howling at the top of his lungs. Chano wouldn't have to be a tracker if that happened. The sound of my crying baby would carry all the way back to the beach. That would be the end of our escape, and I had no intention of that happening. There had been enough failures. We hardly needed more.

By the end of the second hour, I was exhausted and Luis was getting fussy. I'd followed a faint game trail that mostly ran the right direction, though it angled more to the west than I wanted. The worst part was it generally ran downhill. It was probably a trail leading to some hidden water source deep in the jungle, which was okay. What wasn't fine was the fact that I would also have to find a way out of whatever water hole the trail led to. Even walking on level ground was difficult. I couldn't imagine what we would do if I had to negotiate a rocky trail climbing out of a basin. Nevertheless, I stayed on the trail. The thought of stumbling over the fallen logs, vines, and creepers to make my own way was too daunting to even consider. Maybe later.

For now, my first priority was to put as much distance as possible between Chano and us.

A small opening in the maze of vines gave me an opportunity to find a resting place. If we were going to stop, it seemed wise to at least get off the trail a ways. I found a huge, fallen log, lowered my tired body to the damp earth, and leaned back against the mossy surface. I dug one of the little black bananas out of the bag. There were two more left, which would probably get us through to the end of the day. After that, I had to find more food, and more important—water.

The banana was close enough to rotting, I hardly had to mash it. As I fed Luis, I desperately tried to think of what other edible jungle fruit there might be. I hadn't eaten in over twenty-four hours. I would rapidly lose strength if I didn't eat something soon, and if I wasn't able to carry on, then I could not help my son, either.

I scanned the trees and vines in the near vicinity. Nothing of the multitude of plants seemed edible to me. Then I spotted a colorful tree on the far edge of the clearing. A dozen rosy, round orbs hung from its branches. What were they? I hadn't a clue, but

this wasn't the time to be squeamish. I laid
Luis down and limped close enough to hook
one of the branches with a forked stick.
Carefully, I pulled it low enough to reach the
fruit. I bit into one of them. The skin was
rougher than an apple, but inside, it had nearly
the same texture, though it was somewhat
bland. I nibbled at it, then deposited a dozen
more into the diaper bag. They weren't great,
but they were enough to dampen the hunger
pangs.

When I returned to Luis, he seemed
fairly happy. He watched me as I ate the fruit,
occasionally cooing and playing with his toes.
I hoped he'd fall asleep before we again
started down the trail. Whether he did or not
was immaterial. We needed to go.

I shouldered the diaper bag, then
reached down to wrap the blanket around
Luis. The movement probably saved us. Just
as my head dropped below the log we'd rested
against, I glimpsed a pair of legs out on the
trail. Instantly I froze, but my eyes followed
the tracker as he approached the point where
I'd turned off the trail. Twice, I caught a
glimpse of his upper body. The pistol he

carried swung easily in his right hand as his eyes searched for any sign of our passing. Obviously, I'd underestimated our pursuer's ability.

When Chano approached the place where I'd ducked off the trail, he breezed right past it. I breathed a sigh of relief. He'd keep following the game trail—for awhile. But if he was woodsman enough to follow us this far, it wouldn't take him long to realize that my tracks were now absent. I might only have minutes before he back-tracked to the place I'd left the trail. Quickly, I scooped up Luis and fought my way through the liana vines and creepers. Eventually, he would find my tracks, and I couldn't limp fast enough to stay ahead of him. But if Luis would stay quiet, we could at least try to get away.

Panic squeezed every ounce of blood out of my face. If Chano found us, I didn't even want to think about what would happen next. Could we hide? Probably not. My only option was to keep moving and leave as faint a trail as possible. For that, I needed rocky, hard ground. But I didn't have that. My shoes squished through the mud and rotting leaves, leaving tracks a blind man could follow. Fear drove me to a faster pace as I considered my last conversation with Chano. He'd been patient with us because of our monetary value. But something inside me shouted a warning, a message that we were finished. This time, Chano would just want to cut his losses and run. The temptation would be too great to just be done with us. And what better place to make it happen? In this dense jungle, our bodies would vanish within days, long before anyone came close to finding us. I trudged forward, slowed by deadfall and the slippery footing.

The longer I thought about it, the more I knew I was right. To be caught now meant certain death.

Chapter 43

My home had always been the high desert country of Arizona and Sonora, so I knew little of bush terrain and jungles. Be that as it may, by the grace of God we were still alive.

My father had never believed in coddling me just because I was a girl, and though here in the jungle, I was completely out of my element, I'd been raised tough. Mama had often harangued Papa for sending me out with the crew to brand cattle or ride the brush-choked canyons on our ranch as we searched for strays.

"No respectable man will ever want anything to do with her," Mama would wail. "Look at her hands. They are all rope-scarred and hard. What man would want . . ." and so it went. Papa just chuckled, at least most of the time. Sometimes, he gave in to Mama and made me stay at the house, but it was too late to make a lady out of me, and hardly his fault. I was what my papa's people called a tomboy. I'm not sure that was complimentary, but they were likely right.

As I placed one tired foot in front of the other in that faraway Panama jungle, the ranch seemed far away, almost unreal. Here, it was life and death. Not only my life, but my son's as well could be over within the next few minutes. I was under no illusions. When Chano caught us, he would kill us. Nothing else made sense. We had caused too many problems, and finding a way to get us back to civilization would be too much work.

I slogged forward, one limping step at a time, each foot forward a point of condemnation. I'd put my career ahead of my son. Tears streaked my face. Deep inside, I knew it wasn't true, but I was emotionally and physically spent, well beyond what I'd ever thought possible.

I could no longer put one foot in front of the other. I had failed everyone—my husband, Sandy, my ranch family, but most of all, my baby boy. Luis would never grow up with a dad who came home from work and played with him. He wouldn't know what it was like to sit down with both of his parents at the dinner table, to hear them talk about their day, argue, and yes, maybe even have a shouting match. He wouldn't experience the unconditional security other children had whose parents lived and loved together. He would never have the assurance that whatever angry words his parents said to each other, they both loved him enough that no matter what else happened in life, together they would provide a loving home for him. He wouldn't know that the sanctity of marriage was an inviolable principle of his home, that no matter what other bad things happened in his life, he could count on Mom and Dad. They would always be there—together.

I wept harder. How could I have been so selfish, so wrong? I'd listened to the lies. One after another, they paraded like rotten corpses through my mind: "Not to worry." "Kids are so flexible." "He'll be alright." "You need to be happy." And now . . . was I happy? Even if we escaped from this drug cartel goon, I knew that the ache of failure in my heart would never go away. And every day of my life, I would worry about the damage done to my little boy from the divorce. The hurt would be a cancer that he would learn to manage, but the mistrust in his heart would never go away.

It would affect every relationship, most of all with the girl he would one day marry. And God forbid, because of my actions, Luis's children—my grandchildren—would all be affected.

I sunk to my knees, unable to carry on. I wanted to die, and the only thing that made me eventually struggle to my feet was the debt I owed to my son. He needed to live. The least his rotten mother could do for him was to give him the opportunity to survive. And so, I struggled forward against the pain. I would conquer the pain, because in order for Luis to live, I had to.

Night came quickly, as it does in countries close to the equator. One minute, the sun hovered on the horizon, and the next, the light faded like one of those new halogen bulbs that Americans are putting up everywhere in their homes. I'd not prepared for that. We had no water, and I was beginning to need it badly. Though we'd passed several running creeks, I'd been afraid to drink. Unsafe water could put me down as effectively as a bullet, and I wasn't willing to take that chance, at least not yet. Now I wished I'd not been so squeamish. And though in different circumstances, I would have stopped sooner and made some kind of reasonable camp, with Chano behind me, I had no choice but to continue on.

I would have liked to have walked even farther in the dark, just to put more distance between us and the man who would snuff out our lives, but it was impossible and likely dangerous. We were in the jungle, a place where predators come out at night. It was the snakes I feared most. I had a deathly fear of the slithering reptiles. And though I knew there were big cats here as well, they didn't scare me nearly as much as what crawled on the ground. We would stay where we were until daylight.

After feeding Luis the last of the bananas, I ate the other two pieces of red fruit I'd picked. They weren't what I'd call delicious, but neither had they caused any ill effects. When I'd finished them, I wished I'd picked more. Even if they weren't great, they were food, a commodity we desperately needed. Hopefully tomorrow, I'd stumble upon better sustenance for both of us.

I piled up some leaves, then spread out the old coat that had become Luis's blanket. It was a cozy nest, even if it wasn't what he was used to. He fell asleep almost as soon as he'd eaten, which made me both relieved and proud. In the most difficult of circumstances, he was a trooper. I snuggled up next to him, with my body curled around him to give him whatever warmth I could provide. As I lay hoping for sleep to drive away the worries of the day, my mind tried to return to the guilt and shame of what I'd done to my son. But it was as if God suddenly turned the crazy quilt of my life right side up so I could see the finished pattern he wanted to weave. All I had to offer Him was strife and discord, but where only misery and failure had resided, there was now hope.

As I stared up at the brilliant stars, my mind turned from my own failures to the Savior. For a while, that thought dominated. Almighty God was my hope, the only one I had, and if He was here beside us in the Panama jungle, Luis and I were safe.

Finally, I slept.

<u>**Chapter 44**</u>

Dawn came early. The last thing I wanted to do was force my aching legs to hoist my non-compliant body off the ground. Never had I been so sore, but that didn't matter. We had to get moving. The only advantage I might obtain over Chano was an earlier start. He needed daylight in order to follow our tracks. It was my job to leave as few as I could.

I wrapped Luis in the coat and picked him off the ground. Hopefully, he'd sleep at least for another hour. I had no more bananas to feed him, and I was well aware of what would happen when my son woke up with an empty tummy. He would tell the world—starting with Chano. I could not let that happen, because if it did, we were dead.

I set off on what I reckoned was the same southwesterly heading I'd held yesterday. That whole day, I'd failed to hit any game trail that lasted more than a few hundred yards. I hoped today would be different. My injured leg meant any movement off the trail was nearly impossible, so I took every opportunity to follow one of the game tracks through the jungle. I could move faster on a trail, but more important, the footing was more compact which might make my tracks harder to follow. That was of supreme importance. Everything depended on me keeping ahead of Chano.

Several times as I weaved through the trees, I glanced over my shoulder. Mid-morning, I sunk onto a mossy, fallen log, already exhausted. I'd still not seen or heard any sign of pursuit, but something in my heart told me that Chano was close. I dare not stop for long.

A few minutes later, I struggled to my feet and limped down the trail. Luis was awake and fussy, and rightfully so. He was hungry, and he was telling me in the only way he knew how to communicate that he needed food. I didn't have any, which meant that within minutes this escape would be over. Luis would howl. Behind us, Chano would hear him and within minutes, he would sight us. I didn't want to think about what would happen after that. Like a Broadway play, the curtain would come down and that would be the end, only it wouldn't be make believe—for Luis and me, it really would be the end.

Though I tried, one can't hurry with a leg that refuses to cooperate. The terrain was far from level, and though it was more difficult for me, I angled uphill. I'd heard that a wounded bear will do that so he can better scent his pursuer and escape. I was no bear, and I had no way to extend this escape, especially not with a crying baby in my arms. Luis had gone from fussing to a higher volume. He wasn't screaming at the top of his lungs yet. That would be next. My breath came heavy as panic flooded my chest cavity. *Faster—one foot in front of the other.* A glance over my shoulder confirmed my worst fear. A flash of color between the trees caught my eye. I didn't wait to see more. Panic escalated to terror. Any rational response was gone. I left the trail and plunged deeper into the jungle. Horror clutched at my throat. Death was imminent. Frantically, I pulled Luis's head into my breast as I tried desperately to muffle the noise of his crying. Something in the back of my brain said it didn't matter anymore. Chano was too close.

I hobbled in a trotting limp toward a thick grove of bamboo in the distance. Though it wasn't safety, it was cover, a way to buy another few minutes before the man behind me snuffed out our lives. My lungs burned, and I sucked at the humid air for enough oxygen to keep struggling. It wasn't enough, and as much as I didn't want to, I had to slow my pace. Blood ran down into my sock, not that it mattered. Bleeding to death was the least of my worries.

Once more, I glanced over my shoulder. This time, I could see Chano, less than two hundred yards behind me. He'd seen me as well. He shouted. I turned and did the best I could as I stumbled for the protective edge of the thick stand of bamboo. Maybe we could hide. I knew better. Unless it was a stand that covered many acres, it would only prolong the end. Eventually, he would find us, but for Luis, I had to try.

Before I slipped into the bamboo, I glanced back one more time. Chano was coming fast, running at full speed, again shouting. I only had seconds to slip between the stalks and wiggle my way into a safe place —and then I stopped. And laughed. Luis's full-throated roar of anger covered up the sound of my crazy, convulsed chortle. I'd been so panicked, I hadn't even noticed his bellowing. We couldn't hide.

I slid to the ground against one of the bamboo stalks. I'd tried as hard as I knew how. I'd desperately wanted for my son to live. It wouldn't happen, not now. I bowed my head. And prayed. Words from my Catholic youth rolled off my tongue in the language of my mother as I waited for the bullets. "*Padre nuestro que estás en los cielos—Our Father who art in Heaven.*" My tears fell and mingled with those on the cheeks of my son. "*Forgive us our sins*—my sins, Lord, for they are many. The pounding of feet told me I needed to hurry. "*As we forgive those who have sinned against us.*" I slumped forward. "My precious little boy, you are too young to understand what I've done to you, but please forgive me. If we had lived, your mama would have tried to undo the damage she's done, at least as much as she could. And Lord . . ." I squeezed my eyes shut. I had only one more thing to say before the bullets found me. "And Lord, I forgive my husband. We both need Your grace and healing."

I heard the running steps in the leaves before I was done with what I needed to say to God. I didn't look up. Within seconds of facing my Creator, I wanted desperately to have a clear account with God. But then I was finished, and unaccountably still alive. Luis had suddenly quieted, and I opened my eyes to face the gun.

My mouth dropped open, and I stuttered gibberish at the bulky figure in front of me. "Frederick? How—"

"Why did you run? I called to you and you wouldn't stop." He stepped forward and gently lifted Luis from my arms.

"I thought it was Chano. I didn't know it was you!" It didn't seem a very intelligent statement, but it was the only thought that would come to my frozen brain.

"Chano? The guy in the yellow shirt?"

I nodded.

Frederick almost contemptuously waved the subject away. "One of the other guys took care of him." He squatted beside me, a sudden look of concern on his face. "You're bleeding."

"I suppose I am, but I doubt it will kill me. At least it hasn't yet. Do you have any food?"

"Of course. We'll get you back to the crash site on the beach. The chopper is there."

"No, I mean now—for Luis. He hasn't eaten today. I had some bananas, but they're all gone."

Frederick was already on the small portable radio. Obviously, he wasn't alone, and I heard him bark orders like he was the General in charge of World War III. Suddenly, it hit me. I was alright. And more important, our son was going to live, and hopefully grow up to be like his dad. While Frederick gave instructions on the radio, he held Luis close to his massive chest like he'd never let him go. Maybe he squeezed him too hard, because though Luis had been silent when Frederick took him from my arms, he suddenly let out a wail. And that was only the first. He'd had enough. Frederick chuckled and stood, rocking him gently. The sight made me want to cry, but I couldn't even do that. I was too tired and emotionally exhausted for mere tears. My head slipped off the narrow stalk of bamboo. I didn't care. I slumped to the ground, my face half-buried in dry leaves and maybe some mud. It no longer mattered.

Frederick laid a hand on my shoulder. "Hang on, Dina. The guys are only minutes away. You won't even have to walk out of here."

That was nice to hear, because I couldn't have done it. Maybe it was the loss of all that blood, or perhaps I was just reacting to all the strain. A film of dark purple quickly turned black in front of my eyes. I had something I needed to say, and I fought the darkness away. "Frederick?"

"What, Dina?" The gentle way he said my name made me remember why I'd loved this man.

"I'm sorry."

"Sorry?" He cocked his head, puzzlement in his eyes. "This wasn't your fault."

"No, Rico." I used the name that was only mine to call him. "Not for this. For walking out on our marriage. Our son needs both of his parents. God gave him to us, and I think he deserves to have a mom and a dad. I just wanted you to know that."

Frederick never answered, but he leaned forward and gently combed through my hair with his fingers. He'd not touched me that way ever since—well, it had been a long time, and more my fault than his. Maybe it was too late to start over, but I was going to try.

Frederick and I might never know love for each other again. What mattered is that we both cherished our son with a fierce and unconditional love, enough that we would commit to providing the security of a home with both parents present. God hadn't given me even a glimpse of what that would look like, but I knew in my heart that He'd asked me to do it.

My eyes closed against the pain and weariness, but I was at peace—with my husband, my baby, and my God.

The End

<u>**Author Notes**</u>

Sacrifice was an exciting, though arguably dangerous story to research. Clearing Mexican Customs, then walking across the border from laid-back Douglas, Arizona, into the tense undercurrent of fear that, at the time, defined Agua Prieta in the Mexican state of Sonora seemed a step too far for a writer of mostly fiction.

Too much of Mexico has succumbed to a legitimate fear of the cartels. But that's why we were there, to gain authentic background material. The week before, a shootout between the two major warring cartels had left one of the buildings in the downtown area with a bullet marked facade, one more testament to the many deadly altercations between the Sinaloa Cartel and their new rivals, the Jalisco New Generation Cartel.

To you, my valued friends and readers: I hope you have enjoyed this story, In our on-line world, authors live or die on book reviews. If you enjoyed *Sacrifice*, please consider posting a review to whatever book site you enjoy.

With appreciation - David Griffith

<u>**Author Notes**</u>

Sacrifice was an exciting, though arguably dangerous story to research. Clearing Mexican Customs, then walking across the border from laid-back Douglas, Arizona, into the tense undercurrent of fear that, at the time, defined Agua Prieta in the Mexican state of Sonora seemed a step too far for a writer of mostly fiction.

Too much of Mexico has succumbed to a legitimate fear of the cartels. But that's why we were there, to gain authentic background material. The week before, a shootout between the two major warring cartels had left one of the buildings in the downtown area with a bullet marked facade, one more testament to the many deadly altercations between the Sinaloa Cartel and their new rivals, the Jalisco New Generation Cartel.

To you, my valued friends and readers: I hope you have enjoyed this story, In our on-line world, authors live or die on book reviews. If you enjoyed *Sacrifice*, please consider posting a review to whatever book site you enjoy.

With appreciation - David Griffith

Vengeance is Mine
The Freedom Series, Book 2

Dina Rodriguez cut her first tooth on trouble. Born to parents embroiled in one of the most secretive CIA operations on the Mexican border, she's seen the dark side of her late father's efforts to keep America safe.

The Rodriguez ranch straddles one of the best smuggling corridors in Mexico. Until now, they've maintained an uneasy truce with the drug cartels, but when Juana Altamirez disappears, trouble descends like a six-taloned buzzard.

Juana's husband Raul has been Dina's mentor and friend since childhood, so when he leaves to search the vast canyons of the Sierra Madre for his kidnapped wife, Dina starts her own perilous journey of discovery. She pleads with her husband for help, but with an agent mired in the most daring and dangerous infiltration of his career, Frederick is once more unable to respond to Dina's need. Is this the end of their already tumultuous marriage? Dina has to decide.

ALSO BY THE AUTHOR:

<u>THE BORDER SERIES</u>

All books are available in paperback & e-book formats.

Subscribe for email updates or order at www.davidgriffith.ca